AMPHIBIAN

AMPHIBIAN

TYLER WETHERALL

virago

VIRAGO

First published in Great Britain in 2024 by Virago Press

1 3 5 7 9 10 8 6 4 2

A CIP catalogue record for this book
is available from the British Library.

Hardback ISBN 978-0-349-01792-1
Trade Paperback ISBN 978-0-349-01793-8

Typeset in Bembo by M Rules
Printed and bound in Great Britain by
Clays Ltd, Elcograf S.p.A.

Papers used by Virago are from well-managed forests
and other responsible sources.

Virago Press
An imprint of
Little, Brown Book Group
Carmelite House
50 Victoria Embankment
London EC4Y 0DZ

An Hachette UK Company
www.hachette.co.uk

www.virago.co.uk

For my mum.
I miss you every day.

'But if you take my voice,' the
little mermaid said, 'what am I
left with?'

HANS CHRISTIAN ANDERSEN,
The Little Mermaid

Let me sing to you now, about
how people turn into other things.

OVID, *Metamorphoses*

I

(preparation)

TADPOLE

My body is stretched out before me like a tongue. Pale pink and improbable as a salamander.

I take a breath and sink below the water's surface. My ears fill with the rumble of the tap.

Here, I am a creature, not a girl.

I am a tadpole with fledgling legs kicking.

I have gills and a tail as flat as a newt's.

Once, I told a girl at school I had webbed toes and made her cry. Somewhere out there a girl believes Sissy Savos has webbed toes.

My lungs tighten for want of air, and still I wait. If every time I wait a little longer, one day I'll hold my breath long enough never to drown.

Mou says we came from the water. She says in the long-ago we grew stumpy little arms and we pulled our pupal bodies from its dark soupy depths. Our flat frog-like faces gasped for air and our lungs burned, as we blinked at the new world, devoid of birdsong.

I let out my breath slowly and sink deeper, the hard knobs of my spine knocking on the base of the tub. By the end of this story, I'll have turned into something else, something frightful. As in: something full of fright.

My lungs have emptied. Panic pulses through me. Get used to it, I think. Mou says there's nothing humans can't get used to. We're resilient, she says, convincing herself of the fact.

My head bolts from the water, gulping air, like my amphibian ancestors did before me. I blink at the bathroom around me, a pea-green suite my mother hates.

I am a girl again.

I PULL ON the oversized T-shirt I wear in place of pyjamas – Mou doesn't see why we need special clothes for sleeping – and crawl into the snug in the corner of my room. Mou was already in bed when I got home from school today and she won't get up. I don't want to think about that just yet.

The snug is small enough for two me-size girls sitting cross-legged, though it's always just me. There are shelves for my clothes and belongings, and a basket for toys I've outgrown.

Lying on my back, I look up at the sticker of Luke Perry's face on the underside of the shelves. The sticker came free with a copy of *Bliss* magazine I read at the doctor's. I peeled his face away with my finger and carried him home in my pocket, until my palms became clammy, and Luke Perry's pilfered face collected pocket fluff, losing his stick in the process. I had to glue him to the underside of the shelf, somewhere only I knew to find him.

The girls at school have crushes. Lydia sent a birthday card to Mark Owen from Take That offering him her virginity the day she turned sixteen on the condition he wrote back. He never wrote. My Luke Perry sticker is different. I don't care about Luke Perry. I don't want to write Luke Perry a birthday card offering my virginity. I've never even seen his TV show. In my daydreams he's not called Luke. He's called whatever I want him to be. He's called Rameses. He's called Adam. He's called Freddie. I find him in the woods and lead him astray. I kiss him and he turns into a frog. I lure him into the water and drown him, tangled in my hair.

In the snug, I play with my two Barbies and imagine the romances they might have with Luke Perry (with Rameses, or Adam, or Freddie). I'm too old for toys now, but it's how I've always done it. The Barbies are a prop so if someone were to see me they wouldn't know what I'm doing. There's never anyone here to see me.

I have to sit just right, kneeling with my heel wedged neatly in the place between my legs. I don't know how I discovered this; it's like I've always known. I also know it shouldn't be done in front of anyone, but I can't say exactly why.

I move my hips back and forth against my heel, rocking slowly at first, and then faster, as my face begins to flush, and the heat rises in me, the urge with it, emergent and rhythmic, until I close my eyes the better to relish the feeling, the rush and the throb, and then I burst open like a supernova. It's the end of all time or the beginning. I float in this other-other, the not-thinking place, washed in pale undulating pink light. Like the light behind my eyelids on a summer day. Other times I see winged horses galloping or rushing waterfalls at night. These are worlds of my making; they're mine. But when I open my eyes, these worlds fall away. I'm just a girl in a snug, holding two Barbies and feeling her pulse beat in every living cell of her body.

MORE!

It's September, the start of a new school year and I'm the new girl. This means I'm strange until proven otherwise, but I won't disprove it. We moved to the West Country from London for reasons I don't fully understand. Sometimes Mou tells me all the reasons before we make a decision. Even reasons for things I don't need to know. This is because she has no one else to talk to, which she tells me also. Other times she tells me nothing, because I shouldn't expect her to have all the answers, okay?

Mou isn't her real name, but the name I have for her, which is mine only. Well, mine and Koko's, but he's not around any more to share it. He called her 'Susie *mou*' – pronounced like the *moo* of a cow – which means 'my Susie'. Other times he called her '*matia mou*', which means 'my eyes' and is another way of saying 'I love you' in Greece, where he's from (making me half Greek, the half that is unknown). When I was a baby, I picked up '*mou*' because I heard it so often and it stuck. I don't tell people this story. When they ask why I call my mother Mou, I lie. Some things are more special when they're kept secret. And furthermore I don't like to talk about Koko.

We left my father somewhere out in the North Sea with the conger eels and the basking sharks he told me about in now barely remembered bedtime stories. *Basking sharks eat baked beans for breakfast out on a broad blue sea*, he'd sing, making it up as he went along. Except the sea wasn't broad or blue. I could see it from my window then, in the breeze-block tower where I was born outside Aberdeen. It was flat and grey and never-ending, and even when I squinted into its depths I could not see the oil rigs in the distance where my father might still be.

At morning break, I circle the perimeter of the playground, trailing my fingers along the fence. Occasionally a splinter snags my skin and I stop to enjoy the satisfaction of picking it out. It's while picking like this that I spot Tegan. She's down by the Wendy houses and there's a little furore around her. It's only my second week, but I know who she is. She's in my class and I've already heard the stories they tell about her, the kids who all came up from the same junior school together. Like the time she instructed the boys to spit in her palm one by one. She said she could tell who would grow up the strongest just by the look of their spit. Everyone thought it was gross, but they didn't say it to her face, because it wouldn't have stopped her.

Tegan is sitting on a bench with a girl beside her, giggling and whispering. There's half a dozen more girls lined up behind them, as if waiting for an appointment. I step closer, leaving the safety of the fence to get a better look. She has a copy of *More!* magazine in her lap. The front is pink and orange, lacquered as lip gloss. Some girls aren't allowed to read *More!* until they're teenagers, because it will make them think about sex before they're ready. Mou doesn't mind what I read, not that I read *More!* anyway.

Tegan permits one girl at a time to sit with her and together they examine the 'Position of the Fortnight'. It's just a drawing of a man and a woman, as far as I can see. But as I watch, it occurs to me the 'Position' isn't what matters. What they're saying to each other isn't important, either. The pleasure is in sitting for a moment in that coveted space beside Tegan. No one suggests she pass the magazine around for everyone to see. No one is riled at the injustice. The point of it all is Tegan.

'Wait your turn!' a girl shouts at me.

I feel a tug of desire to see, to sit, to giggle and whisper beside her – but I won't join the line.

AFTER BREAK, THE kids are rowdy as we wait for Miss Storey to arrive. She's the type of teacher we want to love us: slender with elegant un-ringed fingers and long woollen skirts. She fits our image of what a lady teacher should be. Pretty, but not so pretty as to make us cautious.

I take a seat at my desk, somewhere off to the side with least likelihood of being noticed. I sit close to the fish tank so I can watch the pair of Siamese Fighter Fish called Victoria and Albert. The male spins around the female, wrapping her seductively in the ribbons of his red fins. The female, brown and dowdy, accepts this dance blandly. Albert will hammer his head into the glass if he catches his reflection looking back at him. Sometimes at night, when I don't recognise the girl looking in the mirror, I think about the strength it would take to knock my head against the glass until my skull smashed in.

I told Mou how much I love Albert, and she asked how I could love a fish. A fish offered nothing in return. No affection, no pleasure in being loved. But it's not about that. I love the Siamese Fighter Fish because he is proud and beautiful regardless of anyone's love. He's beautiful without needing to be told, like a god, sure in the knowledge that when he turns in his tank he'll be worshipped.

Tegan walks in and takes her place in the centre of the room. She sits cross-legged on her desk while the other girls chirp and twist around her. Occasionally, one of their voices rises above the group to make itself known, and then there's Tegan's laugh. It's closer to a shriek. Tegan isn't the prettiest girl in class and it doesn't even matter. She's compact, sturdy. Her cheeks are ruddy and her hands square and strong. She isn't the most popular girl either. That would be one of the three Sarahs. Or the single Charlotte. Neat girls who keep themselves clean and play nicely. But it is Tegan who commands our attention. She can be monstrous and strange. She can do things other girls wouldn't dare. I can't imagine what it is to be Tegan.

IT'S RAINING NOW so we can't go outside during lunch. We clog up the classroom instead, our collective boredom steaming up the panes. I long to be outside with my feet deep in the damp earth, my hair dripping wet. I want to slip between the sheets of rain, my mouth opening and closing to the sky like gills.

The other girls are playing 'Never Have I Ever' in the reading corner of the classroom. Never Have I Ever . . . smoked a cigarette? Never Have I Ever . . . kissed a boy? Their Never Have I Evers don't interest me much, until Clara screams.

'She masturbates!'

Her words rise above the classroom din. She is pointing

at Lydia, and we all turn to look. Lydia has a slight overbite, which makes her seem unsure even when she isn't. Her curly hair is tied back in two tight bunches like fists on the back of her skull. Lydia blushes. The blush rises like a tide from under her sweater.

'See!' Clara declares triumphantly. 'She's blushing. That proves it's true!'

'Oh, my God, that's disgusting!' Hannah squeals.

Tegan laughs and rolls her eyes like she thinks they're all embarrassing and childish.

Lydia can take it no longer and runs out of the classroom covering her face with her hands, leaving the other girls to fall about in shock and delight. Even the boys turn and snigger.

LATER, AT HOME, I look up *masturbate* in our old dictionary. I'm embarrassed even on my own, knowing this word is shameful enough to make Lydia run from the room. I pretend to look up words above and below it, for the sake of the girls in my head who are always watching. They're all the versions of me I'll never become, and they can be noisy and judgemental.

I look up *masticate, v.t. to chew*, and *Mataco, n. a people of Bolivia. Mastitis, mastodon* and *matachin*, and then, finally, my eyes land on *masturbation*:

> n. erotic stimulation especially of one's own genital organs commonly resulting in orgasm and achieved by manual or other bodily contact exclusive of sexual intercourse, by instrumental manipulation, occasionally by sexual fantasies, or by various combinations of these agencies

I read it again, and two more times before I start to under-stand. Never Have I Ever. Yes, I have. With the heel of my foot or the edge of my hand. But I never thought to give it a word, certainly not a word I can look up in the dictionary. A word I can call across class, like an accusation. The girls in my head jump up and down, excited and horrified. I shush them and tell them to get back in their places.

I look up *orgasm*, too.

> n. intense or paroxysmal excitement especially: the rapid pleasurable release of neuromuscular tensions at the height of sexual arousal that is usually accompanied by the ejaculation of semen in the male and by vaginal contractions in the female

This is a lot to take on. There is no mention of the undulating pink light. Or the rush and the throb. No mention that some-times it's pale yellow and bright as the sun. Or at other times there are winged horses with hoofs galloping hard, like my hammering heart. There is no mention of anything like that.

Finally, I look up *paroxysmal*, which I can't pronounce and therefore won't later remember, only the vague shame forever associated with the word.

> n. a fit, attack, or sudden increase or recurrence of symptoms (as of a disease): CONVULSION

> a sudden violent emotion or action: OUTBURST

Each word leads to more words, the unknown piling up in terrible pages, until I shut the book with a thump and put it back on the shelf. A dictionary is a book of spells.

A recurrence of symptoms (as of a disease). Am I sick? Or, worse still, dying? Are the feelings that follow a *contraction* or a *convulsion,* some sort of *fit*? Is this why it shouldn't be done in public?

At night in bed, the idea grows so terrible I can't sleep. What if the pleasure isn't pleasure but some sort of trap? Like how scratching a bite soothes the itch, but you're not supposed to do it. It'll leave you scarred. The more I think about it, the more wrong it seems to feel so much that I lose control. It starts between my legs, and then spreads through my body into my belly, where the undulating pink light turns first red and then purple and blue as a bruise.

If I'm sick, I should tell Mou. In the morning, I'll say, 'Mou, there's something wrong with me and I need a doctor.' I whisper out loud to practise: 'Mou, I think I'm sick.'

I've always been able to ask Mou anything. Like when I was six, and I asked her about the neat rows of tampons stacked in a box in the bathroom, like cotton missiles waiting to be fired.

'They're for women to put in their vaginas like a plug to stop them bleeding,' she said. 'When girls become women their womb starts to shed.'

I didn't want to become a woman if that was what it meant.

That night, I climbed into Mou's bed and cried. 'How do I stop it?' I said. 'I'm frightened I'll be the first girl who dies becoming a woman.'

She laughed and said no one had died yet.

But this is different. I'm older now, closer to the moment I might die becoming a woman.

Throwing off the covers, I slip out of bed. The girls in my head are rowdy, delirious. All their fingers are pointed at me and they're chanting: 'Have you ever? Have you ever? Yes, she has! Yes, she has!'

I ignore them, as I fetch my two Barbies from the snug. In the corridor, Mou's door is open, like usual. Her arms are flung over her head, her chest rising and falling with every breath.

'Mou, there's something wrong with me,' I whisper.

She doesn't stir.

I tiptoe onwards, downstairs, gripping the Barbies like bludgeons. We don't own a shovel, so I take a spoon from the kitchen drawer, shushing the clattering cutlery, and head into the garden. A spray of late-summer honeysuckle sweetens the air. We've never had a garden before. It's wild and overgrown, the hedges unruly; I cut the grass with a pair of scissors because we have no mower, but I love it all the same. I like to lie in the long grass and let tiny insects conquer my body.

The moon is full and weighty, watching. I am caught in its beam, a barefoot girl in an oversized T-shirt. The world bristles with my every step. I drop to my knees and dig. The ground, still wet from the rain, gives way beneath my spoon. I'm shivering now, but it won't take long. I don't need to dig so deep.

Mou told me once that in the beginning of humanity there was just one woman. This one woman, all alone, birthed the world and each of us in it. She was Eve without an Adam. She was our first mother. They carved her likeness from bone and stone and tusk and dreams. In this likeness she has giant breasts and no face. She is small, smooth and round, made to be gripped in the night when afraid. And then she was forgotten, or lost, or she was broken apart and died. She was replaced by men and their myths, and first forgotten Eve sank out of sight. She went unloved, untouched, until a man dug her up and named her Venus. Mou showed me her photo in *National Geographic*, a figurine of a faceless woman with giant

13

breasts and no feet. She said this was the true story. This was the only story I needed to know.

I can't tell Mou my secret. I can't tell anyone.

The hole is deep enough now to reach my hand in up to my wrist.

I make a promise. I promise I'll stop. From this moment on, I won't make my body explode like a supernova. I won't visit the other-other or feel the rush and the throb. I'll give it all up for good, as long as it's not too late to save me. I lay the Barbies lovingly in their shallow grave, before burying them for future generations to find, a pair of golden goddesses.

This is my offering.

This is my sacrifice to first forgotten Eve.

THE MAGIC TRICK

In assembly, we sit in rows cross-legged on the floor of the Big Hall, our bare knees bashing against one another's. Mine are still muddy from the night before. I cover them with my hands, but there's dirt beneath my nails, too. The girl beside me stares. 'You're dirty,' she hisses, shifting her body away from mine. 'Don't you shower?'

I pull my sleeves over my hands.

When the rest of the school bow their heads in prayer – 'Our father who art in heaven, hallowed be thy name' – my eyes wander to Tegan's blonde crown. I wonder if she's praying, and if she isn't, what she thinks about. I wonder if she has dirt beneath her nails.

Sometimes a bird flies into the rafters of the Big Hall, and I look up to watch it. This is more like worship. The bird takes a stately swoop, driven by urges known only to itself.

IN THE LUNCH hall, the gelatinous stew has skin so thick it peels away like a scab.

'I'm a vegetarian,' I tell the lunch attendant. 'My mum wrote a letter.'

The girl next to me, whose name I don't know, sniggers. She has a cute girl nose. A button nose, which you can undo or do up. A nose that might fall from her face if a thread came loose.

'My mother says vegetarians are just fussy. It's natural for people to eat meat. That's why we have canines. See?' The girl bares her teeth.

I don't see.

'The Korowai of Papua New Guinea eat people. I read it in *National Geographic*. They think that's natural. Who says they're not right?'

I think I've made my point, but she pulls the face they make when I say something weird. It's better to be weird on purpose than have them accuse you of it, as if you don't already know.

DURING THE BREAK, Tegan and the boys slip away behind the old school buildings at the bottom of the playground. None of the girls are invited, not even Hannah and Clara, Tegan's best friends. Normally, the three of them hang out in the Maze, a part of the playground with high hedges that hide it from my view. But today Hannah and Clara have busied themselves making friendship bracelets, their fingers nimbly knotting threads to pass the time. They're jealous. I can tell by the look of them. Not jealous of Tegan being with the boys, but of the boys getting to be with Tegan.

Some of the girls have boyfriends. Kissing takes place on the bench by the Wendy houses, the same bench where I saw Tegan with her copy of *More!*. But this is different. This is just Tegan and a whole gang of them. Too many for kissing. Certainly for kissing all at the same time.

I follow them to the long narrow alley down which they disappeared. It runs the length of the Big Hall. They're up ahead. One of the boys calls back, 'Fatty won't fit,' and Fatty, whose name I'm yet to learn, gives an affected 'ha' to disguise his hurt. That 'ha' echoes along the brick walls, 'ha, ha, ha', to where I stand.

I squint down the alley. I want to know what a girl like Tegan does. I want to know her. I step inside, and the temperature drops immediately, the air damp against the thin layer of hair down my nape. I can't see for a moment, my eyes unadjusted to the shadows, but I hear Tegan's laugh and the boys jostling, their jibes magnified in the confines of the alley, until their babble is carried away beyond my reach.

I shuffle forward until I emerge into a scrappy field the other side, dotted with the occasional limp daisy and the dismantled mechanics of a trampoline. The others are entering some old tennis courts at the bottom of the field. I catch up, used to being unnoticed, and slip in behind them. I keep my back against the fence, wrapping my fingers around the wire and ivy. The playground up top has brightly coloured tarmac and neat white lines that are not to be trespassed when playing games. But here weeds grow wild and cracks have formed in the broken ground. The white lines don't mean anything any longer.

'Show us, then!' William shouts, his face scrunched and combative, a curl of brown hair plastered against his forehead in the autumn sun.

Congregated in the middle of the courts, the boys form a circle around Tegan. Her occasional shriek of laughter slips between their grey-shirted backs to where I stand. People don't make Tegan laugh: she chooses to laugh. If you tell a joke, you do it as a service to her, and she rewards you with that bright cackle.

'Okay! This one!' Tegan says, and there is an exchange of items in their hands, but I cannot see beyond their shuffling elbows. The boys all take a step back. A cloud passes over the sun and casts the courts in shadow. There is a loose circle around Tegan now, and she holds up a small round stone for the boys to see, a magician capturing her audience. She puts her hands up her skirt, and there is a moment when Tegan appears to concentrate, her eyes turned skywards. Just as the sun reappears from behind the clouds, she raises her hand into the air, and opens her fingers, one digit at a time. Her hand is now empty.

The boys are silent for a moment, and then they approach, all at once, checking her pockets, patting the ground around her in case she dropped the stone and they had not seen. In case she cheated. They demand she open her palms, while they paw at her for answers. She even drops her knickers to show it isn't in there. The stone has gone. She disappeared it.

'What've you done with it?' one of the smaller boys asks, disbelieving, quickly followed by another: 'What do you think she's done with it, you eejit?'

The circle loosens again. They stand around her, shoulders back and jaws slack, eyeing her with a sense of cautious awe.

'How far up does it go?' Chris asks, serious now. Chris doesn't have command of the group the way William does – he wouldn't punch a boy in the side of the head if he took a dislike to him – but something about his seriousness means the other boys listen to him.

Tegan shrugs.

'Tell us, go on.' He sounds earnest. I want to know, too.

'No.'

'What if it gets lost?' says another boy. 'Will it come out again?'

'Yeah, it goes straight up and out her mouth!'

They all laugh.

'Do it again!' William demands, the tone shifting. He stoops to pick up another stone, this one heavy and angular, and he steps forward from the circle to offer it to her. 'But with this one.'

I want Tegan to do it again, and maybe this time it will make sense, and I feel a rush of excitement I can barely translate. But I also want Tegan to stop and walk away from the boys and this court, and back to the place where the rules are laid out in neat white lines. I want both things with equal intensity, one measured by desire, the other by fear.

Tegan eyes the angular stone disdainfully. 'No.'

'Go on, what's the difference? Dare you.'

He tries to force the stone into Tegan's hand, but she backs away.

'I won't,' she says, and crosses her arms to fend him off.

'See? She's a liar,' William says, turning back to the boys. 'She didn't really do it.'

Tegan scowls. Her eyebrows are so pale against her face they're barely there. All her anger is in her eyes. For a moment I'm frightened Tegan will be defeated. She must be, too, because a flash of dread crosses her face. She looks around in desperation, which is when she sees me. 'I won't,' she says, 'because it's Sissy's go now.'

The boys all turn and see me for the first time.

'Sissy, your turn!' Tegan calls, and I hate her.

I look towards the gate in the corner, wanting to run, but it's too late now, because William is stalking towards me.

'What you doing following us around like a sheep?'

He begins his attack, turning his anger from the unknown place between Tegan's legs to me, the weird new girl. 'Shoo!' he says, flicking his hands at me. When I don't move he takes a few steps closer. 'Fuck off, then!' A ripple of exhilaration passes through the group at the curse. 'No one wants you here, sheep,' he repeats, the word losing all its meaning, now menacing in his mouth.

I lift my head to meet his gaze because I won't show him I'm afraid. I won't be defeated either. And then he rushes me. I dodge, wily, as I am, but I'm fair game now, and another of the boys comes at me from behind, locking his arms around my chest, his smile against my cheek. 'Let me go!' and I struggle free, only for another set of grabbing hands and grimaces to come at me. 'Herd her, hey, sheep! Baa!' A boy lifts my skirt, laughing, and I pull it down, but with my hands occupied, another boy pins my arms behind my back, bleating and bleating, and the whole time there is Tegan's laugh, that cackle, ringing out among their clamours of sheep, sheep, and their grabbing, grabbing hands. 'Show them, Sissy, go on,' Tegan is saying, her presence now only audible between the crowded faces of the boys. I free myself for a moment, only to be shoved from behind and I stumble. I slip away, slip into the darkness, the same dark beneath the surface of the North Sea; my hands stop my face hitting the ground, and then, still unseeing, I find the stone.

When it happened, I didn't think or choose or mean to – if my action had intention, the intention was only to defend myself, which is what I will say later, when called to account for my behaviour. 'I didn't mean to,' I will say. And it's true, I didn't know what I'd done, not until I heard William cry out, and only after that did I feel the hard edge of the stone in my hand meet with his head, again, and the smooth crack of bone that came with it.

The boys fall away, making room for William, bent double, his head clutched in both hands. They've all stopped still. Their grabbing hands hang at their sides.

I get to my feet. Miss Storey is standing in the gate looking at us, her height a sign that the rules have returned. 'What's happening here?' she says.

I drop the stone. The same angular stone Tegan had refused.

William rights himself, wincing, as blood gathers thick and fast between his fingers. Miss Storey examines the wound. A gentle hand on his shoulder.

'She did it!' The small boy they'd called an eejit points to me, wildly. 'The new girl!'

Tegan catches my eye, and gives me a sideways smile, as if she's really seen me for the first time.

Despite myself, despite it all, I smile back, a smile no one sees but Tegan.

We were not defeated.

We share this first smile like a secret.

'You're not to play in here, you know that,' Miss Storey says. 'Now, everyone, come along. Sissy, straight to the head-mistress with you!'

We file past Miss Storey as she holds the gate open: William, still bleeding; me, still smiling; and Tegan, still with a small round stone somewhere inside her.

ALL THE WINDOWS in Mrs Greidinger's office are closed, brewing a mothball stuffiness that accumulates around her person, like old age. There is a mole on her cheek, which I have never examined up close. A heart-shaped smudge I want to reach out and touch. I imagine it to be soft. Fuzzy like a mouse. Mrs Greidinger's mousy heart-shaped mole moves as she speaks.

'Miss Blackmore, you're in big trouble,' she says.

Blackmore is Mou's maiden name. She insisted I take it when we moved here, saying a mother and daughter should have the same name. I couldn't object: it would suggest allegiance to Koko. Sissy Savos is the girl I might have been had we never left Koko behind.

'Big trouble, indeed, young lady,' Mrs Greidinger repeats.

She's going to call Mou to tell her what happened. I feel bad for making Mou worry. It's my job to make things easier for Mou and I failed.

Back in class, I feel Tegan's eyes follow me to my seat by the fish tank. None of the other girls know about Tegan's trick, I'm sure of it.

I draw in the margins of my workbook to occupy my thoughts – a make-believe creature with wings and flesh-eating claws. I'm back on the courts, except this time, when William tries to grab me, I rise up above him, my wings beating hard, and flames erupt from my mouth, swallowing him whole, until he is nothing but a jangly set of teeth on the gravel, and no one remains but me and Tegan, sharing that secret smile.

'Hey.'

Her face appears on the other side of my desk, interrupting my daydream. She's propped up on her knees, resting her chin on her hands, her eyes, bright and blue, meeting mine. She has a fleck of amber somewhere near her pupil.

'Did you see?' she says, excited, confidential. The other girls stare. They don't know why Tegan is talking to the new girl.

'See what?'

'Look who's missing.' Tegan nods towards the group of boys at the back, who are oddly quiet in the absence of their ringleader. 'He's still with the nurse. Apparently you gave him concussion.'

'William? Crap. He's going to kill me.'

'I heard he attacked his big sister with the garden shovel. She's not been right since. She can only smile with one side of her face.'

Tegan does an impression of a girl with a wonky smile, which makes me laugh, even though it's cruel.

'Why'd he do it?' I ask.

'He was sick of her beating him up. Makes sense, I guess. His dad probably beats him up, too. It runs in the family, you know,' she says sagely.

I look at the boys one more time, and they all look away.

'Hey, you're bleeding,' Tegan says.

She takes my hand and examines where the gravel has scraped away my skin. This gesture of kindness leaves me giddy. It was Tegan who made the boys turn on me and now Tegan is here by my side, my hand in hers.

'Are you being nice to me so I don't tell the others what you did?'

Without warning she spits on the graze. It's warm, and then it stings. I snap back my hand, the spit still in the scoop of my palm.

'It's antiseptic,' Tegan says, as if I shouldn't mind.

She has dirt beneath her nails, too.

'Sissy! Tegan!' Miss Storey calls, now standing by the blackboard waiting for class to begin.

After class, I gather my books quickly. I push through the boys who, on this occasion, step aside to let me pass. Tegan wants to talk to me. I want this, too. More than anything. The curious look that passed between us down on the courts, an understanding of sorts. But it's just this wanting that makes me walk out all the faster. It is too dangerous to want a thing there might be hope of having. Better to want faraway hopeless things. Like wings. And fathers.

BACK HOME THAT evening, Mou tells me that Mrs Greidinger gave me a detention and I should feel very lucky it wasn't worse. We're eating dinner around the white plastic picnic set we have in place of an ordinary dining table.

Mou is a collector. Records. Cake forks. Anything with birds on it. Trophies that other people have won and discarded, as if the glory of the prize can be transferred from them to her. She hates to see joy go to waste. Mostly she collects scraps of paper with some sentence or other in which she recognises a part of herself. She cuts the sentences from second-hand books and old magazines, and gathers these scraps in piles around the house. She tries to make paragraphs, or whole passages, and maybe one day a book you can read from start to finish. She calls it poetry collage, a poetry of chance. 'Like life itself,' she says.

When we moved here, there were so many boxes of records and trophies, and so many bird teapots and ornaments, that there was no room for things like beds and desks and kitchen tables. Those things are replaceable, she said. She bought everything we needed from the Royal Society for the Protection of Birds charity shop in town, where she volunteers a few days during the week while she's looking for a real job.

Now our home is full of other people's things, the curtains

carrying the dust of other people's bodies, and the cutlery the memories of other people's dinnertime fights. I think of this every time we eat on the white plastic picnic set. Mou says it's like eating *al fresco*, even in our dull oatmeal kitchen, beneath a bulb as bright as the dentist's light and just as cruel. Mou hates the light so much she's collecting lamps now, too.

Mou says the school gave me the benefit of the doubt because I'm the new girl, which, she explains, means they're choosing to believe something good about me instead of something bad, even though they think the bad thing is just as likely.

'Can't both things be true?' I ask.

'That's not the point,' Mou says.

'What is the point?'

Mou sighs like she does when she feels she ought to tell me off but she isn't sure why. Mou isn't like the other mothers even though she tries. She's young and pretty for a start. We look nothing alike. Her skin is white and pale while mine is muddy olive; and her mouth is bunched up in a closed rose-bud, while mine is a flat line. Mou is petite, and I'm almost as tall as her already. 'You have your father's height,' she once said, and I looked away, embarrassed. There's a postcard on my mantelpiece of the village where he was born, which he sent one Christmas with a note calling me '*koukla*', which means everything to me and nothing at all. The houses are as white as temples, clustered on a rock amid the blinding blue sea. Mou glances at it every time she passes, like it carries hurt I couldn't possibly understand.

Mostly Mou and I are a team, just us, and that makes it special. She can place her hand on my chest and know what I'm feeling. But sometimes Mou cries at the kitchen table late at night, saying, 'I don't know how to do this.' She says it's because she ran away with Koko at seventeen years old and never finished all the growing up she was meant to do. Once she stayed in bed for what felt like weeks. She slept and she slept and she wouldn't get up. Or she lay on her back with her eyes open, the curtains drawn, not speaking. I climbed into bed and tugged at her arm, but it didn't make a difference. I sat on the floor and bawled, and she still didn't move. She wasn't my mother any longer. She was a stranger. The un-mother I blamed for everything my own mother would never do. Eventually the school called because my clothes were dirty and I never had money for lunch. We moved house again shortly after that.

Now each time she gets up late or goes to bed before sunset, I'm frightened it's happening again, and it's my job to make sure it doesn't. It's a sickness, Mou said later, when she was trying to explain, and it's secret. Being a sickness meant it wasn't her fault, and being secret meant no one could know.

'The point is,' Mou picks up again, 'Mrs Greidinger is an idiot. Whatever the reason you felt the need to thwack that boy in the head, Sissy *mou*, I just hope he learned his lesson.'

I smile. At moments like these I'm glad she isn't like other mothers.

I didn't tell her why we were down on the courts, because how do you put into words what we were doing down there? There's a place inside Tegan where she hides a stone and we all want to know about it? This is the second thing I've kept from Mou this week.

THAT NIGHT I cast a spell. I can hear the quiet rumble of Mou's medicated snore in her bedroom next door. Some nights she takes a pill to sleep. She says it's like pressing reset on her mind. Like when an appliance doesn't work, turning it off and on again can fix it. In the morning what's broken will be mended. The pills are round and bright blue. They're all past their sell-by date and Mou rations them because she doesn't want to go to the doctor to ask for more.

In my own bed, I pluck a single hair from my head. I hold it while looking to the top right-hand corner of my brain to concentrate. This is where the memory of my father lives and first forgotten Eve. I make a wish and then I tie the hair in a knot to seal it. I wish for Tegan to be my one friend. I tie a second knot. I focus on it deeply, because half the success of a spell is believing in it. If Tegan will be my one friend, I promise I'll ask for nothing further. A third. If Tegan will be my one friend, I'll want nothing more. I place the hair beneath my pillow, knotted with a wish.

DETENTION

The story of the stone-throwing new girl spreads through school. It changes with each telling. In one version, I was standing when I threw a stone, unprovoked, with eagle-eye accuracy. In the other, I bashed William on the head while we scrambled around on the ground in response to a punch so hard in the ribs that Lydia swore she saw my bruises in the changing room before PE. Neither version is accurate, but I remain silent. Tegan, on the other hand, fuels both with equal vigour, unbothered by the truth. She hasn't said another word to me. In all the stories, I may as well be someone else. Sometimes, though, I feel her watching – a peculiar tingling down my spine – but when I turn, she's looking away, so I can't be certain.

William lurches at me in the corridor to prove he's not afraid. 'Sheep!' he shouts.

'Troll!' I shout back, raising my fist as if to hit him. I think of his sister and the shovel, afraid of his revenge. There are ways I might hurt him in return.

I've only hurt someone on purpose twice before. I stabbed a sharpened pencil into a boy's palm. He watched me sharpen the pencil and then he held out his hand and said, 'I dare you to stab me.' He didn't think I was capable, so I did it. But the teacher didn't believe me. The pencil lead was lodged so deep in his palm the doctors couldn't get it out. For a lifetime, that boy will tell the story of how a girl called Sissy Savos stabbed him in the palm with a pencil. I doubt he'll tell the part where he asked me to. I don't talk about the other time. Mou asked me not to.

After school, my detention requires me to spend an hour in the library helping with the books. This isn't punishment. All our books at home have sentences or whole pages missing where Mou has found a passage she likes for her box of scraps. These books are almost entirely whole, which make them unlike real stories that always have gaps in them.

Normally I'd take the bus home, but with detention I finish an hour later, so Mou has to collect me. I wait for her on the brick wall by the side of school, kicking my legs, imagining the type of tail I'd like. Soft and striped, like a lemur's, so it curls up behind me, or something scaled and strong with short fins for propelling me through water? When I was small, Mou took me to see *The Little Mermaid*. At the end of the movie, the lights came up and Mou was sobbing into her popcorn. 'But it's a happy ending, Mou,' I said, and she just shook her head. Later, she read me the real story, and I understood why she was crying. The movie got it all wrong. I read it again and again until I knew it by heart. The little mermaid traded her voice and her tail for the prince – that much was true. But in the real story she gives up everything and gets nothing in return. In the real story, she's turned to foam on top of the sea because the man she loved didn't love her in time. I've never even kissed a boy. If I'm not loved in time, will I become foam on top of the sea? I wouldn't give up my tail in the first place.

The light is fading and still no sign of Mou. I imagine her appearing around the corner, her forgive-me smile on her face, like it's okay to forget your daughter. Like it's happened just once. I feel a wave of anger then. She appears with her forgive-me smile, except I'm not there. I've gone missing. I'm dead.

'Hey there,' a voice calls.

A blue car has pulled up and a woman is getting out. She's magazine pretty, glossy and impenetrable. She's wearing a black tube dress with a short denim jacket, and heels so high she's standing on her tippy-toes, like a ballerina.

'What's your name, sugar?' she asks, and I see she's still part-girl.

'Sissy,' I say.

'Hi, Sissy, I'm Haley.' She looks up at the darkening sky with a scowl. 'Does your mum know you're out here by yourself?'

'She's held up at work,' I lie. Another part of my job is to protect Mou from what other people think. I know Mou shouldn't forget me. 'She called the school to tell them.'

Tegan appears from the side entrance and takes us in as she approaches.

'Hey, missy,' Haley says, and she kisses Tegan's cheek.

'Why you still here?' Tegan says to me.

'Detention,' I say, with a pointed look to remind her of the role she'd played in it.

She breaks into a smile – not remotely chastised. 'Oh, yeah.'

Haley opens the car door. 'Hop in. I'll give you a lift home.'

Tegan is in the front seat already, and I want very much to go with them, so I climb into the back, and just like that we're off.

From where I'm sitting, I can see the sides of their faces and I realise then they're sisters.

'How did you do in the exercises we worked on?' Haley asks Tegan, as we drive. 'Did it help?'

Tegan nods, and shoots a shy glance at me. She has catch-up classes. Now I know two of her secrets.

WE PULL UP outside a small row of shops on the edge of town. Haley has to grab some things and when she's done she'll give me a lift home. I follow them into a door next to Chicken Cottage. The smell of fried chicken follows us up the stairwell to the first-floor flat, making me both nauseous and hungry.

Inside, furniture is crowded together and strung with clothes, hung out to dry. The radiators are covered with brightly coloured lace thongs. High heels are stacked in a wine rack. A man is playing a video game on the TV. Gunshots fill the room alongside the percussive sound of his thumbs against the controller. Tegan flops down on the sofa.

'Hey, squirt,' the man says, except he's not really a man yet. He's part-man, part-boy, like Haley is part-woman, part-girl. His hair is sculpted in neat spikes stiffened by gel and there's the faintest layer of fuzz on his chin. His eyebrow is pierced and the skin is red raw around the metal.

'Don't call me that, dickhead,' Tegan says, reaching out a foot to shove him. 'Do we have to watch you play? Yawn much.'

Haley hands me the phone to call my mother. I call the bird shop, but they say Mou wasn't in today, which I already knew. And then I call the house, though she won't answer. Mou doesn't like to answer the phone unless she knows who's ringing.

'This is Peter,' Tegan says, as I take the seat beside her on

31

the sofa. On the TV, the barrel of Peter's gun kills everything it passes. Bodies hit the ground and then magically disappear. 'You can ignore him,' she says. 'He just hangs around, like he owns the place.'

Peter stands and throws the controller down on his chair. 'All yours, squirt. Enjoy your playdate.'

As he walks away he ruffles Tegan's hair. She grabs his hand and launches forward to bite it. Peter stumbles onto the sofa, so I have to lean away not to be embroiled in their tussling. There's a pained look on her face, and I think to fight him off, but then I see he's tickling her and the pained look is laughter. She releases the grip of her teeth and falls away from him into my lap. Peter wipes his hand on his shirt and examines the neat imprint of her bite. 'Trouble,' he says, looking over his shoulder as he walks away.

He calls to Haley before opening her bedroom door, 'You'd better be topless in there,' and then walks in.

Tegan composes herself, throwing her hair over her shoulder, just like her big sister. She switches the TV to a different channel and an afternoon soap opera comes on.

'Is Peter your brother?' I ask, confused. I don't have brothers and I don't know any boys outside school.

'Ew, no way. He's Haley's best friend. They used to go to school together before she dropped out. I'm going to leave home as soon as I'm sixteen, like Haley did. Maybe she'll be living with Ryan already – he's her boyfriend – but if not, we'll be official roommates, not just sisters. Wouldn't that be cool?'

Yes, that would be cool. I learn that since Haley turned eighteen last month, their mum lets Tegan stay over sometimes during the school week. Their parents live on a cow farm in the countryside and it saves Tegan hours on the bus travelling back and forth and the money for the bus fare. It's a trial run, Tegan tells me.

'Mum might change her mind 'cause she's a bitch, not because she actually wants me there.'

'Wouldn't she be upset if you left for good?'

'Who cares? It doesn't matter once you're sixteen. You can do whatever you want. It's the law. You can move out. You can get married. You can drink alcohol. You can have sex. All the good things happen at sixteen. I can't wait.'

Tegan is twelve already, a year older than the rest of us. She was kept down a few years ago. No one knows why and they won't ask her. She has that way about her. Like you mustn't ask what she might not want to reveal.

She looks at me then, probing.

'What is it?' I say, embarrassed under her gaze.

'Why do you always hang out by yourself? That's why everyone thinks you're weird.'

I shrug. 'Maybe I am weird.'

I examine a hole in my tights that frames a neat circle of flesh beneath. When I look up, she's smiling. Sometimes, when she smiles, a single tooth latches on to her bottom lip. I haven't noticed this before. Later I'll learn it's called a snaggletooth, which is also the name of a deep-sea fish that uses its bioluminescence to lure its prey. The TV hums in the background and the sound of Peter and Haley's conversation fades. Tegan and I look at one another, that same strange something between us. She reaches for my face and, instinctively, I pull away. I'm frightened, unready for whatever this is.

'You're scared!' she says, delighted.

'Am not.'

'Don't be scared. Last time I saw you scared you broke William's head open. I like my head, thank you very much.'

I laugh then, trying to relax. This is what I wanted, I tell myself.

'It was pretty cool, right?' I say, proud of the violence that bonded us, but Tegan isn't listening. She's playing with my hair, as if it's her own, as if I belong to her already. I don't understand what's happening, but we've slipped into another place, the place we occupied for a moment down on the court, a place we'll come to share in which the outside world no longer matters. A place that is wholly ours when nothing else is. She pulls my hair this way and that, and we're both smiling, laughing a little, and I think, Is this it? Is this what it is to be friends? She kneels up beside me the better to reach my head, and we're so close, closer than we've ever been. She leans back occasionally to examine her work, pleased or displeased with what she's done.

'Ow,' I say, unused to having my hair styled. Mou has never cared how I look.

'Hold still,' she says, now fully absorbed.

She tugs on my roots as she secures my hair with a band from her wrist. She sits down beside me. Her eyes trace my face.

'See? You could be pretty if you wore your hair differently. It suits you up like that.'

I frown, pulling the band from my hair to let it fall down. I give the band back to Tegan, who plays with it for a moment, and I think it's done. We won't be friends. This was a test of my compliance and I failed it.

'You're right,' she says, taking my hand in hers. 'It looks better the way you do it.'

*

34

IN THE CAR, Tegan sits in the back this time. I try to adjust to this new reality, in which Tegan chooses to sit next to me.

There's a bag of clothes on the seat between us.

'Hand-me-downs,' Tegan says, by way of explanation. 'From Haley.'

Without siblings, I've never had a hand-me-down. I examine a baby blue cami on the top of the pile.

'Have it,' she says. 'It would look nice on you.'

'Are you sure?'

Tegan hands it to me. 'Why not? You like it?'

I fold the top in my lap, my very first hand-me-down. I look out of the window to hide my pleasure. We pass an old burned-out factory where older kids hang out drinking, the boys' jeans low on their hips and the girls with purple hair and piercings. The tinny din of a tape deck blasts out music. Tegan eyes them keenly until they pass. We drive through the centre of town, over the bridge, and out to where Mou and I live, in a small enclave of houses near the railway.

As we pull up, Tegan turns to me. 'Come over again tomorrow, yeah?'

Just then, Mou runs out of our front door, panicking. I jump out of the car, not wanting Haley to realise my lie.

'Mou!' I say.

She looks up, confused for a moment about how I've materialised from nowhere. Then Haley and Tegan are out of the car too, standing, looking just like each other with their arms crossed, sharing a sisterly scowl.

Mou tugs at her hair. 'Sissy, what are you doing here? I was just on my—'

Haley steps forward to explain, but I want to save Mou from her disapproval. 'Mou, I told them you were stuck at work. I said you called the school and told them so.'

35

Mou looks at me and I can't bear it. Of all the looks my mother gives, this is the most painfully aware.

'Oh, good, all right then, I was ...' Mou starts as if to ramble.

'Thank you very much for the lift,' I say to Haley, wanting this interaction to end.

There are some introductions, hellos and goodbyes, but my mind is humming, until they're back in the car and it's over.

'I'm sorry, Sissy,' Mou says, as we watch them drive away.

'It's okay.'

'It's not okay. You shouldn't have to lie for me. I don't know how I lost track—'

'Mum!' I say, because calling her that is the best way to get her attention. 'Please, don't.' I turn away and let myself into the house.

IN THE MIDDLE of the night, I wake up to find Mou on the edge of my bed, her eyes glistening.

'What's wrong?' I say, still half asleep.

'It's going to be better, okay? I promise I'm going to do better here. I'm going to find a real job and we're going to get back on our feet and make a proper home here. We have a garden, don't we? I always said we'd have a house with a garden, so that's one thing, and ...'

'Mou!'

'Yes?'

'I'm asleep.'

'Yes, of course, you are. I love you – you know that, don't you? You're all that I have. Just us.'

I nod. 'I love you, too.'

I turn on my side, my back to her, and close my eyes. I'm

awake now, but I want her to go away. If I don't see her like this then maybe it doesn't count. She sits for a few moments longer. Then her weight lifts from the bed, and she's gone, evaporated into thin air.

THE MUSIC BOX

The following morning, Mou walks me to the bus stop at the end of our road. There's a chippie, a post office, a pub and a corner shop, which I avoid because the shopkeeper's teenage son stares at me whenever I go inside. I'm unused to this kind of staring and unsure what I did to bring it on.

Further up the street is Señoritas with its lipstick-pink sign. The first time we walked past, I asked Mou what happens inside. 'It's a massage parlour,' Mou said, then thought better of it. 'It's a massage parlour where men pay women for sex.'

'How do you know?' I asked.

Mou had to think about this. 'Real massage parlours don't blacken their windows.'

I always slow my step when we pass now, hoping for a glimpse behind the closed door. I create imaginary lives for the women I've seen come and go. They're called Xanadu and Cheetara and they're not mothers or daughters or like any women I know. They're candy-pink women. Barbie dolls, grown-up and working for a living. Just walking past Señoritas gives me a thrill.

The bus kids have avoided me since the stone incident, so

I sit on my own. It smells of cigarettes smoked long ago and the Impulse body mist that all of the girls wear. Some of them have bus boyfriends, boys from the other school up the road, like Hannah, who goes out with Marlon, who's thirteen. They sit together every day, and get off the bus at the same time. She says he walks her home and they kiss in her front room while her mum is busy making tea, but none of the other girls have seen this, so they haven't decided if it's true.

The bus kids have their own rules. They scream and shout and tease Mr Bens, the bus driver. 'What's for dinner, Mr Bens?' they heckle. 'All of the pies?' He still plays the local pop radio station to please them, singing along to the Spice Girls and Robbie Williams under his breath, and this act of appeasement makes me mad. On the radio today, they're talking about a teenage girl who's gone missing in a neighbouring town. They keep interrupting the music to give us the latest report, but none of the kids pay attention. 'The police are appealing for help from the public . . . '

I don't pay attention either. Today I'm not thinking about the bus gossip that passes between the seats. I'm thinking about after school when I'll go home again with Tegan.

ALL DAY I feel nervous. Alert. As if something grand is about to happen. Tegan and I don't talk or even look at one another, but I feel that same electric pull. We are enmeshed in something strange and secret. There is a sense of expectancy I can't explain.

We meet at the same spot we did before. Most of the other kids take the bus or get picked up at the main gates by parents, but Tegan waits around the side each day for her sister.

'All right,' she says, without looking at me.

'All right,' I say back, deflated by her apparent disinterest. Haley's car pulls up. Tegan gets into the front and me into the back. I'm surprised to see Peter at the steering wheel. I'm not meant to get into cars with strange men. It's one of the few rules Mou has. But when do men go from strangers to friends?

'Where's Hayz?' Tegan asks, unfazed.

'On the phone. I said I'd come and get you.'

Tegan fiddles with the tape deck. From where I'm sitting, I see there's a little pus now around Peter's piercing. He catches my eye in the mirror and I look away.

'What sort of name is Sissy, then?' he says. I'm flummoxed, because he knows who I am.

'My parents named me after Sissy Spacek.' Mou and Koko went to see *Carrie* for their first date. 'She's an American actress.'

Peter smiles at me. Two dimples appear in his cheeks. 'She was the psycho in that Stephen King movie, right?'

I nod. I don't tell him I haven't seen it. 'She has telekinetic powers.' I like to say the word out loud. I like to imagine I have telekinetic powers, too.

'Is that what you call it?'

Tegan presses play and a woman starts singing sexily. Peter turns it off almost immediately.

'Oi!' Tegan presses play again.

'I'm not listening to that crap. Put something else on.' Peter stops the tape and throws it on the floor at her feet. Tegan slaps at him, which Peter deflects with his arm. 'Hey, not while I'm driving.'

'I thought you said I look cute when I'm angry.'

'Stop!' Peter gives her a look I can't see.

'Boring,' she says, and Peter breaks into a reluctant smile, his dimples deepening.

Tegan puts another tape on, which Peter likes better, and he drums along on the steering wheel.

She turns around from the front seat, looking directly at me for the first time all day and her sudden focus is disorientating. I'll get used to this later, how she can switch in a moment and make you feel like you suddenly exist. How she can be one person and then another in the time it takes to blink.

'I'm going to be a singer or an actress when I leave school,' she says. 'Or maybe before, because once I live with Haley properly, I'll have to get a job so I can help out with rent. How about you?'

'I've not really thought about it,' I say, which is a lie. I want to be an archaeologist, like the men I read about in *National Geographic* whose job it is to dig up goddesses from the ground, but I also know I'm meant to want to be a vet, a pop star or maybe a nurse, so I don't say anything.

Tegan turns back to the front.

'You happy with the music back there?' Peter says, and I realise he means me. I nod eagerly, pleased to be included.

A melody comes in and Tegan starts to sing. She doesn't sound like herself when she sings. She sounds suddenly vulnerable. Peter joins in with gusto, and they exchange a look. Together they sing, until he breaks into a wild falsetto and Tegan rewards him with a giggle.

HALEY IS ON the phone when we get to her flat. Peter disappears into her room, and greets another man, or part-man, or still boy. I don't know. This other man, I'm told, is Haley's boyfriend, Ryan, but he never leaves her room, and I get the impression Haley keeps him apart.

Tegan and I sit side by side on the sofa like last time. She turns on the TV, and flicks through the channels, unable to settle on what to watch. Now we're here, I can't think of a single thing to say. Haley paces back and forth from the bedroom to the kitchen gathering belongings and pulling hard on a Camel Light. Her body shifts in a black dress in ways I can only hope mine might one day. Haley is talking about a girl called Angelina, and what Angelina did last night, which no one must know. It's impossible to watch the television, when she's moving back and forth like this, saying, 'I haven't told a soul,' but I hear her tell at least two. 'He'll flip if he finds out. What was she thinking, going home with Mr Hands-Down-His-Pants-Dick-For-Brains?' And then, an afterthought, 'She's worth so much more.'

Tegan plucks a cigarette from a packet on the coffee-table, and when her sister is out of sight, she paces, pretending to chain-smoke anxiously, talking on a finger phone, with such an uncanny talent for mimicry, I have to cover my face to stifle my laughter. 'You won't believe what Angie's done, you won't fucking believe it,' she says. Haley reappears and Tegan jumps back down beside me. We giggle into each other's shoulders.

'What are you up to?' Haley says, but already she's back on the phone.

Things feel easier now we've laughed. Tegan makes us tea and gets us each a KitKat from the cupboard. We never have KitKats in the cupboard at home. She shows me how to suck my tea through the KitKat like it's a straw, leaving our fingers and faces chocolaty.

'What's the worst thing you've ever done?' Tegan asks, wiping her hands on her school skirt.

I shrug. 'I don't think I've done my worst thing yet.'

'Was it hitting William?'

'No! That was self-defence.'

Tegan laughs. 'Why didn't you just do it?'

'Do what?'

'With the stone, like I did. That would have really shut his fat gob.'

I don't want to tell her I don't know how. Not fully. Like how I know the way home but I couldn't point it out on a map.

'Harder to hit him in the head that way,' I say instead, and Tegan laughs. 'What's the worst thing you've ever done, then?'

'I can't tell you mine,' she says, serious now.

Here she can be quiet and strange, but perhaps at school she's quiet and strange, also, and it's everyone else who makes noise around her. Only her laugh is loud.

'How about this? If you tell me a secret of yours, I'll tell you a secret of mine,' Tegan suggests. 'It doesn't have to be the worst thing you've done. It can be anything, even something stupid, just something you've never told anyone else.'

We agree to write it down so it's a more solemn exchange, more formal, and she fetches us a pen and paper.

I tell her about the pet gerbil at my old school, which I accidentally decapitated in the hinge of the hutch when it tried to escape. I felt so bad. I placed the gerbil and its head back inside and told no one. They had an investigation at school, and I didn't confess. Tegan was the first person I ever told that it was me who killed the gerbil. I wrote on my piece of paper: *I killed the class pet.*

'Isn't it a sign you're an actual psycho?' she says. 'That's what psychos do, they kill their pets first.'

I shrug. 'It wouldn't surprise me.'

I go to open her piece of paper and she stops me, holding her hands over my own. 'No,' she says. 'I'll tell you one day, but not yet. Once we're better friends. I think we'll be better friends, don't you?'

There were only a few words on her piece of paper and I'm reluctant to give them up.

'But you said—'

'Please.'

I nod. I understand.

'You're good at keeping secrets, I can tell. I bet you have tons of secrets. I feel like I could tell you all of mine already and you'd never tell a soul.'

'You can tell me anything. I'd never tell. I promise.'

I mean it more than I've ever meant anything before and Tegan takes this with the earnestness in which it was offered.

'I have an idea,' she says. 'Come with me.'

Tegan drags me into her bedroom. There is a vanity table against one wall with a three-sided mirror. A few perfume bottles and lipsticks are displayed in a semi-circle like offerings at an altar, half-empty Haley hand-me-downs.

'I'll hide it in here.' She indicates a small music box. She unclasps the box and a ballerina pops up, turning in circles to a song. She hides the note inside the mechanism. 'When I'm ready, I'll give it to you to read.'

She looks at me, willing me to agree, and I nod, excited by the promise of a future friendship in which she'll share her secrets with me. She closes the lid to the box and smiles.

With that done, the excitement of the pact still with us, we stand around, unsure what to do next. Tegan plays with the items at her vanity table, examining each one in turn. She wants me to look and be impressed by her tokens of adulthood. There's a poster of a topless man on the wall, his thumb hooked through the loop of his Levi's jeans, pulling them down to show us his white pants.

'He's lush, right?' Tegan nods at the man. The Levi's man nods back, making me uncomfortable.

I sit on the edge of her bed, feeling suddenly claustrophobic. The promise in the music box is enough for one day, I think.

'I should probably go home soon.' I'm pre-empting my exit. 'My mum will want me back for dinner,' I say, which is a lie.

'Don't go yet! How long do we have?' Tegan asks, as if there's something she's been wanting to do all this time. She doesn't wait for an answer. 'Come and look!' Tegan beckons me to the vanity table.

Standing beside her, I follow her gaze to our reflection in the mirror, our faces repeated in triplicate around us. To get our image in together we must stand close, our sides pressed up against one another. I am a little taller than Tegan, but it never appears that way. I have 'bird bones', my mother says, meaning my bones are as delicate as a bird's, not that one day I will have wings, as I had hoped when I was small.

I look at my face first. My eyes are murky grey, like an overcast day, and my skin seems insipid next to the pink of Tegan's cheeks. Tegan seems brighter than me in every way, her hair blonde rather than my ashy brown, and her eyes sky blue and always searching. Her edges are more defined.

'We're not so different, are we?' Tegan says, and I look again.

The path of our eyes loops around each other's face. And through her eyes, it becomes true. We both have long noses, unlike the other girls with their neat buttons, and our hair hangs straight down the sides of our face. I catch my reflection in Tegan's eyes, and for a moment I am lost in the infinite repetition of one another, looking back on ourselves from the future, the rest of the world evaporating to insignificance and time flattening to a mere second from the creation of the universe to its eventual demise, and through it all we're shining. Her fingers entwine with mine, and I know she sees it, too. My eyes focus again on her face, which is smiling.

'You saw?' she says.

I saw.

'I WANT TO show you something.' Tegan rummages beneath her bed for a few moments and pulls out a photo album. She takes a seat beside me on the bed, and we shuffle backwards until our backs are propped against the wall. We share the weight of the album between our laps. Tegan turns the pages, giving me nuggets of information about each photo. They are the usual family photos, Christmases and birthdays and holidays by the sea, but there are so many more in her family than in mine.

'Is that you?' A blonde little girl carries a baby with a fat fuzz of white hair.

'No, that's Haley. She carried me everywhere.'

A younger, blonder Haley hugs the baby Tegan tight to her chest, a scowl on her face and a look like she'll never let go. A gaggle of boys is visible in the background, one face grinning and disfigured by the photo's crop.

'And them?'

'My brothers.' Tegan turns the page. 'That's Mum and Dad when they were young.'

Tegan's parents are wrapped together in a tartan blanket. They are smiling like they have been caught in a private moment. Her dad nuzzles his head on her mother's chest, and her mother's face is turned upwards towards the camera. I wish I had a photo of Mou and Koko rolled up in a picnic blanket like this, happy as a sausage roll. 'Are they in love?' I ask.

'Don't know. They used to fight all the time. I was hoping they'd divorce and then we could leave the farm and live somewhere less shit, but that was a while ago.' She paused. 'What about your parents?'

I shake my head. 'They're separated. I don't see my dad.'

'Do you miss him?'

I think of the Dad-shaped figure that populates my most precious daydreams. The height of him beside me and the faint smell of turpentine he used to clean his hands or the cedar oil he ran through his hair. When I look up, there's a shock of black curls and the sensation he's smiling, but his face is out of reach.

'I didn't know him much. But I'd like a dad around, if only to make my mum happier.'

'Your mum's so pretty,' Tegan says, as if that's a salve. 'Why's she unhappy?'

'She's not,' I say, defensive now. Mou's sadness is my secret to keep. 'It's tough being a single mum,' I say, which is something Mou tells me on those mornings she doesn't have enough money for my lunch or when she doesn't have the energy to get out of bed. I'm not ready to tell Tegan these things, not yet.

Tegan nods solemnly. I look down at the photo album, wanting her to continue with her life, not mine.

'Who's that?' I point at a Staffordshire bull terrier. He's standing to attention, his broad shoulders proud and his tongue lolling to one side beyond his control. A dark-haired boy's arm is wrapped lovingly around him.

47

'That's Harvey.'

'I wish we had a dog.'

'He's dead,' Tegan says.

'Oh. Sorry.'

'It's okay.'

Another photo: three boys standing in a row wearing football shirts, different versions of each other, of themselves.

'Your brothers? There's so many of them. What are they called?'

'That's Kevin,' Tegan says, pointing at the youngest. 'He's a dick. And Tom. Who's probably a dick, but he's always in his room, so who cares?'

'And him?'

'That's Andy. The eldest.'

Tegan's arm tenses beside me as if the thousands of hairs we share between us just bristled. She stops turning the pages. I feel a rush of panic, because I already know what's coming next and I don't want to hear it. 'Andy's dead, too,' Tegan says. 'I only know three people who've died. My grandpa Jack, Harvey, our dog, and my brother Andy. I knew them all since I was born and they all died the same year, when I was nine and Haley was fifteen.'

'Did they die together?' I ask, and immediately regret my curiosity. It feels dirty and unfeeling.

'No, Grandpa first, on New Year's Day. And then it was Andy who killed the dog, before he went off.'

'Why?'

'It was his dog really, but still. He was part of the family. He killed him for nothing either, just some stupid thing. He took him out to the yard, and hit him over the head with the cricket bat, but he kept missing, 'cause Harvey wouldn't keep still. Haley didn't want me to see and covered my eyes, but I

48

could hear, all the same. When Andy was done, he left him there, bleeding, and went to his car and drove away. Haley wanted to dig a grave, but the ground was too cold, it was so hard. So we left him out in the woods for Dad to find.'

I don't want to hear any more.

'It wasn't Andy's fault,' Tegan adds. 'He wasn't himself when he did it.'

'I'm sorry,' I say, because I don't know what else to say to a story like that.

Tegan stares blankly back at me, like everything she just said never happened. Like we were sitting here the way we were a minute before.

'No matter,' she says, looking away. 'Just a stupid dog.'

I want to ask, Why me? Why was I chosen for her story? But I don't. I want more to go home.

'It's dark outside,' I say. I want to be anywhere but in this room.

'Yes, it is,' Tegan replies, her brightness depleted.

'I need to get back,' I lie. I feel guilty, like she opened a door and invited me in, and instead I turned away. She closes the photo album.

Next time, I think.

'Next time,' she says, as if she can hear my thoughts.

HALEY HAS TRANSFORMED herself into a night creature, her eyes so dark around the edges she's staring out from an abyss. She offers to drop me home on her way to work. She wheels a small suitcase out of her room, where I catch a glimpse of her boyfriend Ryan lying on the bed behind her. He is a real grown man, not even part-boy any more.

When we leave, Tegan is back on the sofa with Peter.

49

Her knees are pulled into her chest as she watches him play Nintendo. He's killing everything in sight.

'Look after each other!' Haley says.

As we walk out of the door, Tegan doesn't say goodbye. She doesn't even look up when I go.

THE CHANGING ROOM

Mou is up before me. This is a bad sign. It's my job to bring her a cup of Nescafé in bed – black, two sugars, no chatting until she's finished – and wake her up. But when I come down for school in the morning, she's at the kitchen counter, buttering slices of bread with gusto, shopping bags overflowing around her. The shopping bags mean she isn't sleeping. They mean she went to the supermarket some time between me going to bed last night and getting up again.

'Sissy *mou!*' she says, too brightly, looking up at me in my school uniform. 'Get out of those stuffy clothes and put something fun on. We're going to the beach.'

'What about school?'

I feel foolish about my exit from Tegan's last night, about the atmosphere I sensed in the room, which in the light of day feels imaginary. There was nothing to be afraid about. Nothing to cause me to balk. Today, I want to show her that I can be her friend. But Mou has other ideas.

'Look!' She gestures out of the window with the butter knife, before returning to her sandwich-making. 'It's beautiful outside! Soon it'll be cold and dark and the days will be short and miserable. I called you in sick.' She registers the look of shock on my face. 'What? I want to spend some time with my beautiful daughter. Is that a crime? You wouldn't make me go to the beach by myself, would you?'

MOU STILL DRIVES the same red Vauxhall Nova from the 'car days', as she calls them. They came before London but after we left Aberdeen. They were never just days, but weeks, or maybe even whole months, when we did our living and eating and sleeping in our red Vauxhall Nova, the floor littered with pages dislodged from the *A–Z*. Mou said the sun would guide us. It was an adventure. We were exploring. Searching for a new home across the country. Eight limbs, four wheels and a car radio. The rest of it doesn't matter, Mou said, and it was true. Just us.

During the car days we would celebrate each milestone by pulling over and blasting the Clash or the Damned out of the windows, and dancing around the car shout-singing along to Mou's favourite bands, who all sound angry and happy at the same time.

By the time we reach the beach at Weston-super-Mare, the morning sun has disappeared, leaving the day dull and unassuming. A few dog-walkers cut solitary figures across the sand. Fat gulls gather around the beach debris, picking from the collection of nets knotted with driftwood and listless seaweed. It's low tide, leaving great swathes of grey as far as I can see. It's the opposite of the postcard on my mantelpiece, a place I've only visited in my dreams.

Mou and I sit on a wall and eat our sandwiches, looking out across the mudflats and the murky water of the Bristol Channel. A pair of bored donkeys flick their tails and the

Ferris wheel stands motionless in the distance. This sort of bleakness isn't good for Mou.

'Grandma Jean took me here when I was a girl,' Mou says. 'We came out for the weekend from London. There was a place where you could rent pedalos, and we took a boat out, my sister and me pedalling, and Mummy sat between us. She was shrieking the whole time, thinking we were going to capsize, which made us laugh our heads off, and that made Mummy shriek even more, shouting, "Watch where you're going!" as if there was anything to hit. I'm sure she was doing it just to make us laugh. That was before things got bad with me.'

Mou's focus is far out to sea. A school of sailing dinghies circles in the distance, tiny white flags waving.

'I told your dad that story back at the beginning, when we were first in love. One day Koko surprised me, driving us here, and we took out a pedalo, which was where he proposed. He nearly fell off the boat trying to get down on one knee,' she says, smiling. 'He didn't have a ring. I think it just occurred to him there and then. He wasn't a planner really, your dad. Neither of us. We were thrilled and went round telling anyone who would listen that we were going to get married, running up and down the pier. We were so young – I can't have been sixteen yet and Koko just nineteen – people probably gave us funny looks. He drew a ring on my finger using a marker pen from the chippie. I kept calling him my fiancé. Each time I said it, we'd start laughing again, like it was the best joke.'

Mou pauses. I'm fearful if I say anything I'll break the spell and she'll stop talking. These are precious stories I'll magpie away and bring out later to examine in more detail.

'I thought you weren't married?' I prompt.

Mou looks at me, as if she's forgotten I'm even sitting beside her.

'No, we weren't. It never happened, did it? We just stayed fiancés or whatever you want to call us, and then one day, we started saying we were married because people asked us fewer questions that way. When Koko first went out to the rigs, he said it was because he wanted to make enough money for us to have a proper wedding, white dress and all that malarkey. Bloody hell, to think of that now. And then, of course, he was going to buy us a real house with a front door and a little garden where you could play, not just those God-awful towers we were in up north, where each time you played on that swing-set, I was scared you'd get a needle through your foot or something. I doubt you remember that place.'

'Blue doors?'

'Yes, that's right.'

'It was high up. There was a path around the outside and a fence to stop you falling. I used to dangle my legs over, looking at the tiny people below.'

'You'd sit out there like that for hours when Koko and I were fighting. I'm sorry you remember.'

I made friends with each of the families who lived behind those blue doors. My favourite was Mrs Adebayo in 36E next door. She and her husband came from a faraway city with a name I couldn't pronounce. They had a daughter, but she was taken from them. I never knew who took her or why. Or if they were the same people Mou was frightened might take me. Mrs Adebayo and her husband fought late at night in a language I didn't understand, and afterwards I would hear Mrs Adebayo weeping through the walls, which needed no translation. Each morning she emerged swathed in bright yellow cloth sculpted carefully over her head, and together we looked down on the world below. And then one day, when I wasn't there to sit with her, Mrs Adebayo jumped right over the edge. I imagined the yellow cloth of her headscarf coming loose as she fell, circling in the air above her body, like the brightness of her spirit departing. Mou said some people are so unhappy it makes them sick, and death is the only cure they can imagine.

'It's okay,' I say to Mou, throwing a crust of my sandwich for the birds. 'I'm glad I remember.'

Mou puts her arm around my shoulders. She gives me such a tight squeeze that I drop the rest of my sandwich and a gull swoops down to grab it, flapping in our faces. It makes us both jump up and scream, then fall about laughing at our fright, a good belly laugh.

'Hey, Mou, can we find the pedalos?' I ask.

We go off hand in hand in search, but there are no pedalos, and Mou wonders if maybe it had been a different beach, it was all so long ago. In forgetting, she seems to lose herself, and stops skipping alongside me or gathering me up in the crook of her arm when the wind blasts cold sea air at us. It makes me mad. She took me out of school and away from Tegan just to drive me to this bleak strip of sand full of memories, and walk around silently staring, like a ghost displaced from its haunting grounds. I should be cheerful to please her, but I don't feel like it.

On the drive home, I imagine Koko and Mou's younger selves, skipping down the Grand Pier, smiling and simply happy. I like to imagine this time in my mother's life, when she was still Susie, a woman I never knew. I see my father circling her ring finger with a black pen. He's looking down at her and she up at him, like a scene in a film I might have watched – but then the gull swoops down and breaks it, and all I see in that black ring is her sadness, which stays with us all the way home.

THE NEXT DAY at school, I get to class before Tegan. It's good we had a day apart. Perhaps she felt foolish to have shared so much with me. Today I'll make it right. I could tell her about Mou and her sadness. I could tell her about Koko and the sea. That's all to come later. Everything will be different now, I'm sure of it.

These are my thoughts when Tegan walks into class. There is always a moment when the room adjusts to her presence, and in that moment, she takes her place at her desk in the middle, without even looking my way. She greets Clara and Hannah, and sets about gossiping, and then it hits me: she isn't going to say hello. She won't even acknowledge my existence.

I can't take my eyes off the three of them, giggling and twisting around one other, entangling their limbs like the plaits they tie in each other's hair. I bet Clara and Hannah don't know about Tegan's dead brother or Harvey, her dead dog. I bet they've not met Peter or even been to Haley's flat. Clara throws me a nasty glare and I avert my stare. My desires feel transparent, projected on the blackboard for all to see.

Miss Storey comes in and the class quietens. We learn about the last Russian tsar and his family, all of them murdered, and I imagine killing Tegan. I change into a snake and wrap my coils around her so tightly that I squeeze her to death. As I'm doing it, I say, 'Now, watch! This is the worst thing I've ever done.' Or, perhaps, I only *nearly* kill Tegan and then spare her, so she'll be forever in my debt. The scene has to be witnessed by a crowd. It's not about the act of killing, not really: it's about the reaction of horror and awe. To be seen as something more powerful than a girl.

IN PE I stand by the wall between one telling-off and the next. The teacher, Miss August, sounds like an engine starting when she shouts. She's scraped her hair back with a Minnie Mouse hair bobble a girl left behind in the lockers.

I hold a rail or a rope or stand in line for the springboard but never jump. The other kids leap about me like deer.

I am held back when the bell rings.

'You need to take part, if you want to fit in,' Miss August says, her Minnie Mouse bobble wobbling. 'Just be more like the other girls,' and then, smiling, 'Don't be a lemon!'

Of all the things I might be, I am not a lemon. I pull at the elastic of my too-small gym shorts and wait for it to be over.

In the damp, chlorinated stuffiness of the girls' changing rooms, a chemical fog lingers around the showers, clogged with hair. Tegan, Clara and Hannah always occupy the same spot on the bench in the corner. Clara is plump with a pudding-bowl haircut but a brazenness that keeps her from being bullied. Hannah has less capacity for cruelty, but no will of her own. Her hair is always pulled back perfectly in a ponytail and she has a spray of freckles over her nose. She could be a Sarah or a Charlotte, if she wanted, but she won't abandon Clara – they've been friends since kindergarten. I find her prettiness unsettling. Like her arms might pop from their sockets if I pulled too hard.

I shuffle into my uniform facing the wall. I hate changing in front of the other girls in case there is something about my body I haven't yet seen. A mark? A sign? A mistake? The webs between my toes. The nub of a tail where it shouldn't be. Gills in place of breasts to let me breathe. I have no gills. No breasts yet either. Tegan, being the oldest, was the first to start wearing a bra, and within days all of the girls had white Tammy Girl bras to match, whether or not they were needed. My bare chest now seems both babyish and obscene.

Clara catches my eye and glares.

'What are you always staring at?' she says. Her gaze lands on my bare legs. She laughs, turning to the others. 'Look at her legs! They're like some sort of animal's.'

I've never noticed the downy dark hair on the ridge of my shins before. To cover them, I pull on my tights quickly.

Clara's showing off for Tegan, just like they all do. She wants Tegan to know she's not afraid of the stone-throwing new girl. She wants to make a scene. When I don't respond, she starts on me again. 'Why are you always following us around like a sheep?' Clara says. William's refrain has escaped the confines of the tennis courts and found its way here. 'Get away from us, sheep. No one wants you here.' The girls around me stare, Tegan too, unblinking. She's waiting to see what I'll do. 'Fuck off, sheep!' Clara says.

I turn back to the wall and pretend she's not there. I hold my breath to stop myself drowning. I am not a sheep. Nor a lemon. I am amphibian. I am something found on the bottom of the ocean floor. I'll swap my (hairy) legs for a tail and swim back into the water from which we all came.

Clara emits a gloating bleat. 'Baa!' It comes back to taunt me, ricocheting off the wet walls.

The other girls laugh, and Hannah, emboldened by Clara's success, takes up the call. 'Baa!' She bleats a note higher, giggling. One of the Sarahs joins in, and then more follow suit, and soon there is a chorus of bleats and laughter behind me.

My fingers stumble on the buttons of my shirt. My sweater

gets caught over my head. I will not cry, I promise myself; Tegan is in the corner watching. I won't show her I'm afraid.

'Baa!' the chorus continues. When I turn from the wall, there is Clara, making that ovine noise with a smile spread across her face, like a tear in fabric. I am struck for a moment by the look of her, one hand on her plump middle, belligerent in her white training bra, with stitches where her breasts will one day be, just buds now, but more than I have. The waistband of her skirt is rolled over twice, like the girls do here to make their skirts shorter, and her mouth is agape in that incessant bleat, so I can see down into its dark pink depths and I shudder. I shoulder my way out past the other girls, now standing and staring and bleating together.

From the doorway, I catch eyes with Tegan in the corner. She doesn't look away. She isn't with the other girls, but she isn't with me either. She could save me and she won't. A flash of defiance. I don't need her help. But then the chorus builds around me and I must leave before I break my promise not to cry. Their bleats follow me down the corridor, occasionally picked up by a passer-by.

All the way to my next class, I think about that look and I understand something new about our friendship. It exists in the same place as what happened down on the courts. Ours is a friendship never acknowledged, but shared between us, like a secret. It is the note inside the music box. It's hidden, but that doesn't mean it doesn't exist.

Back in the classroom the kids who occupy the same social stratum as I do are already at their desks. Amelia, with her ponytail down to her waist and her small sad pink eyes always blinking away tears. Baz, the fat kid, whose name I now know, and the girl who arrived from South Korea for a year whom no one has spoken to. I sit in the corner and busy myself doodling. I don't look up when the others arrive. Whereas before, my gaze would wander in Tegan's direction during class, from now on, I'll not once let our eyes meet. I won't look, or listen, or even long for it to be any different. I'll remove myself completely from her influence. As long as I don't exist for Tegan at school, Tegan does not exist for me. This is the only way for us to be friends. I'm sure of it.

OLD MEN PRETENDING
TO BE BOYS

We take our places on the sofa. We watch *Blue Peter*, then *Neighbours* and *Hollyoaks* – our favourite for all the kissing that happens, which we rate out of ten.

'If you could snog any of the boys, who would you go for?' Tegan asks, even though she knows my answer already. None.

After *Hollyoaks*, I usually go home for dinner with Mou. I don't have to, but I pretend so Tegan thinks Mou is strict. I imagine being strict is what a mother should be. This is another way I protect her. Tegan's mother won't let her wear make-up or swear or talk about boys. Mou wouldn't care if I did any of these things, not that I do.

We play thumb war to see who will make the next round of tea. Tegan sucks her thumb while watching TV, so it's damp and crinkly against my own. Sometimes we don't even play. She holds up her damp, crinkly thumb and I hold up mine and we sit like that until one of us gives in.

We flick through the *Sun* newspaper, which Peter leaves on the coffee-table. We open it across our laps and use it to shield us from view so Haley won't see we're looking at the breasts of the topless women on page three. Lucy and Melanie and Cheryl smile back at us, their peachy skin rendered grainy on newsprint.

'Barbie's day job,' I joke.

'If Barbie had nipples,' Tegan says.

And we giggle behind the paper like old men.

Tegan likes to imagine what type of breasts she'll have when they're fully grown. She casts herself as a Barbie doll on page three, her freshly imagined breasts on grainy display to be lusted over by workmen drinking their tea.

'I want mine to be ginormous,' Tegan says, and we both agree that's most likely. She's already bigger-busted than the rest of us and all the boys know it.

The sofa is our universe. It is both private and a window to the world. We watch whatever TV we want and observe Haley and Peter's comings and goings, mysterious and adult as they are. Ryan stays in Haley's room, just another male presence, circling the periphery of our world.

Sometimes Peter or Haley sits with us, most often Peter, as he waits for Haley to get ready, and he and Tegan bicker, though I'm coming to learn they enjoy it. At other times, Haley wedges her body between us on the sofa so we can share her equally. She paints her nails with a clear varnish that makes her gag when she chews them, and yet she chews them still, almost as soon as the varnish dries. She sits between us, eyes vacant, teeth clenched, talking and chewing and gagging, and asking us questions without waiting for the answers. I think she's magnificent. She's already loved. She'll never become foam on top of the sea. She's beautiful and indifferent. She and Tegan share this quality of seeming to be wholly unavailable to the world around them. To everyone except each other.

And then she leaves, and it's just Tegan and me again.

We use a cushion to cover our faces. We bring our heads close together, so we breathe in each other's whispered words like air.

The next day at school, we'll pretend we don't even know one another. I'm so good at pretending for those hours that she barely exists. Mou is the only person who knows that for the past few weeks I've gone home with Tegan after school most days. This happened because I wished for it. I made a sacrifice to first forgotten Eve and she granted me this wish. Only I know this to be true. It is another truth I mustn't speak aloud for fear of breaking it open like a shell that promises the sea.

TEGAN AND I lie on Haley's bed watching her get ready for work. I'm holding a cuddly lion cub called Blondie. It was a gift from Andy. He said Blondie would look after Haley when she slept. I only learn this later, or maybe I already know by the way she clings to this toy, long after she's emptied her life of other childish things. Blondie is ragged and threadbare from loving, soft only in her protected crevices, the creases of her ears and armpits. Blondie has a mane. She is a girl lion posing as a boy. Haley is this way, too, and maybe that's why I love her. She's compact and fierce.

Tegan told me Haley barely speaks to her mother any more. By 'any more', she means ever since Andy died. Haley calls her mother 'Brenda', which Brenda hates. When Haley drops Tegan back at the farm, she doesn't even go inside. Tegan sometimes calls her mother 'Brenda' too, but I suspect never to her face. They each say 'Brenda' like they're really saying, 'I hate you,' and every time I think about Mou and what it would take for me to feel that way.

'What's that for?' I ask, as Haley blends in a cream, draining her cheeks of colour.

Tegan observes, but acts like she knows it all already. She's dangling her head off the edge of the bed, watching the world upside-down.

The foundation gives Haley a dewy sheen, as even and smooth as plastic, the blusher bronze warrior streaks across her cheeks. She reaches over and blushes my face, too.

'See? Stunning!' she says. 'We should dye your hair blonde. Just some highlights. If your mum would let you.'

'Then you'd look like our sister, too!' Tegan says, draping herself over me. Tegan is always this way with me now. A little finger looped around my own, her legs thrown over my lap while we sit on the sofa. It is the most I've ever been touched by another person and every time I want to stay completely still for fear she might part herself from me.

Haley scores the pale strip of skin between her eyeball and the lash with black eyeliner. Her lid flutters against the instinct to open, to protect itself against the sharpened point.

Last week, Haley took us to Pizza Hut. She'd got a big tip at work and wanted to treat us with it. The waiter flirted with us all as he brought out free dessert, but his eyes were on Haley only. Even Tegan is invisible when we're with Haley. When we left, the pizza boy was waiting around the corner smoking a cigarette. He reached out and grabbed Haley's hand, pulling her towards him. She laughed and reclaimed her hand, but she didn't stop smiling. 'Come on, baby!' he said. 'Drop your little sisters at home. My shift is nearly over.' I wanted to kick him. He kept reaching for her hand as if he had the right to touch her, and I wondered if she'd given him that right in the restaurant when I wasn't looking. She walked towards him then, and I thought she was going to kiss him; he thought it, too, because he shut up. Tegan and I exchanged a look, and Tegan rolled her eyes, pretending this wasn't both frightening and thrilling. I couldn't hear what Haley said in his ear, but the power shifted from him to her.

'Are you going to see the pizza boy again?' Tegan asked, as we walked home. She wants to live through Haley; she wants to hear every detail of these men and their desires. But Haley just shrugged. There are others like the pizza boy. Whistles follow her down the street, delivery boys and taxi drivers and business men on their lunch breaks with wives and children at home. They all want her and she wants them back, but not for the same thing. She flashes a look and takes a slow drag on her cigarette, smoke sidling up her face as she smiles. (Later Tegan and I will practise this slow, sidling smile.) We never get answers to our questions. We don't see the men again. They come and go, their numbers tucked into a pocket and later discarded. Sometimes I think Haley devours these men. She eats them immaculately, like she eats her pizza. She never bites into it directly; she tears off mouth-size morsels and places them between her lips with the tips of her fingers chewed down to the quick. This is how she eats a man: one mouth-size morsel at a time.

Haley turns to Tegan and me, her face freshly painted. 'Will I do?'

HALEY IS ON the phone with Peter. Tegan and I are slumped on the sofa, listening.

'But, Peter, you said . . . ' Haley is furious.

'Tell him I don't want to see him anyway,' Tegan shouts across the room with all her might. She's furious, also. 'I'm old enough to look after myself.'

Haley hangs up and looks at Tegan with a sigh. 'He has a date with what's-her-name, the girlfriend with the cut-up arms.'

'Amanda,' Tegan says. And then looks at me. 'Amanda self-harms.' I have no idea what this means, but it sounds adult and glamorous.

'And I know you're old enough, missy,' Haley says, 'but if Brenda found out I left you alone that would be it for you staying here. I'm not going to fuck this up.' This last part seemed as much to herself as to Tegan or me.

'But how would she even find out?' Tegan says, kneeling up to get her sister's attention. 'I'd never tell. Sissy neither.'

Haley looks at the clock on the wall, her fake black lashes batting fatly around her eyes, like butterfly wings. 'Maybe I'll call in sick.' The prospect terrifies her, and she's working out which is more terrifying: to call in sick or leave Tegan at home alone.

'Sissy could stay!' Tegan offers. 'I wouldn't be alone then. Sissy's mum leaves her on her own all the time. Doesn't she, Siss?' This was true but I'd never told Tegan, which meant either Tegan knew things about me some other way, or she was lying, and the latter seemed more likely. 'You don't mind, do you, Siss?'

I shake my head. Tegan and I exchange an excited look. Haley thrusts the phone into my hand, and without time to think about what's happening, I'm calling home to ask for permission. Haley and Tegan gather around me, like we're in on a conspiracy. 'Don't mention about me being at work,' Haley whispers, cringing. I don't expect Mou to answer, but she does on this occasion, perhaps because it's dark and I'm not yet home.

'Hello?' Mou's voice, always cautious when talking on the

phone, as if she's entered a house where she doesn't belong. Mou says she's glad I have a friend, which I choose to take at face value, and like that it's settled.

Haley shows me the list of phone numbers on the notice-board in case of various emergencies and the ready meal waiting in the fridge. When she leaves, she kisses us both on each of our cheeks, four tiny kisses. 'Thank you!' she says just to me, as if passing a baton of adulthood my way, and I swell with pride.

She fetches the small suitcase she keeps in the corner of her room, and wheels it out of the door, calling behind her, 'Look after each other!' I want to ask what's inside her suitcase, but the way she drags it behind her, its one wonky wheel wob-bling, makes it seem private, part of the adult world I'm not ready to unlock.

TEGAN AND I leap across the furniture, shrieking, playing the floor is lava until we collapse in a heap on the sofa once more.

'A whole night!' Tegan says, and the thrill of it does a backflip inside me.

We settle in, watching the evening TV that comes on past the time I usually leave. A vampire slayer called Buffy is in love with a vampire and her best friend is a witch. I tell Tegan I can read palms and she thrusts her hand out to me.

'This is your luck line,' I say, making up what I can't remember from a witchcraft book Mou found for me in the charity shop. 'It means you're fated.'

I hold her hand to the light, tracing the lines of her future, like rivers on a map. I want to do this for ever. I want to sit here for ever with her hand in my lap.

'Fated?'

'Fated for something. Like destiny. Luck is following you through life. Maybe you'll be a Hollywood star.'

'How do you know?'

'See? I don't have one.' I show her my palm, an empty space where a luck line should be. 'It's a very special line.'

I tell her what she wants to hear. I want her to believe in me. She looks at the line, seeing it for the first time. The line is a promise.

'How many boyfriends will I have?'

She proffers her hand, again and again, as if each time the reading might reveal something new I haven't yet seen. She always wanted to know what the future held; she wanted to be there already.

'This break in your life line means something big happened when you were younger, like a major change or a death.'

She snatches her hand back.

'It's not for real,' I say, but I know what I did. I want to prove I'm powerful, so like all good charlatans, I used what I already knew. We have never talked about Andy or Harvey the dog again. The knowledge sits between us sometimes, like a companion we choose to ignore. We don't talk about what happened down on the courts, either, with the boys and the stone and the place deep inside her. I have questions I know she could answer and for that reason I'll never ask them out loud.

WE GO ON Haley's computer and wait for the dial-up tone to open a portal to the adult world. The boys on MSN Chat, Tegan tells me wisely, are most likely old men pretending to be boys. We say we're sixteen-year-old twins. We say our names are Tallulah and Tatiana. We reinvent ourselves as these make-believe women. We tell each of these boys (who are probably old men pretending to be boys) a different story, and each of them believes us for the time we're chatting, the same as we believe them. We're trapped at home by a cruel father and ask them to save us. We're already married and we're looking for an affair. In all our guises, we want to be loved. To be desired. And we want to hear the ways in which they will love and desire us if we were theirs. They all offer to rescue us. They all describe the things they would do to us, sometimes without our asking.

One old-man-pretending-to-be-a-boy writes, *I want you to sit on my face until my beard is wet with your cum. Will u?*

We squeal and run around the room covering our mouths and our eyes to un-hear and un-see what he has said. I cannot imagine what he's describing, but he has a beard! And that's enough to be horrified.

A little box pops up then with the name Eric666, and Tegan takes my place at the keyboard. I perch on the chair beside her.

Hello sexy, Eric666 writes.

'You know him?' I ask.

Tegan's concentration is fixed.

I'm with my friend. She wants to know what you look like, she types. 'We chatted a bit before.'

It hurts more than it should. I thought we were discovering a world together, but she's already crossed this terrain.

Eric tells us he's twenty-one years old, five foot ten, with short brown hair and hazel eyes.

My friend thinks you sound lush, Tegan types, and I shove her.

What about u? he writes.

If you love me, u have to love her 2

We both giggle, but we're electrified. The room has reduced to this box on the screen.

Tallulah and Tatiana, I can love you both, he writes, and we fall about giggling.

He calls us by our make-believe names on every line that he writes.

Tallulah and Tatiana, I can only imagine how beautiful you both are. Will you send me a photo of you together?

We are thrilled to be called beautiful. To be treated as one.

'Shall we do it?' Tegan asks. I look at her, astonished. She's smiling. That tooth latched onto her bottom lip.

'We can't! He'll know how young we really are,' I say, but Tegan doesn't care. She can believe whatever she wants to believe, and all I can do is distract her. 'Ask for one of him first. Just in case he's an old man pretending to be a boy.'

Give me your address and I'll send you a photo, he replies, and something shifts inside me. I'm no longer excited. I want to close the portal to the adult world and go back to playing pretend.

Tegan starts to type Haley's address.

'Teg,' I say, and she looks up at me, wildness in her eyes, 'don't,' and I'm not laughing any more.

She pauses for a moment while deciding. And then she keeps on typing. I reach for her hand to stop her just as she hits send. There it is on the screen: Haley's address in a box being read by Eric666. Tegan switches off the computer, and turns to me, all intensity gone.

'Don't worry, Siss. He lives in London. It's not like he's going to come all the way here and grab us.'

She says this last part like he's the bogeyman of our childhood nightmares. Like I'm the one being foolish, not her. And I believe her. Tegan is full of desires. I am full of desires, too, but I won't act on them. Tegan wants it all, and sooner, and more than the last time. She wants it now. I look back at the black box of the computer screen, and pretend the danger has vanished.

TEGAN GIVES ME an old T-shirt to wear in bed and I change facing the wall, shy again now. There's animal hair on my shins. I've been told. My body defies my desire to be invisible. When I asked Mou for a razor, so I could be hairless like the other girls, she said, 'You're half Greek,' as if that explained it. But why did it have to be the bottom half? 'Puberty is vicious,' she said, as if talking about a wild animal I'm yet to tame.

I follow Tegan into the bathroom. She brushes her teeth first.

'Let me do yours,' she says, and I open my mouth.

She clumsily moves the brush over my teeth, occasionally jabbing my gums, between our laughter.

'Ow!'

'Stay still! This is hard.'

The contours of each other's mouths are new territory to explore.

I brush hers, too, until we're just dribbling toothpaste smiles.

In bed, we lie face to face, eyeing each other, like we're trying to learn about one another just by looking. Tegan is different with me than she is with the other girls. At school, she wants you to love her even when she's cruel. She wants you to prove it. Like the time Lydia came in with her hair down. 'Your hair is perfect. You should wear it like this always,' Tegan cooed, wrapping her fingers in Lydia's curls, as if they were her own. Lydia visibly softened. She stopped wearing her hair in tight bunches for a few days, letting it

71

bounce proudly against her face. But later that week Tegan was sour about something. 'Shit, Lydia, isn't it time you did something about your hair?' Lydia's jaw dropped. 'My sister has straighteners. You should get some.' I don't like Tegan when she does this. Lydia begged a hairband from Hannah so she could tie her hair up after Clara refused, revelling in Lydia's distress.

But Tegan isn't this way with me. When she talks she takes my hand in hers and it's always warm, and I want to pull her right into me. I want to be the same girl. I want to be her. It was me she chose as the repository for her secrets. She chose me.

'I can't sleep,' Tegan says, though we've barely tried. 'Will you tell me a story?'

We bury our heads under the covers and I tell her the story about the little mermaid.

'It's not like you remember it from the movie,' I say. 'The little mermaid was the youngest of six sea princesses, and the prettiest of them all.' This pleases Tegan. 'When they each turned fifteen, they were allowed to swim to the top of the ocean, sit on a rock in the moonlight, and see the human world on land.'

'Are you sure it wasn't sixteen?' Tegan asks.

I shake my head. 'For mermaids, it all happens at fifteen.'

'I guess it's not like they can have sex anyway.'

I nod, and continue with the story.

'The little mermaid waited as each of her sisters turned fifteen and swam to the top of the ocean, returning with stories about the wonderful world on land. When her time finally came, she rose to the surface and it was everything she had hoped for. A great ship passed, and on it there was the most handsome prince. She couldn't take her eyes from his face, watching him all through the night. But then a massive storm hit, capsizing the ship and drowning the whole crew. The little mermaid dashed through the wreckage to find the prince and carried his body to the shore, covering his face with kisses and saving his life.

'She returned to her sisters in the morning, to the sea palace where they lived. But as time passed, the little mermaid grew sad. She couldn't get the handsome prince out of her head. She longed for him, longed to cover his face in kisses again. Eventually her longing was so great, she visited a sea witch, asking if she could trade her fish tail for two legs. The sea witch gave her a potion to drink ... '

'It's not so different from the movie,' Tegan says. 'She just wanted to get laid.'

'Just wait,' I say, and continue. 'The sea witch said, when she drinks the potion, she'll feel pain like a sword passing through her and every step she'll take on her new legs will feel like treading on sharp knives. But worst of all, the sea witch demanded she trade her voice for the magic potion. If the prince fell in love with her, she would regain her voice and win an immortal human soul. But if the prince married another girl, the mermaid would turn into foam on top of the sea.'

'Can't she just be a mermaid again?'

'No, that's not the deal,' I say. 'The mermaid was so in love with the prince she agreed, sticking out her tongue so that the sea witch could cut it out. The little mermaid woke up on the marble steps of the palace, naked, with two legs and a pain through her middle, just like the sea witch had described. The prince found her and took pity on her, dressing her in expensive robes, and treating her like a devoted pet, even kissing her and stroking her hair, but he never considered her

73

for a wife. Eventually the prince fell in love with a beautiful princess from a neighbouring kingdom, and on the eve of his marriage, the little mermaid knew the next morning she would die.'

'But the prince changes his mind, right?' Tegan says.

'That night, as the little mermaid looked out over the water, thinking about her death, she saw her five sisters rise to the surface. They had traded their hair with the sea witch for a magic knife. If the little mermaid plunged the knife through the heart of the prince, when his warm blood fell on her feet her legs would fuse back into a fish's tail and she could live out her three hundred years underwater. The little mermaid took the knife into the prince's chamber, where his bride-to-be was sleeping on his chest . . . ' I feel Tegan listening in the hot damp of our duvet tent. She wants the mermaid to stab the prince. I want it too. We're baying for blood. For the mermaid's sweet revenge. 'The knife trembled in her hand. She gazed at the face she'd fallen in love with, and then she hurled the knife into the ocean. She took one last lingering look at the prince, and threw herself into the water to become foam on top of the sea for evermore.'

Tegan sits bolt upright, throwing the duvet from our heads.

'That's not how it ends!' Tegan shouts, and won't let me go any further. 'Why didn't she kill the prince and go back into the sea with her sisters? That's what I would have done, no matter how fit he was. He didn't even love her.'

'I know,' I say, glad she shares my indignation. 'I'd never trade my tail for legs.'

'All because she fancied a silly prince. We should do our own version where she kills him. That was rubbish. Tell me another one.'

Tegan asks for story after story. She wants to talk until we fall asleep mid-sentence. She will do this every time we share a bed, until she's heard all my stories, and still I'll find more. Eventually, she asks, in a voice so close to sleep I can't tell if maybe she's already dreaming, 'Tell me one about Eric666, about when he comes to visit us here. Make it a good one.'

My heart stops. I open my mouth to keep talking, but I cannot. Words have power, I've learned that. Between my words and Tegan's will, we might just conjure him. The black box of the computer screen with its green cursor flashing, like a door we neglected to lock at night.

'Siss?' Tegan asks, but I pretend to be asleep.

I'm alert to every shift of her body, until I feel her soften beside me, and it's just the proximity of her person, breathing and dreaming and painfully alive. She sleeps deeply, as if exhausted by being Tegan the rest of the time.

I wake in the night to the sound of Haley returning, wheeling the little suitcase behind her down the corridor, and it sounds so lonely. She's finished for the night – she devoured the men while we were dreaming. One mouth-size morsel at a time.

II

(cleansing)

THE GIRL SNATCHER

When the girl goes missing, the town closes ranks around its daughters. I remember the girl from the neighbouring town now, who many dismissed as a runaway – shacked up with some bad boyfriend in a dingy Portakabin, they said. But this latest girl, she's one of ours.

The girl was snatched on a Saturday night. Her mother's face is on TV, wrung out with tears, like a sodden rag. I watch the news with the sound off, because Mou says the bad things might pollute my brain. I still watch, though, because she also says it's important to have an idea of what's going on in the world.

Even without the news, I'd have heard about it. Posters go up on streetlights and in car windows. People trade stories in the line at the supermarket, in the ladies' loos, outside the school gates. Kids pass notes in school. Someone scrawls on the wall of the bathroom cubicle: *I am the missing girl.* And I believe the scrawler. We are all the missing girl.

Mou and I weren't part of the community before, but in the flurry of concern, they folded us in by accident, like a stray hair in cake mix. People stop us in the street to talk about it, people who have never talked to us before. 'A girl has gone missing,' they say. Those without daughters of snatchable age enjoy this feeling. Parents with daughters, like Mou, are looked at with pity, as if our snatching is inevitable. But us daughters, we're barely looked at, and if we are, it's with sadness first and then suspicion, as if we're at fault. Girlhood is a dangerous thing, their eyes say.

The missing girl lived up a lane with only one streetlight illuminating the way, and it was almost dark, but not quite, which makes it more frightening, because I feel safe in the almost dark. A petition goes around to erect a second streetlight on the lane. 'It's something to do,' says the anxious mother who tells me and Mou outside the chippie.

No one knows what happened but everyone has heard something, and these somethings accumulate beyond our control. The girl was on her way to meet friends. The man was in a mask. He had a hook. Not all of these things can be true. The girl was made to get on all fours, her tights, torn and discarded, like the skin of a snake that has already moved on. The one piece of truth is the most awful: the man who snatched her is on the loose.

HER POSTER IS on the noticeboard at the library that weekend. I know her face as if she's my sister or best friend. She is so pretty, prettier now than she will ever be.

'I'm sure they'll find her soon, dear,' says the librarian, smiling gently.

Tegan and I don't see each other at the weekends, because she's at home on the farm, so it's just Mou and me. Mou's friends in the bird shop told her that the library is looking for a part-time assistant. Mou says this would be a dream job. She has to catch up on all the reading she missed by not going to university. We used to have a book club. There were just two members, me and Mou. Our meetings were conducted with a great degree of ceremony and many official announcements. 'Commencing the fourth instalment of the multi-annual, exclusive literary sojourn for the year 1997 ... ' Mou would go on like that, until I began to giggle.

We took turns choosing books. I put forward *Lord of the Rings, Northern Lights*. Mou always chose books about women who are unhappy, preferably unhappier than her so she could feel, relatively speaking, lucky. We haven't had a book club since arriving here. Being at the library is a good sign, like maybe Mou is starting to feel more like herself. She dispatches me to explore while she talks to the woman at the front desk.

Somewhere between Young Adult and Fiction, I find a display table on Myths of the Ancient World and linger. There's a picture book called *The Trojan Horse*, which seems for kids younger than me, and a weighty encyclopaedia of Greek mythology. I don't know anything about being Greek. The only thing I have that Koko gave me is a piece of smoky quartz from the Isle of Arran and a piece of obsidian, jet black and dense as the night sea. Sometimes I slip one into my pocket for safety: the crystals have powers. Koko told me so, sitting on the end of my bed in the long-ago, and that makes it true, and this truth comes from a time before doubt, so doubly true. These simpler, doubly true truths are inscribed in my memory and recited by night. The things my father told me are finite, and – just like the crystals – that makes them precious. I display my crystals collection on the mantelpiece of the defunct fireplace in my room next to his postcard from Greece, which is all I've seen of the country. These books are different, though: their stories are ancient.

81

On one of the covers there's a picture of a girl running, the cloth of her robes flying as she looks over her shoulder in fear. She seems more frightened of what's behind her than the fact that her arms are stretching into branches and her feet are rooting in the ground.

'Sissy!' Mou shouts, followed by a shush from the librarian.

Later, in the bath, I try to read my new book, making soggy fingerprints on the pages. It is a book of fables and much of it is beyond me. But then I reach the story about the girl on the cover. Daphne is her name. She was changed into a tree to escape a man who loved her. She didn't love him in return; she didn't want to love any man at all. But once she became a tree she could no longer run from him, and he made her branches into a crown.

I skip forward, and there are more stories about girls and how they change. This changing happens with or without their asking. It is both punishment and crime. I read about a girl who was raped and turned into a nightingale that cannot sing. Rape is the worst thing, and by being the worst, it's beyond comprehension. But the voiceless bird is real. The girl who changed into a bird and the girl who changed into a tree, they're just like the little mermaid, silent as foam on top of the sea. Transformed for being loved or not loved at all. Each fable ends and there is no redemption. It just moves on to the next.

I drop the book on the floor by the bathtub and look down at my body beneath the surface. I have two hard nuggets where breasts might one day be. I pull on the curl of hair that has so recently appeared between my legs, and feel alarmed at what my body is setting itself to do, in spite of me or my desires. I check the skin between my toes in case I have webbed feet. I check the base of my spine for signs of a tail. I don't know how to love or be loved in the right way and there's nobody here to guide me. I don't know what I'll become when I'm done changing. If I'm not loved in time will I turn into foam on top of the sea? If I'm loved too much will I transform into a tree? Was the missing girl loved in the wrong way, too soon, or too late, or not enough? Was she forced to change against her will?

I FIND MOU in her room. I ask if I look as a girl my age ought to look. I want to know if I'm at risk of snatching yet or if that comes later.

Mou is busy choosing an outfit for her job interview at the library. They said she could come in next week and meet the manager. She pulls all of her clothes out of her wardrobe and lays them on the bed to assess.

'You're beautiful, Sissy *mou*,' she says, while picking at a stain on a blazer. That's not what I wanted to hear.

Mou turns to me, holding up the blazer against her body. It's several sizes too big. 'Does this look like a hangover from the eighties?'

'No, Mou.' I have no idea what she means, but I know what *she* wants to hear.

I skulk away to my room and examine my face in the mirror. I look for the woman I might one day become. Or the bird. Or the tree. I wonder if I'll come out of this unscathed. I ask Luke Perry in the snug if I look like a proper girl yet, a girl of snatchable age, and he says proper girls are of no interest to him. Proper girls are busy becoming women. He likes mermaids. Or creatures that live at the bottom of the sea. But the little mermaid never got to go home, I say. Neither did the girl who transformed into a tree, or the girl who was turned into a nightingale. Once they changed, there was no going back. Once they changed it was for ever.

MOU AND I are eating crudités and tinned bean salad for dinner. Mou likes to be healthy, but she hates to cook. She calls the rectangular slices of cold vegetables crudités to dress them up as something better than they are.

Until the sleepover, Mou hadn't asked many questions about Tegan – other people's children don't interest her – but she's curious about Haley. She asks what Haley does if she isn't at school.

'She works in a bar,' I say, chewing on a carrot rectangle. 'Do you think I'm pale?'

'I remember now. She said so on the telephone. Which bar? No, Sissy *mou*, you have beautiful skin.'

'I don't know the bar's name. Haley said I should get some sun on my cheeks. She says with my complexion I'd get a great tan. She goes on a sunbed once a week.'

'It's just a thing people say. And those things give you cancer. Why doesn't Tegan live with her family?'

'She does. Some nights and at weekends. Her parents live on a farm in the countryside.'

'Right.'

'It's too far for her to travel each day. Her dad has cows. Maybe it's because we don't eat meat.'

'Why did Haley leave home?'

'Tegan says you can do what you want at sixteen. It's the law.'

'That's nonsense. There must be a reason.'

'I don't know, Mou.'

'Don't you want to be vegetarian any more?'

84

Mou and I never talk about just one thing at a time. We always talk about at least two, if not three or four.

I shrug. I want to add that Tegan isn't pale. Her cheeks are rosy and it's probably because she eats beef from her farm, but this feels like a betrayal. Mou and I decided to be vegetarian together after the BSE scare a couple of years ago. BSE made cows across the country go mad and fall over. Some people went mad, too. It was because humans made the cows become cannibals.

'Where does Tegan go when Haley's at work?' Mou's tone has shifted. 'Does Haley have a boyfriend?'

'Don't know,' I say, and I get up from the table to protect Haley from these questions.

LOVE US BEFORE
WE'RE READY

The following week, Mou walks me to the bus stop on the morning of her job interview. She's occupied with anxieties about her attire, whether her dress is too short, or too tight, or appropriate for this type of interview at all, which I suspect it might not be. She's wearing a blue floral dress she found in the bird shop and the oversized blazer with the stain on the front. Dressing-appropriately-for-an-occasion is one of the life skills Grandma Jean rates highly, and therefore one of the skills Mou avoided learning.

Every few steps she tugs her dress down over her tights. When she isn't tugging at her skirt, she's tugging at her hair. She made an effort to brush it this morning, but it won't be smooth by the time she reaches the library. Anticipating this, she put a hairbrush in her handbag, along with a lipstick, which she always carries, just in case, but has never once used.

'You'll do great, Mou,' I say, as I get on the bus, and she waves at me gratefully.

*

HANNAH HAS COME to school with a hickey to prove Marlon loves her. She twists her neck this way and that in the classroom, displaying her wounds like a necklace. I don't look directly, but I'm jealous from a distance – jealous of being loved until it hurts. Her bruises are so thick she could have been strangled.

'Look! The girl snatcher got his next victim,' Tegan declares, revelling in the murmur of shock around her. All last week the school was abuzz with talk of the missing girl. Older kids who knew her walked around bleary eyed and teary, but not Tegan. She traded horror-story endings with anyone who dared.

Marlon is thirteen, and he says the girls in his class are doing it with their boyfriends already. Tegan says Marlon might dump Hannah if she doesn't do it. She also says Hannah shouldn't do it for that reason. They're having this conversation in the middle of the classroom as we wait for Miss Storey to arrive. Hannah is speaking quietly, casting furtive looks around her, but Tegan and Clara amplify their voices. They talk about it like it might actually happen.

'How do I know if I'm ready?' Hannah says.

'You're ready when a bloke wants to do it with you,' Tegan says, and Clara guffaws. Tegan glances at the Sarahs and Charlotte. She wants to see they're outraged by the potential for sex before it's legal. We're all meant to wait for someone we love and that's all we know about it.

When I was six, Mou gave me a book called *The Nature of Sex*. It was shortly after I asked about the tampons. She said it was best to learn these things early, so they come as less of a shock when I'm older, but she gave me the book and forgot to explain what anything meant.

In the book, a drawing of a man impregnates a drawing

of a woman. In my memory it's the same as the drawings in *More!* magazine, except in *The Nature of Sex* neither the drawing of the man nor the drawing of the woman was smiling. They were expressionless as boiled eggs.

Shortly afterwards, a friend came over to play. I whispered in this friend's ear, 'Do you know what sex is?' She shook her head, eager for my knowledge. I was too embarrassed to say the words out loud so I wrote what I learned from *The Nature of Sex* on a piece of paper. *When a drawing of a man lies down with a drawing of a woman, he puts his thing inside her.* I didn't say what thing. I didn't need to. I didn't say where he puts it either. That part was unclear.

The friend read my note and looked at me, horrified. 'Dirty liar,' she said. So I showed her the pictures in my book and she cried.

That evening, the friend's mother telephoned Mou to tell her what had happened. The mother said the friend was not allowed to come to our house to play any more. She had assured her daughter that I was a dirty liar and the sex I described did not exist. She said other things, because when Mou hung up, she burst into tears, too.

'Mou?' I said. 'I'm sorry, Mou. I didn't know it was a secret.'

Mou stopped crying and looked at me. She laughed, quietly at first, and then louder. I tried on laughing for size, but it felt wrong. Dirty liar, pretending to laugh.

'You know what that frigid so-and-so said to me?' I didn't know what 'frigid' meant then. For a long time, I thought frigid was her name. Mrs Frigid Soandso. 'She said, at the very least, tell your daughter it's an act shared by a husband and wife.'

And Mou laughed again. I wanted to ask if Mrs Frigid

Soandso was right. Was it an act shared by a husband and wife? Was I a dirty liar?

The girl never came to play again because I'd told a secret I wasn't supposed to.

Even though we're nearly teenagers now, the teachers at school never mention sex. We have not yet had a lecture on Saying No, or what we're Saying No to, or why. Certainly, no one has told us we might want to Say Yes, and what it might feel like if we did.

I imagine losing my virginity. It's abstract, like a maths problem. What do I become once it's lost? A woman? I know my virginity is to be lost to a boy, but does the boy keep it and, if so, what does he do with it afterwards? Do boys collect virginities like shells picked from a beach, displayed in a jar on the mantelpiece, their origins later forgotten? If virginities can be lost, can they also be found? Can they be returned, with a note reading, 'I'm sorry for taking what wasn't mine'? Do boys have virginities? What is lost for them? What do they give in return?

I know the act of sex is more tangible than this. It involves putting one thing inside another. Like pushing your thumb into the centre of an orange and feeling it come apart in your hands.

'It will fuck her up if she does it,' Tegan says, later that evening, about Hannah on one of our long, rambling telephone calls, in which we talk about the day's events as if we experienced them together. I agree it's definitely too soon. 'She's too frigid anyway,' Tegan adds.

Mrs Frigid Soandso, except now I know what the word means. It's what they call you when you don't want to do it, but a boy does. The girl who turned into a tree to escape being loved, she was frigid, I guess. And if you do want to do it, they call you a slut. The little mermaid would be a slut, if she wasn't half fish. I'm learning you have to walk the line between wanting and not wanting. Between being loved and loving too much.

Miss Storey walks into the classroom and Hannah pulls up her collar to cover the bruises on her neck.

'All right, children . . . ' Miss Storey begins.

TEGAN AND I perch on the edge of the bathtub at Haley's, side by side in our underwear. Mou relented and bought me a training bra from Tammy Girl. I only have one, though, so I wear it every day and wash it by hand at weekends.

Tegan draws a line through the white foam with the razor, her bare leg revealed beneath, like earth under snow. 'Like that,' she says, handing me the razor.

I'm nervous. 'Mou says once you start shaving, you have to shave for ever.'

'Yeah, that's the point. Come on! It's the only way the other girls will stop teasing you.'

There's another way, which involves her claiming me as her friend, but I'll never say it. I don't want what isn't freely given.

I draw the razor up my calf shakily. The freshly shaved flesh stings with the promise of womanhood, as my half-Greek legs transform, the animal hair left behind in the foam. But then a sharp pain. A line of blood trickles down my shin, and we both scream. I clap a hand over the wound, too afraid to examine the damage. I hop around in the bathtub, while Tegan tries not to laugh, coaxing me to show her what I've done. She isn't squeamish. Give her a wound and she'll poke it. She scrapes the sleep from my eyes in the morning. Later, she'll ask to pick my nose, and I'll say yes, because I never knew how to tell her no, and why would I? After she takes out her finger, she'll say, 'Haley thinks people make a lot of fuss about sex, but really it's no different from picking someone else's nose.' I'll clench my nostrils. 'Does that mean we just had sex?' and she'll laugh. 'Totally.'

I remain half shaven, half Greek. I flush the morsel of flesh away with the bathwater, a blood sacrifice to first forgotten Eve.

Haley barrels in, dropping her knickers and peeing with a sigh of relief.

'You cut yourself!' she cries, when she sees my shin. She fetches me a plaster and puts it on for me, and this gentle mothering makes me want to stay here for ever, in this very bathroom with them both by my side.

TEGAN PULLS A small blue envelope from its hiding place inside her bedside table. She hands it to me and waits for my reaction. I sit beside her on the bed and examine her offering. It's already been opened. It's addressed to *Tatiana & Tallulah*. I gasp and cover my mouth. Eric666 climbed out of the computer and now he's here with us in Tegan's room. She nods feverishly, sharing none of my trepidation.

'What did he say?'

'Read it!'

Inside the blue envelope is a blue piece of paper folded into a neat square, like a note passed in school. I scan the letter. His handwriting is tight and the paper is torn in one place where he pressed too hard with his biro. His girlfriend cheated on him, he writes, and now they've broken up. He's lonely. He hopes we will help him get over his ex. *You told me you like kinky things,* he writes. *Tell me some of the things you like and don't like, and this friendship can grow into something special.* I don't remember telling him we liked kinky things. I don't remember that being something we typed. At the end he asks to visit us. Signed Eric W.

'And look!' Tegan pulls a photo from the envelope. Eric W is dressed in rugby gear. He looks part-boy, part-man, like Peter. He's smiling with his arms thrown around the shoulders of two other part-men who have been sloppily cut from the image. 'He's fit, right?'

'You think that's him?' I ask.

Tegan told me men on the internet lie, but I can't imagine fully the ways in which they might.

'Maybe it's his son,' Tegan says. 'That would be fucked up.' Tegan swears like an adult. She likes that people don't expect it of her.

His dark curls are stuck to his forehead with sweat. His shorts are muddy, his thighs thick as tree trunks and covered with hair.

'Let's arrange to meet him, but hide nearby, so we can see what he really looks like.'

'But then he'll know we're liars,' I say. 'Are you going to write back?' Already I know Eric666 belongs just to Tegan.

'I'm not,' Tegan says, and then, with a smile, 'Tallulah might.'

That night in bed I think about Eric666. I don't want any part of it. I want Tegan not to want it either. She isn't interested in boys in our class, not really. She's interested in boys with facial hair and broad arms. Boys who hang in the skate park on a Saturday afternoon, Lynx-laced and sweaty. Older boys behind the steering wheels of cars. Boys like Peter. Like Eric666. Boys who will love us before we're ready.

THE MAN IN THE CAR PARK AT ASDA

It's Saturday, and Mou and I are hanging around in our house uniform: oversized T-shirts, slouchy socks and no underwear. We never have guests so there's no need to get dressed at a weekend, and Mou says it's good for us. 'Gives everything a bit of an airing.' We turn up the heat so we can stay in our uniform and be warm despite the cold weather. We're halfway through my first term at the new school and I've been friends with Tegan for over a month now.

'I think Mrs Durant next door isn't well,' Mou says, talking over the TV. This is another thing she does. She can talk through whole TV shows from beginning to end, and then she'll turn to me and ask what happened. We've dragged the duvet from Mou's bed down to the sofa to have a sofa picnic, which involves staying on the sofa all day. 'I saw her yesterday, and there was something in her look. Some days I don't think she leaves the house. I should probably go round and talk to her. I'm sure that fella of hers—'

'You mean Mr Durant, her husband?'

'He's a toerag.' She shudders. Mr Durant once offered to

mow our lawn, but Mou refused. She told him she preferred it wild, then made an audible comment about men and their lawns. 'Imagine having to kiss that face? That's probably why she's such a pain – she's lonely. I should bake for her, that's what I should do. A nice cake, and then invite her round for tea, Jesus, for a bloody G and T, loosen her up, the old bat, and she wouldn't be stuck in there with that toerag. That would be a nice thing to do, a cake . . . '

Mou has been like this ever since the job interview. She was meant to be volunteering in the bird shop today, but she called in sick so she wouldn't miss the call from the library if it came.

I nod, feeling disturbed. Last week, Mrs Durant came over with a date and walnut cake. I answered the door, and told Mrs Durant that my mother wasn't feeling up to visitors. I knew better than to let her in. I took the cake from her, said thank you, and shut the door.

The cake stayed on the counter, its icing sweating slightly, until Mou came down from bed. She refused to eat the cake. It's a sign they think they're better than us. 'With their fancy bloody cake and their fancy bloody lawn, and they can keep their fancy bloody life and shove it up their fancy bloody arse. You hear that?'

She took the cake into the garden and demonstrably crumbled it on the grass for the birds. I was sure Mrs Durant could see from her kitchen window, so I rolled myself up in the heavy curtains in the front room. From between the dark folds, I watched as Mou stalked the lawn in her weekend uniform, her T-shirt occasionally blowing up to reveal her pale grey bum cheeks beneath.

The birds didn't eat the cake from the patio, though, because there are no birds any more, Mou said, and then she stood at the window weeping because all of the birds have died.

At night, foxes rifle through our rubbish bins and scare me with their screams. Mou says they scream because the female foxes have teeth in their vagina, which bite down when they make babies. This makes so little sense to me and yet means so much. I think about it every time I hear them. On the night after Mrs Durant's visit, the foxes weren't screaming through their gritted vagina teeth or rattling the bins out front: they were right next to our house, eating Mrs Durant's date and walnut cake.

WHEN MOU OFFERS to make Mrs Durant a cake, I wonder if she simply forgot the cake that came before, or if it's a cake to say sorry for the crumbling of Mrs Durant's cake, or if something else is happening in Mou's brain to make sense of it.

I know some children whose parents can't care for them are taken away and raised by other people in place of their real parents. I've known this for as long as I can remember. This is our greatest fear. When Mou is most frightened, she tries to act Proper with a capital P to disguise what's wrong.

Back in the car days, Mou made me practise what I should say to other adults if they asked why I wasn't in school or where we were going. Other adults wouldn't understand that we were on an adventure, she said, and they might try to separate us. Late at night, when she and I were wrapped up in our sleeping bags, she would whisper to me about who may or may not knock on the window and try to take me from her, and what we should do if it really happened. But the only man who came wasn't after me.

We'd been in the car for some time, longer than days,

certainly weeks, maybe months since we had left the towers up north and Koko with the conger eels and the basking sharks. Mou was sleeping in the passenger seat, reclined as far as it could go, with her sleeping bag zipped up to her chin, because it was cold by then, which means we must have been in the car through the summer and out the other side. I was in the back seat in a sleeping bag of my own, with my two crystals from Koko beneath my pillow for safe keeping. Mou left the window open a crack for fresh air, so we didn't suffocate like forgotten dogs.

Mostly, no one bothered us, though sometimes a security guard or policeman knocked on the window, and Mou would say we had been driving through the night to move house; she was too tired to drive safely, so she'd pulled over for a nap. Her husband was driving the moving van, she would say, and this imaginary husband was waiting for us in our imaginary house. I didn't understand then why she invented a husband and a home in these moments, when the rest of the time she was busy saying these were things we didn't need. We only needed our eight limbs, four wheels and the car radio. Just us.

On this occasion, we were sleeping in the car park at Asda, and we woke to a man knocking on the window. He had heavy eyebrows over bloodshot eyes. A grey beanie pulled low on his forehead. Mou, still groggy, unzipped herself from her sleeping bag and wound down the window. She assumed he was a security guard, asking the same questions they always asked and she would give the same answers she always gave. She told me this later when going over what had happened and why, and where we had gone wrong, and in what ways she should be sorry for it.

But the man didn't ask her why we were sleeping in our

car; he asked her for some money, and when Mou started winding the window back up, he put his fist through and punched her once hard in the nose. I screamed and leaped up from the back seat to prise his fingers away from around her throat, where they had lodged themselves. I remember the sound Mou made then, like the last lick of water in a blocked drain. I tried to whack him, but he just pushed me away by my face, until I came around the other side and sank my teeth into his exposed arm. It tasted salty and rank. He cried out and pulled his hand away, which gave Mou enough time to start the engine and drive off. Her nose was bleeding; mine too, as if in sympathy or horror. When we were far enough away, she pulled over to the side of the road, the doors securely locked and the windows closed, and she wept, her tears washing the blood from her face.

That was the only other time I hurt someone on purpose, the time Mou asked me not to talk about. No one else knows Sissy Savos bit a man's arm and it tasted salty.

That was the end of the car days, though. We moved into a flat in London and I went back to school. I was behind on my reading and writing, they said, but I could catch up. Shortly after, Mou went to bed for the first time and wouldn't get up. Or, at least, the first time that I remember.

I used to dream of the man's hand reaching through the window to grab Mou's throat. At other times, I dreamed it was my throat instead, or Mou's hand, or my father's face, or the face of a man I'd passed on the street and stolen for my dream. Mou used to hold me when I screamed, and say, 'I'm sorry, I'm sorry,' again and again. I would wake up with the taste of iron in my mouth and my nose bleeding.

*

THE PHONE RINGS, and Mou and I look at each other. Our eyebrows shoot up. She's at the opposite end of our makeshift bed on the sofa and leaps out, giving me a flash of her entire behind as she scampers towards the phone. I imagine her getting the job and walking back in with a whoop. I imagine her not getting the job and walking upstairs to climb into her bed, and even imagining this makes me sink lower into the sofa with dread.

I hear Mou's muttered voice in the hallway, the sound of the receiver being replaced, and then Mou's footsteps, except they aren't retreating up the stairs to bed, but walking back in with a look of shock.

'I got the job!'

She makes two triumphant fists in the air. I jump up and whoop with all my might, and she breaks into a real laugh then, a laugh I didn't know I'd missed until I heard it. I hug her. It's going to be all right, I think.

'Mou, you're going to work in the library! A proper job! With books, like you wanted! Can we have our book club again? You know you can't cut up the books at the library, right? And you can't talk to people while they're reading or shout out the lines you like ... '

I prattle on like this, while she gently chuckles, all the time thinking, It happened just like I'd imagined. The good thing, that is, not the bad.

THE GIRL WHO
TURNED INTO A TREE

Tegan stands in front of the mirror, turning this way and that, as if each angle might offer a different answer to who she is. She doesn't ask for my opinion even while wanting me to see her in each outfit she tries on.

'Look!' she says.

The girls at school declare themselves fat, just to be told otherwise, or declare themselves ugly as if they believe it. Tegan won't enter into this. She wants me to tell her she looks great without asking.

Haley is having friends over tonight and said we can stay up with them until midnight. We're getting dressed up just to sit in the living room, as far as I can tell. I wear the baby blue cami Tegan gave me with my only pair of jeans. Tegan offers me a skirt to borrow, but I have a strange sort of rash behind my knees, more like blisters really, perhaps from shaving or the soap Haley uses. Tegan takes one look at it and grimaces. 'It's scaly!' she says, and tells me to keep it covered.

Tegan does my make-up. She shows me how to stretch my lips wide in a silent scream so she can apply my lipstick. Her eyes on my lips, and my eyes on her face. The air between us closes, warmed by our collective breath. Tegan motions for me to rub my lips together, and it tastes chalky. My teeth are bright and fearsome against the dark shade. 'It's eyes or lips,' Tegan says, a phrase she borrowed from Haley. 'Otherwise you look like a slut.' We paint each other's nails with glittery gloss. I don't like how it looks, but I like this moment: it's still and quiet, the gentle strokes of the brush against my nails, cocooned by the chemical smell and trance of concentration.

The make-up is new and I don't ask where she got it. I know sometimes she steals. She stole a red lace thong from her sister's room. She showed it to me and wouldn't tell me where it came from, but I had seen it drying on the radiator. Sometimes when we return from the shop she has an extra chocolate bar in her pocket or a magazine she hasn't paid for. Sometimes she tells me the same thing in two different ways, and they can't both be true. As if she's trying on different truths for size. This is also called lying, but I don't like to say it.

We stand side by side to admire ourselves in the mirror. Tegan practises making sexy faces, pouting her lips. Mou says the girls with their mouths open on magazine covers look like goldfish. But I'm learning that what Mou tells me isn't always true. I try pouting. Tegan looks like a proper girl. I'm just a goldfish wearing dark lipstick.

I bare my teeth instead.

'Don't do that,' Tegan says. 'Weirdo.'

And then she bares her teeth back at me.

'Pervert,' I call her, and we laugh.

*

PETER IS STRETCHED out on the living-room floor. His shirt has ridden up to reveal his taut stomach below and a line of hair winding into his jeans, drawing my eyes lower.

'Hey,' he says, and I look away, awash with embarrassment.

Peter sits up to make room around the coffee-table for us to join, and we sit on the floor beside him. The others are on our sofa. Mine and Tegan's sofa, that is. It's no longer ours when they're here.

'Look at you!' he says to me, eyeing my made-up face. 'Doesn't she look pretty!'

I look at my feet. I'm not wearing shoes. They're the only part of my body that feels like me. I wiggle my toes to remind myself I'm still here.

No one else has acknowledged our arrival, and I feel silly and young among this group of proper teenagers, of almost adults. Ryan has his arms wrapped around Haley. It's the first time I've seen him up close. He has a goatee and everything. Sometimes at night we hear him and Haley having sex. Tegan mimics her breathless gasp, until we roll around laughing. But Ryan makes a hot, guttural sound, like an animal in pain. Like she's devouring him alive. Haley slips from his grasp to reach across the table for more wine. Her jeans are so low I can see the T of her thong pointing downwards, like a road sign illuminated in the night. I want to giggle and point like we do to the girls on page three.

There's a Jay or a Jason and a Mark or a Tom, and two girls, Micaela and Sophie, who go to our school as Haley once did. They look at Haley the way the girls at school look at Tegan. If Haley blinks, they cease to exist. Sophie makes occasional smart quips. She's sexy even though she doesn't keep her mouth open like the girls on magazine covers. Micaela has a face like a pudding, so soft you could sink a spoon into it and take a bite.

Drinks are poured and sucked through straws, shots slung back. Jay or Jason empties a cigarette into rolling paper, followed by what I learn is weed. A roll, a lick, a spark, and then smoke fills the room, as thick as fog. It's like a dance, hands always seeking something beyond reach. Tegan kneels up to be part of the action. She plays along like she already knows the words to a song I've never heard.

Peter leans over and winks. He's winking at me, I'm flustered, but, no, he's winking at Tegan, his drink behind his back for her to take a sip. Tegan takes a glug and passes it on to me. I drink without thinking, but it tastes richer than Coca-Cola, more viscous and sweet. Tegan winks back at Peter, as if it's no big thing, this winking, this drinking with boys who are almost men. She flashes me a smile and with it she says, Isn't this amazing? Aren't we cool? And I smile back. Through her eyes, I feel it. Yes, it is and we are. This is it. It's all happening now.

Mou found a scrap the other day she liked so much she stuck it to the wall. It read: 'Perhaps when we find ourselves wanting everything, it is because we are dangerously near to wanting nothing.' I want everything. I want it all now. I want nothing more.

'How could she fancy him?' Micaela is louder than before. 'He's old enough to be her dad.'

'I heard they had to fuck in the dark room to get through the ordeal.' Sophie rolls her eyes.

They're talking about Julie Hendry. She fell in love with the art teacher, Mr Dubin, during after-school art classes, and she told Mr Dubin that if he wouldn't take her as his date to the school dance she would tell the headmistress they were sleeping together. No one knows what happened next, but Mr Dubin still teaches art and Julie Hendry left school. Now he makes all the girls button their shirts before entering the classroom so we can't get the wrong idea.

'He could have lost his job because of her,' Micaela says. 'Being a sex offender would ruin his life.'

'How do you know she was lying?' Haley says.

'*Because!* And, anyway, it's not like she's ten or something. She's perfectly legal.'

'I'd shag our English teacher even if they threw me out of school,' Peter says. 'Miss Kelly!' He whistles through his teeth. 'Every time she turns around to write on the blackboard, fuck!' He pulls on his crotch. 'All the lads in class keep their bags on their laps to hide their boners.'

There's laughter, and more stories, and we never know what happens to the girls at the end. There are gaps in these stories. The gaps are the parts other people don't want to hear. What happened to Julie Hendry? Or the missing girl, or any of the others? They became foam on top of the sea.

Tegan takes my hand and we sneak away to the kitchen.

'They'll never notice.' She pulls a beer out of the fridge and hides it under her top until we're back in her room. We sit on the bed opposite one another and down it in great giggling gulps, belching and shushing each other, expecting to be caught, without anyone here to catch us. We collapse in a pile of laughter. After the beer and the stolen sips of whatever was in Peter's drink, I melt into her. I want nothing to be different. Not a single thing. Together we're animals. We're wolf cubs. We bite at each other's neck and roll in a pile. We are always touching.

'Why do you like me?' I ask.

I know I shouldn't ask her, but I no longer care.

'Don't be stupid,' she says, shoving me and drawing me

towards her at the same time, the push-and-pull that defines being friends with Tegan.

'No, tell me.'

When Tegan thinks she screws her mouth to one side. She is thinking of the ways she likes me, and just knowing this is enough without an answer. I bury my face in the covers to hide my pleasure from her.

'Because you don't care what anyone else thinks,' she says, serious now. 'It's stupid. You aren't the sheep. They all are. They're the ones who do whatever you tell them. You're the only one who won't.'

I like the version of me she imagines. When I'm with her, I believe in it.

'They hate me,' I say, and immediately regret it.

'Who cares? They hate me, too.'

I laugh, because it's true. She whacks me. 'Oi!' I was meant to deny it, but then she laughs, too, as if we've just found the punchline to a joke.

'Are we drunk yet?' I've never been drunk before.

'Come on!'

She takes my hand to drag me back and I follow, the music louder with each step. We round the corner to the living room, and Sophie and Haley have stripped down to their underwear. I'm struck for a moment by their bodies, gyrating along to the song. Is this what I'll become? I can't imagine. Haley reaches for Tegan's hand and then my own, until I'm on the sofa with them, dancing and singing at the top of my lungs. 'My little sisters!' Haley squeezes our hands. I realise she means me, and my face hurts from smiling.

*

THE SMOKE IS so thick I can't see, and everything is moving faster, everything is funnier. I laugh and forget why I'm laughing. Conversations continue without beginning or end, without meaning or sense. It must be past midnight but Haley has forgotten we're meant to be in bed.

The party pairs off in twos and threes. Micaela sits on the breakfast bar with Peter, the straps of her dress down around her shoulders and her pudding face pink and bleary like she might cry. One of her shoes is in her hand. In the other is a whisk she was using as a microphone, but she's forgotten she was singing. Peter is singing still with a wooden spoon.

Tegan lies on her back, resting her head in my lap, so each time she glances in their direction I feel her head shift. She told me that Peter was there for Haley through *everything*, without making it clear what *everything* was. She also said that she and Peter have a special connection. They would be friends with or without Haley around.

'Is Micaela okay?' I ask.

Tegan shrugs, and stops looking at them. 'Hopefully she won't spew on the carpet like she did last time.'

Tegan crawls over to her sister, who's on the sofa with Ryan and another boy, a Mark or a Tom. She sits on the floor by Haley's feet, acting as if she's entirely absorbed by their conversation, as if she's been there all along.

When I look back Micaela is gone. I shuffle around the corner to see if she's spewing on the carpet in the corridor, but she's not. She's being led away by Peter. He's taken her hand. In the other she still holds the whisk. She limps in one shoe; the other is discarded on the carpet, like Cinderella's slipper. Neither Haley nor Tegan has noticed. I wonder if he's going to help her. If he'll hold her hair back while she vomits or unbuckle her remaining shoe before she climbs into bed.

They turn into Haley's bedroom, and I wait a moment before following them. The door is ajar and I can see half of Micaela inside. She is sprawled on Haley's bed. Her dress pulled up around her neck like a noose. One breast exposed. One leg swung open. Peter is there. The half of him I see is burrowing his face deep between her legs. The whisk has fallen from her grip. I'm mesmerised by the scene. He must sense my presence because he turns back to look at me. One eye locks on mine.

'Shut the door,' he says quietly, as if trying not to wake her. The layer of fuzz on his top lip is glistening.

The half of Micaela I can see doesn't move.

I hesitate. Something about this is wrong.

'Siss, I'm just putting her to bed.'

I nod. Then I lean forward and pull the door shut.

Half of Micaela becomes none.

My anger comes too late. He lied: she was in bed already.

I walk back down the corridor to the living room. The ceiling is lower with each step, like the walls are closing in on me. I saw something else happening in there. I saw Micaela transform in front of my eyes. Her roots grew so deep she could no longer move and her legs framed his face like branches. I remember I'm drunk, and feel momentarily reassured that none of it was real. I want to tell Tegan. She will lie in my lap and I'll say, 'I saw Micaela turn into a tree.' And she will laugh. 'No, you're just drunk, Siss.'

Tegan looks up on my return. Not for me, but for Peter. There is a flicker of disappointment on her face, which she quickly disguises, and I choose not to see.

'Siss!'

She reaches out and I go to her.

*

WE LIE ON our backs in Tegan's bed, waiting for the room to still around us. Will the ceiling spin for ever, like I'm falling on the deck of an empty ship? The ship that took my father away. If I turn into foam on top of the sea, will I meet him? Will he recognise me as he sails along my frothing surface?

'Is this how it always is?' I ask.

Tegan shrugs. The bass thuds through the wall from the party still going in the living room next door. Boom. Tsh. Tsh. Boom.

'It's worse if I shut my eyes,' I say, curious about this new sensation.

'I wish I could live here all the time,' Tegan says.

'Yeah. Your sister is so cool.'

'She says I can't because Brenda would lose her shit. I don't think she'd even notice. She's horrid to me when I'm there.'

'Have you asked?'

'Haley says things are bad enough between them without me making it worse. And we should be glad she agreed to me being here so often in the first place.'

'What happened between them?' I ask, but Tegan will change the subject, like she always does. She only ever tells me things in parts, leaving me to piece it together. We have an agreement. I won't challenge her about why she hates going home if she doesn't ask me about my dad. We both struggle to keep our end of the bargain. If I press too hard about Brenda, Tegan pivots. 'Why don't we look your dad up in the phone book or something? How many Savoses can there be?' And I drop it and so does she. Friendship, I'm learning, is as much about what isn't said.

'Peter is going to be my boyfriend,' Tegan whispers.

'What do you mean?'

'As soon as I turn sixteen, just you wait, he'll tell everyone how he really feels.'

If I tell her what I saw, she'll hate me for it.

'He's Haley's best friend,' I say, amid a rising tide of panic. 'And he's got a girlfriend anyway.'

This isn't what she wants to hear. She's coiled venom beneath the covers. I interrupted her daydream and now she'll punish me for it.

'What would you know? You've never even kissed a boy.'

'Have too,' I lie, even though she knows perfectly well I haven't.

'I got off with William Budge once,' she says. 'A couple of times, in fact.'

Normally she acts like the boys at school are all beneath her. And they are. She's telling me this now to hurt me and it works.

'What? Was he your boyfriend?'

'Don't be mental. It was ages ago anyway. Before we were friends. Didn't mean anything.'

'Why'd you kiss him, then?'

'It's just a kiss. It's not like we're married.'

I feel clueless, which is just what she wanted. I look at the topless Levi's man on the wall and think of Luke Perry in the snug at home. On TV, kissing looks expert, the important part hidden between two faces. A tangle of potential tongues.

'It'll happen,' she says, soft again now, my punishment over.

I hate that she knows what I'm thinking.

'Here I'll show you,' Tegan says, and she sits up and reaches towards me. I pull away then, unready to be kissed. 'Don't worry, I'm not going to kiss you, weirdo. You practise like this.'

She takes my hand in hers, gripped by the palm, like she's pulling me up from sitting.

'Now you put your thumb into your mouth and imagine it's a boy's tongue, and I do the same.'

I suck my thumb, and her face is next to mine, sucking her thumb, too, joined by our gripped palms. Her eyes are closed so I close mine, and we roll our heads around, like we've seen on TV.

It takes me a moment to notice Tegan has stopped and I stop too, self-conscious. 'Did I do it right?' I ask, my soggy thumb held in the air, our palms still clenched.

'You did great.'

We dry our thumbs on the covers.

'You don't use your thumb with boys, yeah?' Tegan says, looking concerned.

'Right, yeah.'

She starts to laugh, and soon we're both laughing so hard the whole bed jiggles.

I WAKE TO a crack of light in the doorway. Tegan has rolled into a ball and stolen the covers from me. I shiver, and a shifting shadow catches my attention. There's a figure there. Blinking myself awake, I sit up in bed to see more clearly, and now I'm sure of it. Someone is watching us. I turn to shake Tegan, alarm coursing through my chest.

'Teg, get up!'

But when I look back the figure is gone. The crack of light in the doorway is empty.

'What is it?' she says groggily.

'I thought I saw . . . '

The crack of light goes black.

*

MICAELA IS CRYING on the sofa. She's wearing Haley's sweatpants. Sophie has her arm tight around her. Haley is on the other side, smoking a cigarette, looking ragged. The room is littered with bottles and cans and overflowing ashtrays, and all the boys have vanished with the light.

When Tegan and I come in, Micaela wipes her eyes to hide her tears, but they don't look up at us.

'Do you remember if he used protection?' Sophie says, and Micaela starts sobbing. The sound makes me sick. Her one shoe is on the floor by the breakfast bar where she left it.

'I'm telling you,' Haley says. 'Peter came back in after putting you to bed, which is where I found you. He's not like that. He went through it all with me – he gets it. Let's just call him right now and clear it up, hey?'

Tegan tenses beside me.

'But my knickers . . . '

Haley bites her nails and exchanges a look with Sophie, who has tightened her grip around Micaela. She looks up to see us then. 'Teg, can you get me some painkillers? I've got a bitch of a hangover,' she says.

Tegan practically stomps out the room.

'I'm sorry, I'm such a stupid mess,' Micaela says. 'You're right, Hayz, it's probably nothing. I just feel . . . '

I want to tell them. He led you down the corridor and I closed the door. It was me who left you there. I could have stopped it.

Tegan returns and hands Haley the packet. She eyes Micaela at the centre of this circle of women with open malice.

Haley turns to us. 'Can you two give us a minute?' She pops two pills into her palm and swallows them without water.

I nod, grateful to be relieved from this room with its stale cigarettes and remorse. But Tegan wants to know what happens. I link my arm in hers, and she resists for just a moment, before giving in.

Once we're back in the room, Tegan flops down on the bed. 'She was just wasted. And now she wants to be the centre of attention.'

I can't tell her now. I can't tell anyone. 'What did Haley mean when she said he went through it all with her?'

But Tegan won't answer. I can always sense it. There is a part of her that's off limits. At other times, that part is nowhere to be seen and she wants to tell me everything all at once. She wants to pull at my hand and wrap her arm through my own. She wants to hang her hair over my face to see what I'd look like if I were blonde like her. She wants to talk until she falls asleep mid-sentence. Instead, she plucks out her eyelashes. She doesn't even use them to make wishes.

WHEN WE COME out again, Sophie and Micaela are gone, and some order has been restored. We make ourselves crumpets and sit on the sofa to watch Saturday-afternoon TV.

Haley emerges from the shower, moving with an efficiency that frightens me. She is all tight angles. 'Time to go!' she says.

Tegan sinks deeper into the sofa. She clasps a cushion tight to her chest.

'Come on! I said I'd get you home for dinner.'

'Let me stay, please! I don't want to leave you.'

'Don't start!'

I think there's no way Tegan will persist, but she digs in, her mouth turning down in a sad-clown face I don't recognise.

'I don't want to go.'

Tegan is being childish and it makes me feel superior.

'Tegan!' Haley says, a warning in her tone.

With the next protest, Haley snaps. She takes two strides towards Tegan and hauls her off the sofa by her wrist. The sad clown cries out. Haley's never been anything but gentle and patient, and here she is, calm and cruel, dragging Tegan by her twisted arm out of the door.

'I hate it there!' Tegan shouts. When I think it's over, Tegan turns around, as if to run back inside, and Haley hits her across the face. One solid pink slap, like punctuation.

They are silent after that. This scene has happened before, I'm sure of it.

HALEY DRIVES, HER grip on the steering wheel tight. Tegan sits in the back seat, defeated tears streaming down her face. I feel her distress bundled up beneath the seatbelt beside me, so I slip my hand into hers and hold it tight. Tegan looks down at our hands, then up at me, and squeezes back. We remain like that, our fingers entwined as if in prayer, unwavering in our devotion, until we reach my front door. I give Tegan a final squeeze and say thank you to Haley, feeling a little afraid of her for the first time.

THE MAZE

I bring Mou her coffee in bed on Monday morning. I have to wake her up extra early when she's working at the library. She throws open the curtains, naked, her arms spread wide, pointing her bare breasts towards the sun.

'An Indian summer!' she declares, admiring the brightness of the day.

I say thank you in my head to the library and the ladies in the bird shop who recommended her for the job. When Mou's sad, she leaves the curtains closed all day, like a sign for passers-by to recognise.

She works at the library three days a week, volunteers at the bird shop for two, and on Saturdays she works at a car park, letting cars in and back out. This way we can make ends meet, which is Mou's way of saying everything will be okay. And I believe her. Mou has her job and I have Tegan, and everything will be okay now.

The house is more of a mess than usual with Mou working so much. Her box of scraps exploded over the picnic table, and until she collects up her sentences, we have to eat on the floor in the living room. Each morning, we try to leave enough time for breakfast, but every day we have to do a run-and-a-skip to get me to the bus on time. This is how we walk when we're rushing: run ten paces, skip for three, run ten paces, skip for three. Mou then walks onwards from the bus stop into town. Neither of us does the run-and-a-skip when alone, no matter how late we are.

Today I see her through the bus window as we pass. She is tugging at her hair. I turn to get a better look and she's mouthing words to herself. I can't tell what she's saying. Maybe she's saying, 'Everything will be okay.'

Everything will be okay, I mouth with her.

AT SCHOOL, TEGAN is there before me. I am practised in the art of ignoring her, but today she's kneeling up on her chair and smiling right at me. I don't smile back. That smile must be a mistake. It was meant for someone else. I walk towards my usual desk on the other side of the classroom.

'Sissy!' Tegan calls. 'Where you going?'

The other kids stare, waiting for some cruelty. I'm waiting, too. The Sarahs almost grimace; Hannah looks to Tegan for direction. Clara, ever the brute, grins in anticipation. Even the boys who usually keep to their own quarters have stopped to watch.

'Come and sit here!' Tegan indicates the empty chair beside her that usually belongs to Lydia. 'I've got to tell you what happened with Micaela.'

I take a few steps towards the chair, cautious of its promise.

'So Peter says they didn't have sex, or anything . . . ' Tegan enters fully into the story, her focus entirely on me.

I sit down. This desk doesn't belong to Lydia. I have as

much right to it as her. In fact, it belongs to Tegan. It all belongs to Tegan.

Lydia arrives and stands over me, confused. Tegan doesn't stop talking; she acts as if Lydia isn't even there. Lydia and I catch eyes and I have a premonition that Lydia is me. I am standing in Lydia's place looking back on myself at this desk from the future. I do my best to look sorry. The girls in my head jump up and down in a frenzy. They never saw this coming. Don't be sorry, they say. I harden and turn towards Tegan. I'm not sorry. Lydia shuffles off to the desk in the corner that once was mine.

'Did you hear me? Peter said she took off her own knickers. That's how wasted she was.'

I'm sitting at the desk beside her. I'm where I wanted to be.

'That's great, Teg,' I say, still only half listening. The rest of the class is settling down. 'Micaela must feel relieved.'

'Relieved! She feels like a twat!' Tegan's face is alight. She's drawn a dozen stars up each of her fingers in blue biro. 'She made all that fuss over nothing.'

'Over nothing?'

I'm with her now. The whisk.

'She should be so lucky.' Tegan is triumphant. 'Peter doesn't even fancy her. Apparently he was really upset about the whole thing.'

Miss Storey comes into the classroom and claps. 'In your seats, everyone!'

I look back once more at Lydia. Behind her, the Siamese Fighter Fish turns in his tank.

'DOES THE SHEEP have to come?' Clara whines, as we walk to the playground at lunch.

Tegan ignores her and links her arm with mine. This is how things are and I made it so. I used my one wish on this. It doesn't matter what Clara thinks any more. It doesn't matter what any of them thinks.

Hannah is the girlfriend and Clara the boyfriend. We're in the Maze except not really. We're in a make-believe house, which no one has the imagination to decorate. Hannah and Clara sit on a sofa, which is the only necessary furniture for the scene. The sofa is, in fact, a log. Clara and Hannah make-believe some conversation, and then it's their make-believe first kiss. They don't really kiss. They do it like Tegan showed me. They turn their heads this way and that and pivot their bodies around one another, like a corkscrew, while Tegan and I watch. This is what happens in the Maze, I'm learning.

They pull apart from one another and wipe their thumbs on their shirts.

'I bet I'm a better kisser than Marlon,' Clara declares.

'And a better boyfriend.' Hannah rolls her eyes in imitation of Tegan. 'I'm so horny,' she moans, laying herself over the log decadently. This is Hannah's new thing, Tegan told me. She said she offered to have sex with Marlon and now he won't do it with her. No one believes her: she only says she's horny to cover up that she's not.

'Do it again, but more real,' Tegan says, bored of their chatting.

Hannah and Clara resume their positions, and Hannah fashions a new line of dialogue. She introduces a make-believe husband who is waiting for her at home; some other things happen, which are of no real interest, but Clara begs her to stay, asking for one more kiss before she goes, and Hannah keeps saying no. I'm embarrassed by it. In junior school, the kids played kiss-chase, but we're too old for that now, too old for make-believe, too; yet in this hidden corner of the playground this game has persisted at Tegan's will.

Tegan isn't giggling like the other girls: she's concentrating. In her eyes, it's not a game: it's practice. She's practising for the moment when she's on a sofa with a real boy. Or maybe these things have happened already. I don't know. Hannah and Clara's faces are pinned together at either side of their closed fists.

'Our turn now,' Tegan says, without warning. She drags me into the middle, and the others move aside, giving each other a look that speaks all of their grievances with my arrival in their gang. I don't want to play, but I'm thrust from observer to performer against my will.

Tegan begins without consultation on a new line of pre-tend. I don't know my role, whether I'm the girlfriend or the boyfriend, but it doesn't matter, because she's pulling me down to the ground, and this is what it's really about, I realise. The others laugh at first, but then we roll over, on top of one another, and the rest of the Maze disappears. There's only this moment, which lasts for ever, and even as it's happening, I don't want it to stop. I want it to go on for longer, to go further, to draw closer, and inwards, and down. I don't acknowledge this or admit it later, but I feel the same urgency, the rush and the throb. It's the same. The buried Barbies beneath the back lawn break free. The girls in my head chide me: Don't go too far, they say. Don't get carried away. Just one more moment, I think ... but then there's a hand on my shoulder pulling me back, and there stands Miss Storey, her slender face a graveyard, trembling and horrified.

'What on earth are you doing?' Miss Storey says to Tegan. Adults talk to Tegan differently. They talk to me as a child, but they talk to Tegan like they see the woman she will one day become.

'We were just playing,' Tegan protests, clambering to her feet.

'Good Lord, that's not a game! You're never to do that again! Do you hear me?'

I want to say we weren't really kissing. Then I wonder if we were and I didn't notice, or if at this point there's really a difference.

She looks at us like we're monstrous, like we aren't girls at all. 'You're not to play that, do you understand?'

I nod and I don't understand.

'I came to check on you,' Miss Storey says to me, as if I'd let her down somehow. 'I saw you go off . . . ' She shakes her head. 'Now go on! Join the others.'

She shoos us out of the Maze. As we walk, Tegan glances back over her shoulder and gives me the same sidelong smile she did down on the courts. That smile wills me to break the rules with her; it says there are no rules we need to follow. Tegan rolls her eyes, and I can't help but laugh, the shame flitting away like shadows in the sun. It's not us who don't understand. It's them.

PROPER WITH A CAPITAL P

On Halloween, a third girl goes missing. The local paper runs an offer for cut-price rape-alarm kits and they sell out within two days. Mothers buy them for their daughters in droves. They print posters for this girl, too, and pin them to lampposts beside the posters of the other missing girls, who still haven't been found. This one has braces, like a good teenage emblem.

She was snatched on her way to a costume party. She was wearing a cape and devil horns. The police issue a warning: girls of snatchable age should not go out unaccompanied. Parents of daughters of snatchable ages should keep a watchful eye.

There was another man who snatched girls, they say on the TV, though he preferred grown women. He did his snatching in a different way. He got into the front seat of their cars and made them drive somewhere quiet. I don't like to think of what he did to them in the somewhere quiet. Even though they say it's unlikely to be the same man – one man wearing a mask and liking the girls he snatched to be not yet grown-up, and the other man liking the girls he snatched to be women and driving cars somewhere quiet – they repeated their warnings from the first girl snatcher. We should lock our car doors, just in case. We should beware of strangers. They didn't catch that first snatching man either.

THIS DOESN'T GET through to Mou. Not really. She's too busy making ends meet, but they're meeting in too many places for her to keep track. The first week she was at the library, she came home with a book for me. I gave it to her to read after me, but she returned it and no further books came. We never had our book club, either.

There is nothing to eat in the house, except a can of baked beans that expired last year and some fancy pasta shells that came in a gourmet gift basket we won at a pub raffle; we keep saving them for best, but best never arrives.

'Mou, there's nothing to eat,' I say.

She doesn't answer. She's at the kitchen table busy writing lists of the ways in which she will do better tomorrow.

She will no longer tug her hair in case she goes bald.

She will wear lipstick of the Proper colour at the Proper moment.

She will buy clothes that make her look like a Proper woman, a Proper adult, a Proper mother.

She will be a Proper woman, a Proper adult, a Proper mother.

She will brush her daughter's hair before bed.

She will tell her daughter she loves her every day.

She will eat breakfast. Her daughter will eat breakfast, too.

She will buy a Proper dining-room table, not our white plastic picnic set.

She will buy a book in which to put her scraps in a Proper

order and then the house will be organised, and everything will be better.

She will stop telling lies for no reason. (I've forgotten my glasses. I used to live in Bangkok. On Tuesdays, we play bingo with other people's grandmothers.)

She will stop speaking to herself while walking.

She will stop looking at the stars while weeping.

She will not stand in the garden at night without remembering how she got there.

She will warn her daughter not to stand in the garden at night without remembering how she got there either.

She will warn her daughter not to tug her hair until she goes bald.

She will phone Grandma Jean.

She will forgive Grandma Jean. (Maybe later.)

She will do these things in the space between now and tomorrow morning when she will wake up a better version of herself.

'You've forgotten something,' I say, looking into the empty cupboard.

'What's that?' Mou asks, her eyes wide.

'To go to the supermarket,' I whine.

She nods, looks back down, and writes *go to supermarket* at the bottom of a list where she'll never find it.

MOU SAYS GRANDMA Jean is as mad as a bag of cats. On another occasion, she said Grandma Jean is a cold-hearted bitch. Grandma Jean calls Mou 'Susanne', like it's a command. When Mou is with Grandma Jean, she becomes Susanne: quiet, meek, says please to cake. Susanne might also thwack you around the face with a coffee cup on a Sunday morning, which is exactly what she did to Grandma Jean at sixteen years old, which led to all the quarrels in the first place, or so she told me.

It was the first time Mou took to her bed, after she met Koko, after he had proposed to her on the back of a pedalo with a black ring around her finger like an omen. And after he left again on the same Greek shipping freighter that had delivered him to her in the first place. When Susanne still wouldn't get up, Grandma Jean had thrown back the bed covers and said, 'Enough of this nonsense,' which was when Susanne came to life and thwacked Grandma Jean around the face with the coffee cup. Grandma Jean hadn't flinched, despite the scalding from the hot coffee and her daughter's temper. Susanne folded herself back into bed, pulling the quilt over her head, and imagined the ways in which a girl might die of a broken heart.

The next time Mou woke up, she found a doctor with plump hands and the faint smell of Germolene sitting on the end of her bed.

'Do you know who I am?' the Germolene-smelling doctor had said, which Mou did not.

'You're a figment of my imagination so I won't entertain you,' she said, absorbed instead by the patterns on the quilt, which, after a week of not eating, shifted and changed like the surface of the ocean that had taken Koko away. The next time the doctor came, he brought two other men, who had not sat quietly at the end of her bed and had not gone away when she asked them to.

Mou told me all this during the car days, those long rambling hours driving with no destination in mind, when she talked so much she could have told me her whole life story twice (though she skipped the parts I most wanted to hear, like why she left Koko and where he might be now).

Mou never forgave her mother. Grandma Jean's father had grown up in an institution in Scotland, because he and his father were psychiatrists. Grandma Jean remembers visiting her grandfather, and playing amid the grounds where the patients could wander in white robes between the purple spray of bell heather and moss. There was a mound in the middle of the garden, which allowed the patients a view beyond the perimeter wall to the glens. The patients gathered on the mound and stared out at the distance, accompanied by the haunting sound of the organ from within the grand house, intended to soothe their thoughts.

Mou says Grandma Jean was capable of calling the Germolene-smelling doctor to take her away because she had a rose-tinted view of psychiatric institutions from those early childhood memories. Also, because the people we love are sometimes the ones we most hate. And, she says, because there isn't always a good reason why people do terrible things to one another.

When Koko came back, Mou was waiting for him at the docks with her suitcase, ready to go wherever he would take her. I think of this Mou. This part-woman, part-girl who was my mother, and she looks so brave standing there with her suitcase while a tanker as large as an island barrels towards the shore.

Mou and Koko moved to the apartment in the towers in Aberdeen, and Koko got a job on the rigs, and then I came along before I was meant to, and with me came more sadness. It's a little bit my fault, the sadness, even though I didn't do it on purpose. Mou says I split her in two, which I guess is a metaphor.

She kept the coffee cup, wrapped in a silk scarf at the bottom of that suitcase, and she has it still. It's a reminder, she says. A reminder never to let someone take something you aren't willing to give.

I SLIP A few pounds from Mou's wallet into my pocket, along with one of Koko's crystals for protection. I'm going to walk to the chippie at the end of the road without telling her. Mou doesn't have rules for me, as such, but I know going out alone after dark isn't allowed. It wasn't allowed before the girls went missing, but it must be especially un-allowed right now.

I want to walk to the chippie at the end of the road because it should make Mou worry. I want her to discover my absence, and then to suffer like the crying mother of the missing girl on TV. I'm also hungry. I could tell her I'm walking to the chippie, but she'll only get upset about there being no food. She might try to come with me, and then she'll stand in her room, tugging her hair. There will be no fish and chips that way. And if I tell her, she can't discover my absence later and suffer.

I walk past the rows of houses. Other families are watching TV together. Mou and I watch TV together but it doesn't look the same when we do it.

The chippie is next to the pub. We've only been to the pub once. It smelt of cigarettes and other people's problems with boozy bad breath. The football is always playing and the men look like they might cry at any moment, which I thought was because football makes them sad, but Mou says it's for other reasons. They won't cry and instead they'll end up fighting each other or beating their wives. We're lucky we don't have a man in our lives to sit in a pub not-crying, she says. Or beating us when he comes home to bed.

As I walk, I think about the girl snatcher. It's beyond

almost dark. It's fully night-time. He might be waiting for me in any of these doorways or dark passages. I imagine him snatching me from behind, his weight against me, and its force dragging me down, deep into the ground, where a tree appears in my place, bearing red fruit that never grows ripe. This is a daydream. I don't understand why, but I play it again and again with a different variation each time. I walk faster, trying to think of something else, anything other than the danger lurking, when I hear footsteps behind me. I quicken my pace, scurrying now, but then his breath is on my neck, warm and pungent, until I can't bear it any longer, and I break into a run, tumbling through the doors of the chippie, panting.

The bright lights fizz and splutter, like the fat in the fryer. I look behind me and nobody's there, just fear approaching. The chippie is empty except for the man behind the counter and a teenager waiting on a chair in the corner with hollow eyes. His eyebrow is pierced like Peter's. He's probably only a few years older than me. If Tegan were here she'd say hi to him. She'd ask where he'd been, and if he said one of the pubs in town, she would act like she knew it, like she went there herself. Then she'd ask him to go to the offie to buy us some booze.

'Fish and chips, please,' I say, my voice sounding small.

There are posters of the missing girls next to a flyer for singing lessons and an illustration explaining how to prevent someone from choking.

'Did you know them?' the man behind the counter asks, when he sees me looking.

I shake my head.

'I had a daughter, probably be about your age now.' He doesn't say what happened to his daughter to be spoken of in the past tense. Daughters are dropping dead all around me. 'Where's your mam, luv?'

'At home. We live there,' I say, pointing towards our house, because I want him to know I live close enough to run home faster than he can jump over the counter and get me.

The teenager behind me pipes up: 'Where's my effing chips?'

The man behind the counter ignores him. He acts as if he isn't even there. As if only I can see him.

My fish is frying, but I want to leave. I turn the crystal in my pocket nervously. I wish Tegan were here to make this act of bravery less frightening and I swell with love and pride for my new friend who makes things like this less frightening. I wonder if Mou's noticed I've gone yet. Or if she's still at the table writing her lists and not thinking about where I might be or if I might be in trouble.

Mou told me a story once about when she was a little girl and she got lost in the woods. She wasn't unhappy and she didn't mean to run away. She wanted to make a fort for herself, which she did from twigs and a piece of tarpaulin. But after she'd made her fort, she couldn't find her way home. When they found her, she was dehydrated and confused and they took her to hospital to recover. Grandma Jean acted like nothing had happened. She sat in a chair by Mou's bed, fiercely knitting a scarf. Mou had never seen her mother knit before; she thinks she did it because it seemed the proper thing to do by a daughter's bedside. Her mother never asked what had happened to her in the days that she was missing; it was as if she didn't want to know. The police asked, though. They asked her again and again and they never believed that she had simply been lost all that time.

'Be careful,' the man behind the counter says, handing me

my fish and chips wrapped in newspaper like a present. 'It's dangerous out there for a pretty little thing like you.'

I run all the way home.

When I come through the door, Mou is lying on the sofa wrapped in a quilt. She turns to look at me. She knew I was gone. She hasn't blinked since, hoping the moment would pass sooner.

'I walked up and down the street calling your name. I was watching the clock and when it hit ten thirty I was going to call the police. I counted every second after I realised.'

I go to her, and she pulls me in to her body, close and tight. She smells like musty feathers in an old pillow. Like mothballs and sweat. I hold my fish and chips afloat above her embrace so as not to spill them.

'I'm sorry, Mou,' I say, and I am sorry.

She squeezes me so tightly I can't breathe. She squeezes me as if she's frightened someone might snatch me right here.

'I can't bear it,' Mou says.

I want to reassure her. I am not yet a girl of snatchable age, or maybe I am and don't know it.

'I was hungry,' I say, and immediately regret it, because it will hurt her doubly, and this extra hurt will be my fault too. This is what I wanted: for her to suffer on my account and prove that she loves me, even though I know it to be true.

She loosens her grip all of a sudden, limp with spent fear. I sit up. She places a hand against my chest and listens through her fingers.

'You're cross with me,' she says, and removes her hand, like she's heard enough. 'You're all I have. Do you understand?'

I nod, but I cannot understand. She looks away.

'I'm glad nobody snatched you.' She fusses with the quilt

127

around her legs. She says it as if she's glad nobody got caught in the rain.

'I'm sorry,' I say again, but it sounds insincere now.

'Eat your chips, then.'

I open up the package, but I'm no longer hungry. My chips are soggy with vinegar and regret.

A STAR READYING TO DIE

Tegan is doodling on a missing-girl poster. She tore it down from a lamppost. She's lying on the bed, using her schoolbooks as a hard surface. I'm sitting on the floor by her bed doing actual homework. Everything is different at school. It's exactly as I imagined it would be. Better. Clara still ignores me, and Hannah seems unsure whose lead to follow, but I enjoy it: Tegan has chosen me and their sulking proves it.

Soon Tegan and I will be separated for the Christmas holidays when she'll go back to the farm. We don't want to be apart for so long, so I suggested a spell to bind us. We performed our spell in the cramped confines of a telephone booth by Tegan's house that smelt of stale urine. I plucked a strand of hair from Tegan's skull and she plucked one from mine. It hurt, which was good. That meant the magic would work. We knotted our two pieces of hair together, like I once did alone, all those months ago, and we took a match to the middle. Our knotted hair disappeared in a flash, and the spell incinerated into the air around us, along with the scent of burned hair. We're bound by it now, so the idea of separation seems less daunting.

'What photo would you use if you went missing?' Tegan asks, looking into the missing girl's eyes.

'I don't think you get to choose.'

'She's really pretty, isn't she? I wouldn't want any old picture of me plastered all over town. We should take our best photos and give them to each other, so if either of us ever goes missing, we can give the photo to the police. Promise?'

'Promise.'

Her little finger reaches towards me and I clasp it in my own, a pinky promise, one of many. It's hard to keep track of everything I've sworn to do and not do as conditions of our friendship.

'Maybe I could ask Mou to get us one of those disposable cameras,' I say. 'She keeps asking if there's anything I want.'

'Tell her you want a razor so you don't have to borrow mine.'

'Ha-ha.'

Tegan has never asked why I call her Mou. I don't know if it's because she isn't interested or because she doesn't want to ask for something I won't readily give up, and she senses I might not.

'Do you think he raped her?' Tegan asks.

We're studying common denominators. When the denominators of two or more fractions are the same, they're common. Tegan and I are common denominators. We have become fractions of each other. Everything is divisible by two.

'The girl snatcher, I mean,' Tegan prompts, when I don't reply. She's asked this before, and I'm tired of this line of make-believe. Tegan wants to talk about what the girl snatcher does to them. She wants to imagine it was her. I think about this too, but in my daydreams the story ends with my snatching. ''Cause they found her tights, so he must have pulled them off, right? And what else would he have done?'

'Maybe she changed into a bird. Maybe she's already far away from here.'

Tegan looks back at the poster, as if the image of the missing girl might whisper the answer. She plucks her eyelashes. This means she's anxious. She hands me an eyelash balanced on her little finger.

'Make a wish for me, Siss. A good one.'

We hear footsteps up the stairwell and a part-man's voice arrives in the living room.

'Do you want a snack?' Tegan asks, not waiting for an answer. 'I'm going to get one.'

She jumps up and is gone.

I hear Peter greet her through the wall, 'Hey, squirt,' and I shudder.

I blow Tegan's eyelash from my finger. I wish for the same thing every time. For Tegan to be my friend for ever.

'How'd it go with What's-her-face?' Tegan says. 'Miss cuts-herself-for-attention?'

I pull up my sleeves. The rash, if I can call it that, on the back of my knees has spread to the creases of my arms. I tried applying some cream I found in the bathroom cabinet but it only made it burn. It doesn't itch anyway. It just looks alarming. I pick at a scale of skin, which peels clean away from my body, like I'm shedding. It's so fine, it's translucent. It's barely there.

I yank down my sleeves, disturbed, and examine Tegan's doodles instead. She's framed the missing girl's face in a circle of stars, like a showgirl's mirror. Her grainy black eyes are watching us. This morning, when the missing girl came on the news, Mou said she isn't really missing. Mou had let her second cup of coffee go cold in her hands. She was late for work and seemed not to care. 'Missing girls are always just dead,' she said. 'They call them *missing* so people keep searching. People need hope. They should tell the parents and put them out of their misery.'

'Is that how you'd feel if it was me?' I asked her.

Mou looked like I'd said something dreadful – something that filled her with dread – and I'd meant it like that. She woke me up in the middle of the night again to tell me she missed me. She gave me a few little shoves, and then she started talking about how sorry she is that she's working so much, and how we don't have the time together like we used to now I'm friends with Tegan, and perhaps we should start a new club, not a book club this time, something different, because I was growing up so quickly, and before she knew it, I'd be gone, if I wasn't gone already, and she said all this so fast without coming up for air that I didn't have a chance to tell her to stop and go back to bed. I covered my ears instead. 'Mum!' I shouted. I told her it was the middle of the night, and she looked at her watch, acting surprised.

I'm cross because now I'm tired, but also because she's not meant to wake me up in the middle of the night any more. She got the job and we have a garden and I have a friend, and that means we're done with waking up in the middle of the night or moving for no reason or looking at the stars and crying. She has to wake up in the morning like other mothers and go to work and not forget me after school. I'm also cross because I feel guilty: I haven't been doing my job of making sure she doesn't get sad, because I'm always at Tegan's, and perhaps she woke me up in the middle of the night to remind me of that.

I pull up my sleeves again and peel away layer after layer of skin with satisfaction.

IN THE LIVING room, Tegan and Peter are on the sofa watching TV. She reaches out her hands for me, like she always does, a wordless command. I go to her.

I haven't seen Peter since the party. He nods at me, his attention fixed on the screen. Robots are fighting.

When Tegan goes to the toilet, it's just Peter and me and the space between us that was Tegan, her imprint still in the cushions. Haley is getting ready in her room. She'll go to work soon and give me a lift home, and this thought gives me a moment of relief. I won't have to sit here for much longer with Peter.

'It's cool Tegan has a friend like you,' Peter says, as if we've been talking about it. He's looking at me, but I'm looking at the telly. The robots are rammed together; sparks are flying. 'She talks about you all the time, you know?'

I look to the corridor for Tegan. He's speaking quietly, but I'm still worried she might hear. He's never spoken to me like this before, his voice intimate, like we're friends.

'You seem pretty grown-up. She needs someone like that, someone sensible, because – just between us, right? – she might act like nothing bothers her, but I worry what sort of trouble she'll get into one day, after what happened with Andy and her family being so messed up.'

I've never thought about the fact that Peter knows more about Tegan than I do, but of course he does. He's known her since she was little.

'You knew her brother?' I ask, curious, despite myself.

'Yeah. Hayz and him were super close. He and I didn't

always see eye to eye. He liked to party, hung out with a dodgy crowd. But whatever my feelings about the bloke, it's still fucked up what happened.'

Peter looks at me then, and I catch his eye for just a moment, before looking away, looking anywhere except his face.

'Hey,' he says, and I have to turn back to him, even though I don't want to. He is leaning against the sofa with one arm resting over the top. His arm isn't around me, but it's behind me, which is close enough, and he's looking right into my eyes. 'Me and you are cool, yeah?'

He's talking about the other night. He wants me to say I'll keep his secret. He wants it without having to ask outright.

'I know Tegan would want that,' he adds. The hand on top of the sofa drops down just enough for his fingers to brush my shoulder lightly. 'I'd like that, too.'

I nod. And like that I shut the door on the half of Micaela I couldn't see. 'Yeah, we're cool,' I say, my heart racing. I cross my arms over my chest, sinking away from his touch.

He smiles. The two dimples in his cheeks deepen. I want to stick my fingers right through them until I pierce the flesh.

Tegan has returned from the toilet and she's looking at us on the sofa, assessing. When I spot her, her expression changes, and she flops down between us like she didn't sense a thing. It's me she curls into. It's on my shoulder she rests her head.

'I hope you're talking about me,' she says, prodding Peter with her feet and he grabs them, holding them both in one hand.

'Who else would we be talking about, trouble?'

Haley wheels in her little suitcase. She's in her night-time guise, her eyelashes so heavy she can barely keep her eyes open. 'I'm off to work. Siss, you want a lift home?'

I get up.

'Stay!' Tegan says, a little quiver in her voice. She kneels up and takes my hand. 'This way you're already here tomorrow.'

Brenda said Tegan can stay for the weekend so she and I can go Christmas shopping on Saturday together. We're allowed into town on our own, as long as we're back before dark. I want to stay, too, but I think about Mou at home alone with no one there to stave off her sadness. And then I look at Peter. I can't stand him.

'I can't. Mou wants me home. She's worried because of the missing girls,' which is almost the truth.

Tegan hugs me at the door, like she always does, but she holds on for a moment longer, and I'm filled with the urge to take her with me. I feel it so strongly, I hug her a little tighter. I want to take her from this apartment and back home to Mou, and maybe that would be just what they both needed. I could tell Tegan about the sadness and the sentences, and show her the trophies, and the bird teapots, and she wouldn't think us strange. She would think it delightful. We could dance to Mou's records, the three of us together, shout singing to the open sky. We could have sofa picnics and talk over the TV. Mou would love Tegan, and Tegan would love Mou back, because she doesn't get on with her own mother, so Mou could fill that gap.

But the feeling passes, and with it the certainty that if she and Mou met, they would feel as I do or understand one another.

I pull away from Tegan's grasp.

I walk down the stairs behind Haley.

'See you tomorrow, then,' Tegan says, as the door swings shut.

*

THE NEXT DAY, Tegan is waiting for me on the street outside Haley's apartment, which I think is strange. She's already dressed up in a make-up mask to hide her girlhood. She's drawn a line around the edge of her lips in a different colour from her lipstick. I look ordinary in comparison, childlike and plain.

'What's up?' I ask, when she starts walking immediately, like she's trying to get away.

'Nothing,' she says, not looking at me. She thrusts her hands into the pockets of her bomber jacket. She's all hard edges, which throws me because we've been looking forward to this all week. It's our first outing into town together as almost teenagers.

We pass the burned-out factory where we saw the older kids previously, and Tegan lingers to look inside. The glassless windows frame skateboarders practising their tricks.

'Come on, Teg!' I'm eager for our shopping excursion and for her mood to pass.

We go to the Body Shop. I buy White Musk body spray and bath balls for Mou's Christmas present. Tegan picks things up and puts them down without even looking. She hasn't bought anything for her family yet.

'Where do you want to go, then? How about Woolworths? You could get Haley a CD or something.'

'I don't care,' she says, as if I'm at fault.

'What's up with you? Have I done something?'

We wander down Market Place without purpose. Two lads linger on the corner, eating chicken nuggets with their fingers from a box. They shove the gargoyle shapes into their mouths as if no one is looking. One of the boys eyes Tegan without shame.

'All right, girls!' he says.

Tegan turns to shout back, with renewed vigour: 'All right!'

The cocky boy steps forward: 'Come over here and chat to us, then, if you're up for it?'

These boys seem enormous, lurching animals prowling. There is no Haley here to filter their attention. They look at Tegan like she's something they want to capture. And she acts like she's eager to be ensnared. She walks towards them.

'Teg!' I say, but quietly, because I don't want to play the sensible friend who counters her bravery. I want to be brave, also. Ready.

The boy drops his chicken nuggets, box and all.

'So what you got to say to us, then?' Tegan is all bravado. She acts like she's practised at this. Even I believe in the show. And perhaps she has: perhaps there are things she doesn't tell me. But this aura of experience does nothing to lessen their interest – it reassures them they're not walking on untrodden ground. 'You shout at all the girls?'

'Nah, just you, darling.'

Tegan and the boy, who we learn is called Gavin, shoot barbs back and forth. They have an answer to everything. It's not about what they say but showing they can say it. They are both brilliant. I steal a glance at the other boy. He has wavy shoulder-length hair and a hoodie pulled up over his head. Like me, he lets his friend do the talking.

'We're going to smoke a spliff at the factory,' Gavin says. 'Want to come?'

'Come on, Siss!' Tegan has a delirious expression on her face.

'We have to be home soon,' I say, and cringe.

'Exactly. It's on the way.'

I'm grateful when she lets the boys walk ahead and loops her arm through mine conspiratorially. The interaction has changed her, made her suddenly alive, and the shift in her mood is dizzying.

'Are you all right?' I ask, not for the first time today.

We enter the factory at a side door that has fallen from its hinges. The skateboarders have moved on, leaving the floor littered with beer cans. They constructed a ramp from stacked crates and it acts as a makeshift stage. Tegan runs towards it and the boys lumber after her. The space is cavernous, with no roof. The building's rusted bones frame the sky across which geese flock away from winter.

'Come over here, Siss!' Tegan calls. She's atop the make-shift stage, turning in rapturous circles with her arms spread wide. The boys light cigarettes, watching with side eyes. Under their gaze she vibrates, grows brighter, flickering like a star readying to die.

I wonder if we should be scared here, away from the rest of the town, behind high walls, with these two boys we've only just met. I'm aware this is something we shouldn't do, but I'm eager for the future in which Tegan and I talk about having done it.

I join Tegan. She steals a cigarette from Gavin's hand, like it's completely natural.

'I've been dying for a cig all day,' she says, adopting her imaginary older persona. Here, she's Tallulah. Brazen and already trouble.

'Shouldn't smoke, you know,' Gavin says sarcastically, pulling a six-pack of Foster's out of his rucksack and handing them around. 'It'll kill you.'

'Who wants to get old?' Tegan replies.

'Live fast, die young,' says the long-haired boy, who's called Joe.

Tegan passes me the cigarette, and I concentrate so hard

on not coughing that later, when I play it back in my mind, I'm sure it was the fear of coughing that, in fact, made me cough. The others exchange a smile, and I pass it back, embarrassed.

Gavin rolls a joint, which I now recognise from Haley's party. When it's passed to me, saying no seems impossible. This time, I cough even harder and they openly laugh.

'First time?' Joe asks, and I shake my head, following Tegan's lead. We're pretending to be proper girls, who hang out with boys in abandoned warehouses. Part of pretending is saying yes.

'Want a blow back?' Gavin says to Tegan.

'Sure,' she says, though I'm certain she doesn't know what he's suggesting.

He looms over her, turning the spliff backwards in his mouth, then cups his hands around Tegan's cheeks to blow smoke between her lips. It looks like a type of kissing, and makes me hot on the inside in a way I can't explain. It feels like anger except the edges are softer.

Tegan coughs too, then, and stammers a bit.

'We should get back soon, Teg,' I say, worried for her and what this iteration of Tegan might do. She shakes her head determinedly, her eyes reddening.

'We've just got here,' she says, her voice tight and forced. 'That was intense,' she says to Gavin, who laughs, and she laughs with him. She's laughing at what he's done to her, as if it's a joke.

The world feels woozy when Gavin asks if she wants to see something cool around the side of the warehouse, and woozier still when she says okay. She walks away with him, and I'm powerless to stop it. Tegan turns back once, frightened perhaps, but she goes willingly. Not just willingly, forcefully, like something was already decided. Like it was over before it began.

Joe and I don't speak. I grip my can of Foster's, hating Tegan a little for leaving me like this.

'How old are you?' he asks at last.

'Fourteen,' I say, lying again, my mouth painfully dry. So dry the beer barely wets my lips. 'You?'

'Fifteen. Your friend's pretty wild.'

I don't say anything. Tegan is around the side of the warehouse and whatever Gavin's showing her involves kissing most likely, or worse. I know that's how it works. And I'm meant to stay here and kiss Joe, except I don't want to. Or I don't want to start kissing and for the others to come back and see me doing it wrong. My mouth is too dry for kissing, anyway.

Joe shifts himself closer to me. His hoodie hides a rash of acne across his cheeks. The world around me feels strange, distant. The walls are alive with graffiti. Engorged disembodied cocks dance across every surface. His arm slips over my shoulder as if reaching for a breast, though he won't find one. I hold my breath.

'Do you want to get off?'

It doesn't even sound like he means it. It sounds like he knows it's expected of him, too. I can't form the word 'no' on my lips. Again, it feels impossible. But I can shake my head.

'Cool,' he says, shrugging. The arm slinks away.

He gets up then and walks around kicking cans. I've done a bad thing. I've hurt his feelings. Saying 'no' made him mad. I long for Tegan's return so this can be over and we can go back to imagining it, rather than doing it for real. But when Tegan comes back the flicker of light I saw in her has gone out.

'Shall we go?' I say, expecting her to tease me and call

me scaredy, but she doesn't. Her mouth looks red and sore; her lip liner has vanished. She nods and we leave without saying goodbye. As we walk away, there's a distant sound, and I can't tell if it's birds clattering through treetops or the boys laughing.

'What happened?' I ask. We're walking back quickly to beat the coming darkness and Haley's anger with it. The sun sits on the surface of the earth somewhere and soon the last of the light will be extinguished. 'What did he show you?'

She wipes her mouth with her sleeve. 'We just got off. What do you want – a full report?'

A wall rises between us then and the conversation is over.

WHEN WE GET back to the house, Peter is still there.

'Hey, squirt,' he says, not looking up from the TV. 'Hey, squirt's friend. You look pretty.'

I wonder why he always tells me I look pretty and never Tegan.

She takes my hand and leads me straight into her room. She flops down on the bed, and says loudly, 'Those lads were fit, right?' She starts to talk then. She tells me that Gavin was an amazing kisser and we should hang out with them again; we'll go back next Saturday, and she'll ask if they can get us some vodka and cigarettes of our own. She says these things even knowing that next Saturday she'll be back at the farm and we'll be apart over Christmas. She thinks it would be pretty cool to have a sixteen-year-old boyfriend. She wants to know what happened with Joe, but she doesn't listen to the answer. Then out of the blue she says we should call Eric666 right now: she has his number and he wants to talk to us both. 'Wouldn't that be funny?' and before I can protest, she's moved on. She keeps talking and talking, until finally, she turns to me, her eyes wide and wild, and takes both my hands in hers. 'Can you keep a secret?'

I think she's about to cry. 'Why do you always ask me?'

(What I mean is, why does she ask me but never tell?)

'Well, can you?'

'Of course I can. You know I can. I'd never tell.'

She nods. That's all she wants to hear. It's enough.

That night, she mutters and shudders in her sleep.

'Wake up, Teg. You're having a bad dream.'

She rolls towards me and pulls me close. 'I never want a boyfriend anyway, Siss,' she says. 'I've got you.'

She is my best friend. My only ever friend. We are all that we need. In that moment, I believe it. The rest flitters away in the darkness. We sleep entwined with one another, like we've grown used to, her hair in my face and all over. All through these months, I will find her long blonde hair on my clothes, in my food, and once even lodged between my teeth.

III

(separation)

10

(separation)

UN-SNATCHABLE STILL

I have been in the bath so long it's grown dark. The pea green suite turned slowly grey. The bathwater is soupy, tangled with hair and silty from soap suds.

I am brewing myself, creating a concoction.

I am the same temperature as the water, so if I concentrate I can disappear completely. My boundaries shift and loosen; it's unclear where the water ends and my skin begins.

I turned twelve the day before yesterday. I examine my body for signs of change. I check between my toes, and my fingers catch on what feels like a flap of skin. Lifting my foot from the water for a closer inspection, I spread my toes and the webs of skin spread with them. I yank the other foot out in panic, and it's the same. I clamp my toes shut like a fist.

I am changing, but what I'm changing into isn't clear any longer. This changing hurts. Like the ache at the back of my throat when I try not to cry.

Mou opens the bathroom door, and I plunge my feet back into the water to hide them.

'What are you doing in here in the dark?' she says, switching on the overhead light.

Colour rushes into the world. Alarmed by the brightness, I sink beneath the surface. My webbed toes were just my eyes playing tricks on me, I tell myself, something I imagined.

Mou looks down on me, her face distorted.

'Your breasts are coming in,' she says, except I don't really hear until I lift my head from the water.

'What?'

She nods at my chest. 'Breasts!'

The same two hard nuggets are swollen. 'As if,' I say. I want to show her what's happening between my toes instead. That's the real thing.

Mou closes the toilet lid and sits down. 'Don't worry, I've never had much of them either,' she says, misinterpreting my look of fright. She pulls her shirt tight over her chest to prove the point. 'At least, not until I had you. Breasts are overrated. They jiggle about too much when you run. And a woman needs to be able to run away. You're better adapted with small ones.'

Breasts are the least of my worries. I don't care if I'm mal-adapted and can't run away. I'm not changing how I'm meant to be. I'm not girl, or woman. Not child, or grown-up. I'm changing into something else entirely.

TEGAN INVITED ME to stay on the farm for a few days after Christmas. Mou wanted me to say no.

'Won't it be strange staying with people you don't know?' she prompted.

'Tegan's my best friend,' I replied, as if it's justification enough for leaving her.

Mou called Brenda to arrange the details. I heard her ask where I would sleep and tell Brenda I was vegetarian, which made me cringe. 'They're cow farmers,' I reminded Mou.

'All the more reason. The cows are right there, watching your every bite.'

Tegan and I talk about my visit on the phone most nights. Our telephone is on the floor in the hallway and it only works if you sit very still. Otherwise it sounds like you're calling the future, crackling and distant. Sitting very still like this, sometimes for hours, I imagine Tegan on the other side, sitting very still also, connected by lengths of distant telephone wire stretching over the green fields that separate her from me. She tells me everything apart from what it's really like.

'You're going to hate it.'

'Why did you invite me, then?'

'Because we can hate it together, and it won't be so bad.'

Mou tidied her sentences back into their box and took a few broken lamps to the dump. She wants me to know she's trying. On my birthday, she gave me a leaflet from the local pet-rescue centre. She thought now we're settled, and I'm old enough to be responsible, I might like a small dog. I want to reward her for trying, but the reward she wants is for me not to leave her, and I won't give up seeing Tegan.

This year Mou decided Christmas trees are wasteful, so instead we have a Christmas house plant. We decorated our parlour palm with red baubles and wrapped golden tinsel between its many trunks. But after insisting on it, now Mou is sorry. 'You should have a proper tree, with proper decorations,' she says. I make a show of loving it.

Mou lets me choose one present each year, but she refused to buy me a razor. Instead, she bought me the disposable camera I asked for and another Tammy Girl bra with three pairs of matching pants. I give her the Body Shop basket I'd bought for her in town with Tegan and a Christmas card I'd drawn, like I have every year. She adds it to her box labelled

NOSTALGIA. This box travels everywhere we've been and lives under her bed with the coffee cup wrapped in a silk scarf.

Every Christmas, we call Grandma Jean before lunch. Mou and I sit on the floor in the spot where the telephone works. We sit terribly still, even though I can feel Mou wants to get up and walk around. To be anywhere but here. I listen to their exchange. They skirt so far around the unsaid, there's nothing of substance left to talk about. Mou hands me the phone.

'Wish your grandmother Merry Christmas.' Her accent stiffens whenever they talk.

The last time I saw Grandma Jean was several Christmases ago. She was standing in the doorway of her townhouse in Chelsea watching as Mou struggled to start the Vauxhall Nova. The engine spluttered and coughed and the car wouldn't budge. A postman walked past and offered to help, just as Mou banged on the steering wheel, shouting, 'Fuck, fuck it, fuck, fuck!' and the postman backed away, giving me a worried smile. When I looked back at the house, Grandma Jean had gone inside. Later Mou cried so hard she had to pull the car over to the side of the road.

'You just had a birthday. How old are you now?' Grandma Jean says to me, in a voice I barely recognise.

Mou is crashing around the kitchen, so it's hard to hear.

'Twelve.'

'Oh, my, you'll be a real grown woman soon.'

Unreal. Un-grown. Un-snatchable still.

'Tell your mother you'd like to visit me,' she whispers, as if Mou is listening. 'Do you remember Mephistopheles, my old devil of a cat? He told me to tell you he'd love to see you. He promises to be on his best behaviour.'

When I'm talking to Grandma Jean, it's easy to forget that I'm meant to hate her.

Mou is upstairs making a racket. I hang up and go to find her.

'Mou?' I say, following her up.

She's pulling clothes from her wardrobe and throwing them onto the bed. We're meant to be going to the pub for Christmas lunch, because there's no point in cooking for just the two of us.

'I thought we should get dressed up,' she says, when she sees me standing in the doorway. 'I never get to dress up, but it's bloody Christmas Day, and what better excuse?'

The clothes are piling up behind her.

'This one has moth holes, and, God, I can't wear that, it used to be Koko's favourite ... Did I ever tell you about the first Christmas I spent with Koko? He used to love Christmas. He always said he'd take us to Greece, once we had enough money, and we could see how they do Christmas over there. Something about burning an old pair of shoes and a lot of church. He had a little wooden boat, one of the things he took out to sea with him every time, and he said he used to carry it through the village he grew up in on Christmas Eve and his neighbours would give him small treats to eat. It sounded so romantic. How did I get here? Oh, the dress ... '

I sit on the edge of the bed. I've heard about my father's little wooden boat before, a boat that fitted into his pocket, like my crystals, and it's an object I covet, a treasure I can only imagine. I feel a familiar stab of longing for the version of myself currently sitting around a big Greek family table surrounded by the sea. My father is the sea, distant and mythical.

'How about you?' Mou turns to me. 'Here, try it on.'

'It's too big, Mou.'

'It might fit, if we pin it at the back.'

I pull off my T-shirt, and try on the dress Koko loved. Red flowers embroidered beneath sheer blue taffeta. The delicate straps hang loose on my shoulders and its skirts sit flat without hips to fill them.

'You look wonderful!' She laughs, then launches into her handbag for the lipstick she carries but never wears. 'Here! And take your socks off!'

I shake my head. 'I look silly!'

'Don't say such a thing. No lips? Okay, you're in charge.'

My socks remain on to hide my toes, but Mou has already moved on, squeezing into a black velvet off-the-shoulder outfit from another time in her life, or perhaps an unlikely purchase from the bird shop.

'We need music!' Mou cries, switching on the radio. Gloomy Christmas carols won't do, she says, and insists we carry the record player up to her bedroom instead so we can listen to the Pogues while we're getting ready. It's heavy and cumbersome, and difficult to reassemble once upstairs, but eventually the needle scratches into action, and the Pogues' raspy brogue whines out, maudlin at first, and then near euphoric.

'You're a bum, you're a punk,' Mou shout sings, in her best Irish accent, along to the record. 'Come on! Sing with me!'

She takes my hand and I can't help myself. I sing along, the taffeta rustling as I sway, loving my mother like this, even while knowing we won't make it for Christmas lunch this year.

'You took my dreams from me ...' Mou sings, her eyes closed, as she slips away into the song.

THE FARM

The car lurches over a potholed road towards a distant farmhouse. Mou is muttering to the road. I am muttering to myself. I'm going to stay with Tegan for five whole nights. I'm going to meet her mother and father and brothers. I'm going to help on the farm with the cows, and the pigs, and the chickens. I look out of the window: damp sheep gather against the stone walls, their faces wise beyond their years.

We pull into a cement yard. Toys are abandoned to grow soggy and grey, and doll parts scattered, like a plastic massacre. One soft toy's innards are tufted along a grassy ledge like the white domes of dandelions. The small stone farmhouse is misshapen by extensions on either side, weatherbeaten and defiant, and dwarfed by a barn looming behind it. Cows line up at a metal gate, their warm wet noses steaming. Behind the house is a scrappy copse, and beyond, a colourless sky.

Mou turns off the engine. 'Looks nice,' she says unconvincingly.

One of the cows lets out a startled bellow, followed by the clattering of hoofs. Mou and I look at each other, alarmed, and we laugh.

'Ugh!' Mou rubs her face to free her brain of feelings. 'I was once chased by a cow down a canal path,' she says, and there isn't an end to the story.

I've not been away from Mou for more than a night. And now I'm going to stay in this strange house with these people I don't know, and I'm suddenly unsure.

A dog approaches wagging its tail expectantly. There's a Barbie doll in its mouth, her head pierced in its teeth, her blonde hair matted with saliva and mud. But then I look at the dog, its proud stance. It looks just like Harvey from Tegan's photo album. Exactly like Harvey. So much so that, throughout everything that happens next, my attention keeps returning to this dog, resurrected and panting through clenched teeth.

Mou takes a deep breath and puts on her best smile. She places a hand on my chest.

'Don't worry about me, Sissy *mou*. I want you to have a good time.' She pulls my forehead into her own, and we look at one another, head to head, blurry eyes unified. 'We'll both be just fine,' she says.

The Harvey lookalike barks impatiently, as a woman with bright blonde hair appears from around the side of the house. She waves a hand towards us, which could just as well mean back away and be gone. She has the same strong features as Tegan and Haley, except her chin has been lost to her neck and she's soft in the middle. Her hair has been styled and set but it's off-kilter, as if she's slept on it strangely. She wears a pink nurse's uniform with a pair of rubber boots a size too big. She shuffles towards us in her too-big boots.

We get out of the car to greet her.

'You must be Sissy's mum,' Brenda says. 'I'd shake your hand but just been out back with the cows.'

Tegan comes to the front door and hovers for a moment before joining us, taking careful tippy-toe steps in socks.

'Tegan, put on some shoes.'

Tegan stands by her mother's side, still shoeless. We are shy together in front of our parents for the first time.

'Forgive me, the place is a mess,' Brenda says.

'Not at all.' Mou looks around for redemption but there's none to be found. There isn't another house for as far as we can see, and in the depths of winter the fields have all been cleared of crops, just mud turned over waiting for spring.

'Every year I say I'll fix things up, but what can you do, hey, with an army of kids running riot?' Brenda runs a hand through Tegan's hair, and Tegan flinches. Brenda has cow on her hand, and now Tegan has cow in her hair. Brenda keeps one cow-hand on Tegan's shoulder as we talk. 'Got any more?' Brenda asks, nodding at me.

Mou shakes her head.

'Never wanted another?' Brenda presses.

'Life doesn't always work out the way you want, does it?' Mou says, with more bite than she intended.

'No, you're quite right,' Brenda replies, hardening a little.

Scrambling for niceties, Mou adds, 'I met your eldest.'

'Oh?' I realise Brenda must be thinking about Andy.

'Haley?'

'Oh, yes.' Her face is set in a smile, which is also a grimace. 'Just you wait till your one gets a bit older. A whole world of heartache opens up, I'm telling you. Can I offer you some tea?'

Mou doesn't want tea. She doesn't want to be here. I'm sorry for having a friend and making Mou drive out here so I can see her. I also want Mou to leave quickly so I can be alone with Tegan and we can get on with whatever it is we'll do now we're here.

Mou turns to me. 'I'll answer the phone if it rings.'

I nod reassuringly.

'I'm glad to have met you,' Brenda says, 'our girls being so close.'

Brenda wants Mou to stay for tea so she can ask her more questions about the babies she never had and the husbands she didn't marry, which are exactly the questions Mou hates most. Mou will not stay because she knows this. When Mou looks away, Brenda examines her face closely for signs of age and regret.

Mou squeezes me goodbye and walks back to the car. She smiles from the front seat, a smile that seems not her own, and then she drives away. I feel my mother's sadness. It turns in a circle inside me like a cat settling down to sleep. Once clockwise. Once anti-clockwise.

'Come on!' Tegan says. 'Want to see our room?'

THE HOUSE LOOKS exactly how a farmhouse ought. The walls bulge with a damp sorrow I don't yet recognise, and the timber beams hang low overhead. The sofa sags in the middle from decades of sitting, with legs scratched by the claws of cats, long dead. The tumble-dryer rattles turbulently in the back room, day and night, and every surface is piled with folded laundry. It smells of lavender detergent and wet dog. It is ordinarily old and ordinarily floral. Photos of endlessly familiar faces line the walls. I've met them all somewhere before, or just seen them at times in Tegan.

I follow Tegan upstairs. A boy's head emerges from a doorway, all pimples and rage.

'Kevin, mess with my stuff again, and I'll give you a beating you'll be feeling into your next lifetime!'

Another head appears from a different door, which must be Kevin. 'Wait till Mum hears what you just said!'

Kevin and Tegan could be twins. The same blond hair and eyebrows so pale they're barely there. They're the same height and build as one another. Sturdy and sure-footed.

Tegan turns back to me. 'Just ignore them.'

'Why do you have to be such a twat?' shouts the older one, who I remember is called Tom. He slams his door, but Kevin isn't listening any longer. He's spotted Tegan and me. He flashes a smile, which cracks his face in two. He doesn't look like Tegan when he smiles.

'Who are you, then?' he says, bounding towards us.

'This is Sissy and she's *my* friend. You're to stay away from her!' Tegan grabs my arm and drags me into her room. Kevin is standing in the doorway, staring, still smiling, not saddened by what Tegan said, as she slams the door in his face.

'They're the worst,' Tegan says, her back against the closed door, as if to keep her brothers at bay. And then, brightly, 'What should we do? We have to make the most of every single minute.'

Tegan's walls are plastered in posters torn out from *Bliss* and *Smash Hits*. A thousand bashful smiles follow me around the room, begging me to look at their abs, no, my abs, no, hey, look at mine!

'Hi, Matt and Brad and Jared and Dan,' I say, turning in a circle, exhausted with longing.

'Jared is mine,' she says, licking his paper biceps. 'You can pick any of the others. But hands off Jared!'

These boys are as real to me as any others.

Here we sleep in single beds on opposite sides of the room, rather than huddled together in the one small double, like we're used to. I sleep in the bed that once belonged to Haley. On my pillow is a cuddly toy dolphin.

'Because it's almost a mermaid,' Tegan says, 'and dolphins are horny, you know?'

Tegan's toys are piled in a pyramid in the corner. She ignores them all day and chooses a different favourite each night.

I crash down onto my bed and she onto hers, practising for later.

'But you're so far away!' she cries, reaching her fingers across the abyss that divides us.

BRENDA CHANGES FOR dinner. The pink nursing uniform hangs in the laundry room, like a skin dangling from a wire. She's wearing a sweater and jeans, pulled tight over her bumps and breasts and mum bits. Up close her hair is brittle as icing. I imagine it tastes sweet.

She moves through the kitchen with efficiency, stirring a saucepan with one hand while pulling jars from the fridge with the other, ladling their contents into pots and pans while whisking some cream and taking regular slugs of a large glass of white wine. She is a cog constantly turning, and her brittle hair shakes sugar dusting everywhere she goes.

'Dinner!' Brenda screams, her face turned towards the stairs.

Tegan and I were beckoned by the first scream. It's our job to lay the table. Brenda hands Tegan a stack of plates and me a stack of cutlery, so many it seems impossible we'll all fit.

'Forks on the left, dummy,' Tegan says, following me around the table to swap what I did wrong. I've never laid a table properly before.

Kevin appears from upstairs and loiters around the stove, picking.

'Out of my kitchen!' Brenda shoos him away. 'Kevin, call your brother.'

'Tom!' Kevin shouts.

'Don't shout!' Brenda says, shouting.

Butter and bread rolls and a bowl of salad are ferried from the kitchen to the table by our hands, and the call and response from kitchen to dining room is dizzying. This is what it is to have a family. Just like this.

The back door opens, and a man with large features and a nose as bulbous and strange as a mushroom appears, shaking mud from his boots like bad memories, best left outside.

'The heifer'll be in labour, not long now,' he says.

They don't greet. They don't even look at one another. It's like he's been in this room all along, like they're continuing a conversation that began yesterday or ten years ago.

'Called the vet?' Brenda replies.

The man shakes his head.

This is a father, a foreign creature. He moves through the cramped kitchen, navigating his bulk around Brenda and the simmering pots as if he doesn't really belong here. He washes his hands of the mud and blood and traces of animal, and then takes his seat at the head of the table. I don't know his name and he doesn't introduce himself. I don't think he's even noticed I'm here.

A whimper at the back door, and when Brenda opens it, a creature scampers in and hides in the shadows beneath the table.

Tegan is laughing at me for looking lost. She indicates for me to join her at the table and we sit side by side, as close as we can get.

'See? I told you!' she whispers, and I have no idea what she's talking about.

Brenda takes a seat at the other head of the table, and Kevin opposite us, with an empty seat for Tom beside him. I wonder where around the table Andy and Haley would sit.

The father looks at Tom's seat and over at Brenda.

'Go and find your brother,' Brenda tells Kevin, who rises from the table, while she dishes up. A scoop of cottage pie appears on my plate.

'Sissy's a vegetarian,' Tegan announces.

'Nothing wrong with our meat,' the father says, still not looking at me. He's tearing into a roll with his hands.

'Oh, your mother did say.' Brenda holds one hand to her head, looking exhausted. 'Tegan, you could have reminded me . . . I can't very well make something now.'

'It looks great, really I don't mind. I used to eat meat raw straight from the packet. Honest.'

The father looks at me for the first time then, and smiles a little.

It's true, too. I once ate minced beef straight from the refrigerator before we were vegetarian. I was hungry and Mou was in bed. I remember it was soft and dry as skin.

'Well, just eat around it,' Brenda says, but there's no eating around it.

Kevin returns from upstairs. 'Tom's gone.'

'Gone where?' Brenda says.

'Car's gone.'

Brenda shifts in her seat and the room stills to silence. 'Derek, did you say he could take the car?'

The father, who I now know is called Derek, though still Mr Price to me, looks to either side of him, like he's searching for an answer. Tegan and Kevin catch eyes, their ruddy faces wizened and world-weary as toads. Then they both look away, avoiding their mother's glare and each other's knowing.

'I won't have that boy—' Brenda begins, but Derek cuts her off.

'Brenda.'

There's a moment when the entire table holds their breath waiting for Brenda's response. She folds her hands in prayer, and the silence lifts.

'Let's say Grace,' she says at last.

Everyone closes their eyes. Kevin squeezes his shut, as if that's the only way they'll stay closed. Tegan and I link our arms so we can pray using one hand of hers and one hand of mine.

'For what we're about to receive may the Lord make us truly grateful . . . '

I open my eyes for a glimpse of their faces in prayer. But Kevin's eyes are open too and he's looking at me. He smiles. We're the only ones who can see, which is the same as being alone together. Startled, I close my eyes quickly. He was looking at me in the same way the boy in the corner shop did.

'Amen,' the father says.

'Amen,' we all repeat after him.

When I open my eyes, Kevin is already shovelling pie into his mouth, his lips stained red with the sauce. I take my first bite of meat in years. It's iron rich and cannibal. Pebbles of fat stick in my teeth and I'm not sure I can swallow. The cows can't see me here, I tell myself. Mou neither. Derek, however, is watching. I swallow hard.

'Not so bad, eh?'

'It's delicious!' I fill my mouth again. I am cannibal. Meat-eater. Animal.

'You're the new best friend, then?' Derek asks.

'This is Sissy, Dad,' Tegan says, like he should know.

'Ever asked what happened to the last one?' His face is inscrutable.

I look towards Tegan. She rolls her eyes. 'Dad!'

He lets one corner of his mouth turn upwards. I follow suit and tentatively smile. It's enough for him. He breaks into a chuckle. This is a father, I think again.

'Tell me, Sissy. What does your dad do?'

'He's a sailor. He worked on the oil rigs.'

'Sissy's parents are divorced,' Tegan says, with the same tone she might use to show off about a friend's extraordinary wealth. My parents' divorce makes me exotic, I see now.

'Oh,' Brenda says. 'I'm sorry.'

She reaches over and squeezes my hand. Her nails are cut short and scrubbed until her fingers are red and sore. It makes me think of Haley, chewing her nails down to the quick.

'Good grief, Brenda. It's only a divorce. It's not like the man's dead. I'm sorry, Sissy.'

I'm not sure if he's apologising for Brenda or my parents' divorce.

Just then, a creature nuzzles against me under the table.

'Oh!'

'You don't mind dogs, do you?' Brenda asks.

'I love animals.' The Harvey lookalike squeezes his head onto my lap expectantly. 'What's his name?'

His tail thumps against the floor, a drum beat.

Kevin answers, still not looking up between mouthfuls: 'Harvey.'

I look at Tegan, trying to understand how this could be, and she won't meet my eye. She moves her pie around her plate thoughtfully.

'Harvey?' I ask again, just to be sure, and Kevin nods.

This Harvey lookalike, who is also called Harvey, licks his

lips in my lap. I stroke his head. It's rock solid and un-smashed by a cricket bat.

TEGAN SITS ON the end of my bed. She has toothpaste in the corners of her mouth and her hair is scraped back in a tangled bun.

She plucks her eyelashes quietly.

'Don't.' I reach out to stop her.

I haven't asked her about Harvey. What could I say? Did you lie about your brother killing the dog, and if you did, what else did you lie about? It feels sacrilegious even to think it.

'Tonight I'm going to dream about singing in a nightclub in New York,' she says. 'There's going to be a boy in the audience who looks just like Jared. He's going to wait for me out the back of the club, and even though I'll say I don't want to have sex with him, he'll know better, and we'll do it against a wall in the alleyway behind the nightclub. It'll be amazing. That's what's going to happen in my dream.'

'Shall we write it down so we can compare it with the real thing in the morning?' I say.

I place my smoky quartz on the shelf by my bed. I brought it from home to keep me safe.

'Do you think writing it down makes it more or less likely to happen?' she asks, picking up the quartz to examine its smooth amber surface. She doesn't ask me about it, though, as if she knows some things are too precious for words.

Brenda appears in the door. 'Are you comfortable in there?' she says to me.

How motherly she seems. How un-hateable.

She says goodnight and turns off the overhead light. I'm

playing make-believe home with another family and for now I like it.

'Tell me a story, Siss.' Tegan's voice appears in the darkness, so much darker here than at home. 'Tell me the one about the mermaid again.'

I tell her the story about the girl who failed to be loved in time and turned into foam on top of the sea. And then she asks for another. So I tell her the story about the girl who changed into a tree and about the girl who changed into a nightingale that couldn't sing, and still she asks for more. With each story she imagines herself as these girls, as do I. We imagine each transformation. We imagine all the ways we might love and be loved and the price we might pay. I tell her a story about an ordinary girl who grew scales and webbed feet. I don't say that girl is me. I talk, and talk, until I think she's already sleeping, when she says, 'Tell me the one about your father.'

I stop talking. I want to tell her, but what would I even say? There was a man who worked at sea and he smelt of turpentine and cedar oil. Then what? If I speak of him out loud the little of him that remains might disappear.

I turn to her side of the room. She's already asleep.

THE SOUND OF a car in the driveway wakes me in the night. I look over at Tegan; she's dreaming of Jared. A pair of headlights dashes across the ceiling. It must be Tom come home from wherever he wasn't meant to be in the car he wasn't meant to take. Someone is at the back door waiting for him, because there's a shuffle of feet, like dancing in gravel. Something metal falls and hits the ground. A stumble.

'Stop it!' It's Derek speaking. 'Just stop.'

The shuffling feet fall silent.

'It's not his car.' Now Brenda's voice but packed with rage.

'It's not like he's coming back to use it, is he, Mum?' Tom, near hysterical.

More shuffling, a dull thud, and a grunt. Someone cries out.

'Brenda! Are you out of your mind?'

'I won't lose another. Do you hear me? I will not lose another son.' I feel her voice shake through the air, the particles of dust trembling with pain.

I look over. Tegan is no longer dreaming of Jared. The night light catches the whites of her eyes.

'Teg?' I whisper.

She lies still for a moment.

'Teg?' I say again, and this time, she slips out from under the covers and crawls across the floor, before climbing stealthily into bed with me. There's less room than we're used to and we relish it. We wrap our arms and legs around one another, until we lose our outlines completely. We are divisible only by one.

'See?' Tegan says, into the crux of my neck.

SUPER POWERS

Tegan dresses me for the farm. A thick woollen sweater, a mac meant for a child. Our feet are different sizes so I'm left with my plimsolls, which are immediately muddy and full of burrs.

In the morning, we collect eggs from the chicken coop, removing them from the warmth of the nest and placing them carefully in a milk bucket. Flustered chickens flap around, frantic at losing their offspring. We take the food scraps from dinner out to the pig. The sow is mighty. She's a breeding sow, Tegan says. Male pigs come from neighbouring farms to have sex with her. Her piglets are taken away before they're fully grown.

'She doesn't get to choose who she does it with,' Tegan says, as she dumps a bucket of potato skins and brown lettuce into her trough. The sow greedily eats, her ears flopped over her eyes like blinkers. 'She's a sex slave. Imagine.'

I can't.

Derek is up before dawn to work on the farm. The boys help him when they're not in school. Kevin hangs around in the afternoons, skulking where he's not wanted: in the kitchen when Brenda is cooking; in the yard when Derek brings in the cows; in Tegan's room when he's uninvited. He and Tegan fight scrappily, like cats defending their territory.

'You're such a wanker,' she screams.

'Tegan!' Brenda calls from the kitchen. 'Language!'

'Flat-chested bitch,' Kevin whispers, and then Tegan goes for him, whacking him over the head again and again. He pinches her middle, making her bend double and cry out. He wrestles her to the floor, until she's wrapped in a ball beneath him.

'I hate you!' A muffled shout.

'It'll only end in tears,' Brenda says. There were already tears and it didn't end.

I barely see Tom apart from at dinner. He's either helping Derek, in his room or sitting in the car, which isn't his. No one mentions Andy by name. His door remains locked at the end of the landing. I check the photos and count their framed faces. Tegan. Kevin. Tom. Haley. And there he is. A fifth pair of eyes staring back. They never all smile at the same moment, like the shared pool of smiles wasn't big enough to go around.

Brenda works in a nursing home. She leaves a tray of sandwiches in the fridge wrapped in clear plastic. Each of the family eats their sandwiches alone in different corners of the house. By the time Brenda is home, it's dark and we must be ready to help with dinner.

I see Brenda once from our bedroom window late at night in the backyard. Her cardigan is pulled tight around her, and she's dragging hard on a cigarette, like she's taking her last breath.

*

WITH OUR CHORES done, Tegan and I are left to our own devices. We tramp out into the woods to explore. The days are long and rambling, suffused in a strange winter light. Tegan is always just in front with one arm trailing behind, reaching for me with her fingertips. She laughs the laugh that is just ours.

The countryside is new to me. Insects gather in the morning sun, like fairies communing. I remember a story about two girls who ran down to their garden stream and returned with photographs to prove the existence of fairies. The imaginary could be real, they said. Just try not to believe us. I went fairy-catching too, armed with Mou's camera, but I saw the truth, banging its body against the glass of the jar, cretinous and foul. I took a photo to prove it. Our daydreams are real but they're frightful.

The copse is tangled with brambles that rustle and click with the sounds of creatures. They are the opposite of good children: they can be heard and never seen. Hopeful heads of snowdrops push through the ground of trodden brown leaves and everything drips with dew. The dew is wetter than ordinary water, seeping through my shoes and socks, so I squelch with each step. My borrowed sweater is heavy and thick but this wetter wet creeps through its holes and makes me shiver. Somewhere nearby chimes knock gently against one another in the wind.

Tegan stomps on ahead. In school she slinks, always hanging from the shoulders of friends, or from doorways, across desks, languorous and weary. Like the very act of being Tegan exhausts her. But here she stomps proudly, boyish and brave with muddy knees. It's another thing about her: she never minds getting dirty. Not like the other girls who keep themselves so clean. She has a smell, too, a funk to her, like mushrooms on the forest floor.

At a clearing, a circle of stones pressed deep into the ground forms a pathway and in its middle there's a raised stone platform where a statue once stood. Tegan tells me the woods used to belong to a fancy estate that burned down long ago.

'It looks like an altar,' I say, already imagining the ceremonies we might conduct.

She pokes me hard in the ribs, and then she's off, shouting, 'Tag!' as she disappears into the woods, running and breathless. I give chase. The branches come at my face from every direction, and she's there in the distance, her laughter echoing through the cathedral of trees. We have no destination. No rules. Here we play the games we gave up in school, because it no longer matters. We are children or girls or whatever we want in between. We keep running, the damp sound of our feet against the fallen leaves.

'Tag!'

And we're off again, except she's giving chase. I slow so she can catch me, her arms around my waist, pulling me down and over until we tumble onto the soft earth. The branches form shapes in front of our eyes, as our laughter subsides, and we look out beyond us into the sky. I feel the chill of the earth against my back and I know she feels it, too. I feel the brush of her eyelids when she blinks, like we're one person. Bound. Above, a cluster of starlings darts through our vision, and then they're gone. There is no sun. There are no clouds. There is only the grey as heavy as a blanket laid over our bodies in bed.

'Tell me your secret,' I whisper, her face right beside mine.

'Which secret?'

'The one in the music box. The one you said you might tell me one day.'

'I can't. Wouldn't be a secret then.'

'But you can tell me.'

'I know.'

Our heads are together, our legs spread apart, a two-headed, four-legged star.

'But I'm your friend.'

'You're my best friend.'

'So why can't you tell me? You said you would.'

There is a moment when I think she may and then the curtain goes down, like every time.

'Leave off already.'

She rolls onto her front grumpily, and breaks the spell of trees, and light, and the world feeling like a cocoon around us. But I'm not ready to leave it. She has a secret I need to know.

'Am I really your best friend?'

'I said, didn't I?'

'Then why can't you tell me?'

I'm prepared for her to be cross now. To push me away like she usually would, but she's quiet instead. 'If it's that bad . . .' I begin, sensing an opening.

'I never said it was bad.' Her voice trembles. This fragility appears out of nowhere.

'If it's not bad, then why are you upset now?'

She stacks a pile of small stones in front of her, balancing one on top of the other. The stones stop her crying, I can tell.

'I did something,' she begins, cryptically. 'It might be bad. It might be my worst thing. Or maybe my best. I don't know yet.'

'Then tell me! Let me help.'

'I can't.'

'Why?'

'You wouldn't understand.'

She says it with no malice, though I'm hurt all the same.

I forget mostly that Tegan is a year older than me, and she's kind not to remind me of the fact. But at moments like these I know she's thinking it.

I take one of the stones from the pile. It sparkles in the light. I want to draw her back into me.

'See these sparkly bits?' I say. 'They're different types of minerals and crystals. My dad told me they come from the stars. They were created in the Big Bang and have been here ever since, pressed into the earth like pockets of stardust. Isn't that cool?'

Tegan takes the stone back and examines it more closely. 'It's pretty.'

We sit for a moment. I want to share something with Tegan. I want her to know she can share with me, too.

'I do miss him, my dad. You asked me once, and I said I didn't.'

'I figured.'

'Mou and me left while he was away at sea on the rigs. I don't even know why.'

'You never asked her?'

I shake my head.

'Maybe you should. Your mum seems pretty cool.'

I can't explain. To ask these questions would imply a breach she would interpret as blame.

We sit quietly together. Both at the limit of what we can say.

WE WALK FURTHER through the woods until a stone cottage appears up ahead.

'This is where my nan lives. She's a white witch. Do you want to meet her?'

Tegan enters the house without waiting for an answer,

but no one is at home. Inside, the carpet is hard as wood, worn down by centuries of footfall. The sofa is piled with quilts, in front of a wood-burning stove, now ashes. The windows gape from their frames, sending cold blasts of air around the room, carrying the smell of wild garlic from the woodland outside.

'It's just like your fairy tales, isn't it, Siss?'

She's in one of her reflective moods, when she wants to talk without being interrupted.

'Kevin and me lived here for a bit one summer when I was nine. The sofa folds out into a bed, you see? Like this. Nan would be gone early, because back then she still helped Dad on the farm, so it was just Kevin and me all day. We'd pretend all adults had vanished and it was just us by ourselves with no rules. We'd play house, except in our house no one would fight. That was after Dad had to slaughter the cows and the farm nearly went under.'

'I remember it on the news.' I don't mention that was why we went vegetarian.

'Yeah, the smell was awful. They burned them, you know? Dad was furious. Mum wanted to sell up and leave, start again, but he wouldn't have it. Everything was so bad then with Andy, and Mum and Dad always fighting.'

'Was that why they sent you here?'

Tegan nods. 'And then one day Nan walked us back to the main house. I could tell something was wrong because she held our hands, which she never does. You'll meet her. She's not the hand-holding type. When we got home, Andy was gone, and no one would speak about what'd happened.'

Tegan turns her back on me to examine the glass storage jars lining the shelves, each one full of dried flowers and dust. I don't want to talk about her dead brother. Here in the woods in a witch's cottage, it's too frightening to summon those ghosts.

'I thought you hated Kevin?' I say.

Tegan shrugs. 'He was different then. We were only little. All boys become creeps eventually.'

'What about Peter?' I ask, and even as I say it, I know I shouldn't have.

I feel her tense, like every muscle in her body has stopped moving, and I wish I could take it back. She's stoic in her silence. I look for something else to talk about, anything. There's a black-and-white photo of a couple on the mantelpiece, their faces serious and proud.

'Is this your nan?'

'Her wedding day,' Tegan explains.

The girl sits in an imposing chair with the boy standing behind her against a flat background. Her hair is bound in a fat bun as big as a loaf of bread, which gives her veil a misshapen look, like she's hiding something inside it.

'Why's she wearing black, then?' I ask.

'We were Catholics,' a voice answers from the doorway, and I turn to see Nan. I replace the photo, feeling like an intruder. Nan's hair is now grey, but still bound in a bun at the back of her neck, and her face is the same, just lined with wrinkles, like lacework. She is bundled up in layers of clothing right down to her feet, which are clad in a pair of modern hiking boots. Under her arm she's carrying a basket. She is everything I imagined a white witch to be. Except for the boots, which is all the better. I like her immediately and want her to like me, too.

'Catholics wear black on their wedding day to show their devotion to marriage until death,' she says.

'My dad's Catholic,' I pipe up.

'Really? What kind?'

'Oh, I don't know. He's Greek.'

'Greek Orthodox probably. Morbid bunch, the lot of them.'

Tegan introduces me, but Nan walks straight for the stove, where she puts a kettle on to boil.

'I expect you're cold. City folk complain of the cold.'

'How do you know I'm city folk?' I say.

'Anyone from the country wouldn't come out here in them shoes.'

I look down at my muddy plimsolls.

Nan turns around now. The hand on her hip disappears in the grooves of her sweater. She is a small woman beneath the layers.

'Sissy is a mystic, like you, Nan. She can read palms.' Tegan turns to me. 'Nan's psychic.'

'None of your games, girl.' Nan pulls down a tin of flapjacks.

'Help yourself,' she says, and then she talks as if continuing a conversation we had already started. 'On the radio today there was a man talking about being a Gypsy. The government tried to give his family housing. These government people, idiots that they are, believed Gypsies only lived the way they did because they didn't have a choice, and if they were given a bricks-and-mortar house, the problems with their horses and caravans and crime would go away. Only it didn't work, see. Was in their blood.'

'To be criminals?' I ask.

'No, Gypsies aren't criminals. They have their own code of ethics. To be Travellers.'

'Are you a Gypsy?'

'I'm interested in them. They're a people set apart from others and that makes them kin to me.'

'Nan doesn't like people,' Tegan says.

'I'm done with people,' Nan says. 'Too much fuss. But

you're young. There's plenty of people for you to meet before you can retreat to a cabin in the woods like me.'

We eat our flapjacks, the sweet crumbs dusting the table, and Nan shows us what she's foraged from the woods in her basket: stinging nettles, which she will make into soup; chickweed to throw into salads; and some bright orange mushrooms.

'*Flammulina velutipes* in Latin or a velvet shank mushroom. They're saprophytic – that means they live on dying trees.'

The mushroom's surface is orange and slimy, its stem soft as velvet. 'It's so weird,' I say, running my finger along its gills.

Nan reaches across the table to take my hand in hers. Her skin feels thin as paper. Her thumb circles my palm, around and around, until I feel nauseous and uncertain.

'You two are good friends, I can see that.'

Tegan rests her head on my shoulder. She is doing it for show. She is showing Nan the ways in which she loves me and I love her back.

'This one is a sensitive soul,' Nan says to Tegan. 'Sensitive souls need special care.'

Nan turns to me now, her eyes pressed deep in her face, like precious stones. She looks nothing like Tegan. She is where the darkness in the family comes from.

'You're an only child?'

I nod.

'And you're raised by a single parent?'

'My mum.'

'And how about that dad? You're not in touch?'

I might cry all of a sudden. It's like everything I believe in is real. I want to tell her about the crystal by my bedside and the chorus of girls in my head. I want to tell her about the Barbies I buried in the backyard and the spell I cast asking for

Tegan to be my one friend. I want to show her my webbed toes, and ask, what am I becoming?

'It's all right,' Nan says. 'You can be sad about your dad for as many years as you need to be sad. You can be strong and still be sad. In fact, that sadness might be what makes you strong, you understand? No, I see not, but maybe you will one day. Like the Gypsies have travel in their bones, you have sadness in yours.'

I wonder if Tegan brought me here to be told this, but she looks nonplussed.

'Don't let Nan spook you,' Tegan says.

Nan laughs. 'Nonsense! Anyone can see these things. I see things in you, too, young lady, but I won't tell you what. You'll find out for yourself soon enough.'

'My mum's sad, too,' I find myself announcing and it feels foreign to say it out loud.

Nan and Tegan don't ask any questions. Their silence invites me to speak, but I can say no more. My heart is hammering in my head, beating against my skull with censure. It's a secret, which means no one can know.

Nan gives my hand one more squeeze and releases it. 'You're a good girl.'

I feel cheated, like I brought an offering to her altar and it was taken without reciprocation. I want more. I want Nan to tell me something wise about my mother and her sadness that will make sense of it.

'Now drink up your tea and be gone with you. I have chores to be getting on with.'

Tegan tugs at my sleeve, and even though we haven't finished, she pulls me out of the cabin and away.

*

WE WALK HOME as darkness descends. In the thick of winter it comes on fast before the day is even half over. A gentle drizzle mists our skin, so soft we barely feel it. I wonder why Tegan hasn't talked about Nan before, but then she turns her face to the sky, letting raindrops fall fatly from the treetops onto her cheeks, and I think I know why. It's for the same reason I don't talk about my crystals or my father.

After dinner, we retreat to her room and make a tent under a sheet. She pulls out the sparkling stone she found and examines it. I think of our first meeting, her magic trick.

'Tell me how you do it,' I say, emboldened by all we've shared since.

'Do what?'

'Down on the courts with William.'

She looks confused for a moment and then stunned. 'You don't know?'

She covers her face, laughing, letting the tent collapse around us. I push her, not embarrassed. I feel ridiculous. I feel safe. This is where these questions have for ever been asked.

'Have you never?' There it is again.

'Show me?' I ask, unsure what I'm asking apart from I want to understand. I'm ready.

We lie side by side, her voice guiding my fingers, further, deeper. Foolish and thrilled, I follow her lead, searching for something I've always known was there, but never knew to find. I feel my fingers inside me for the first time, my still cold skin burning from the warmth of my body. A knowledge shifts between my hips. It's been biding its time, a pleasure in waiting. The row of tampons, like cotton missiles, makes sense. And the stone with it. A familiar throb greets me, and I meet it without shame. Desire, like gravity, draws the world down to this place I've only just discovered, but it's a desire without demand. We exchange a look, an opening, but we wait a second too long, perhaps, and burst out laughing instead.

'You've never made yourself come?'

'Yes,' I say, though I've never called it that. To come, like an animal beckoned at will. 'But not like that.'

I show her how I spent countless hours, using the heel of my foot or the side of my hand, with no idea of what I was doing, and she can't stop laughing. I laugh, too. I thought there was something wrong with me, I tell her.

'There might be something wrong with you, but it's not that.'

Her joke passes me by. I am close to epiphany. The two Barbies buried beneath the lawn – I needn't have given it up. Everything falls into place: the rush and the throb; the other-other; the look on the boys' faces down on the courts; the drawing of a man and the drawing of a woman. There's a space deep inside us and it's from here first forgotten Eve birthed the world and everything in it. I was never sick. I am not dying.

'It's like a secret power,' I say.

Tegan likes that.

'A super power,' she adds, with a laugh. 'We can really give the boys a shock now.'

But I don't want to show the boys. I don't want to share this with anyone.

IN THE MIDDLE of the night, I get up to go to the bathroom. I don't yet know my way in the dark, and shuffle blindly, afraid to wake everyone up. A blade of light cuts across the carpet coming from the door to Brenda and Derek's room.

I let myself peer in, curious. Brenda is on her side, a mountainous hip illuminated by the moon. I gently push the door further open. Derek is curled foetus-like towards her. Their breath is disjointed, where one rises, the other falls, against the raspy whistle of Derek's snore.

For a moment, I pretend they're my mother and father. I climb in between them and they don't notice until morning. 'You're too old for such behaviour, missy,' they tease. But my fantasy is interrupted by something in the darkness behind me. I can sense its presence lurking. I turn back to the hallway, reaching for the wall, but my hands meet with nothing, just air. I squint to see, but only the velvety blackness squints back. I think of dead Andy's room, right there, and start to panic.

'Ssh,' the darkness says.

The hairs stand on the back of my neck, like I'm being hunted. Like I'm prey. This is the moment I've imagined, when the girl snatcher grabs me from behind and pulls me down to the ground. But this is real. It's happening.

'It's me! Kevin!'

As my eyes adjust, I catch the white of his hair. I'm afraid still, but also ashamed to have been caught prying.

'I was just going to the toilet,' I whisper.

He steps closer and takes my hand. His fingers are cold against mine. I pull away, but he reaches for me again. We do this a few times more, like we're squabbling. Like it's a game he wants me to play, and I'm ruining the fun. He takes my hand once more, and I let him. I don't understand this hand-holding here in the dark, but I'm cornered, and maybe if I give in, he'll grow bored.

'What do you want?' I say, as an arm slides around me, but then there's a sound from Brenda and Derek's room, and fearful of being caught with Kevin in the corridor, I wrestle myself free, and shove past him.

'Goodnight, gorgeous,' he calls after me, like he could swallow me whole.

Struggling with the lock, I shut the bathroom door, and sit on the toilet, astonished.

MIXTAPES

Tegan won't tell me where we're going. She insisted we wake up extra early to do our chores because she wants to show me her favourite place. I'm glad for any excuse to get out of the house and away from Kevin. He thinks I'm gorgeous. He wants to swallow me whole.

We take a few sandwiches from the fridge, put them into our backpacks and set off into the woods for the day. We walk past Nan's cottage up a steep incline until there's no more path to follow. We wrestle through a thicket at the top of the hill and emerge in a wide open field.

'In the summer it's full of wild flowers,' Tegan says, but the flowers are all gone. All that remains is a handful of sweet violets and the occasional black and wizened sunflower, its seeds eaten long ago by hungry crows.

We follow a path that leads to a hamlet with a pub and a single shop, where Tegan uses her pocket money to buy us a packet of Hobnobs and a pint of milk. A shopkeeper with a single wisp of grey hair greets her by name.

Outside there's a bus stop where the number 68 terminates.

'That's what I take when I don't stay with Haley. It goes

to Buckland Dinham where Clara lives, and from there I get the school bus. I have to get up at six a.m. Shit, right?'

A 68 bus pulls in and an old lady gets out. She looks us up and down with suspicion. 'I hope you paid for those biscuits, young lady,' she says to Tegan.

'Of course, Mrs Bishop. Happy New Year, Mrs Bishop,' she calls after her in a way that sounds like taunting. Tegan has a knack for sounding impertinent even while she's being polite.

We keep walking onwards, taking a bridle path out of the village and into a different type of woodland where the trees are tall, stripped bare and bright white. The wind picks up pace, like waves against a shore. There is a seashell somewhere that sounds like this forest when you lift it to your ear. For a moment, I stop and let myself be completely still. I let my feet sink down into the ground until I cannot tell where the earth ends and I begin. My boundaries are fluid. This is what it is to be alive, I think. Tegan calls my name and I snap out of my trance, running to catch up with her, thinking how lucky I am to be a girl in the woods with my one friend where I belong.

Up ahead, an old caravan has been abandoned, disjointed from the vehicle that once dragged it and propped up with rocks to prevent it from tipping. Whatever path it carved through the woods to get here has long grown over and disappeared. Tegan is waiting for me at the door.

'Before I let you in, you have to promise me you'll never tell anyone about this place,' she says. 'It's secret.'

She looks at me solemnly, a gatekeeper, an oath-maker.

'I promise.' I match her solemnity and add the promise to our collection.

She considers whether I'm adequately serious, then turns to unlock a padlock on the door.

Inside, there's a small gas burner with a kettle and a collection of dirty cups in the sink. Behind the bed photographs are stuck to the wall; up close, I see they're of Haley, Andy and Tegan, younger, fuller in their faces, long hair uncombed. At Andy's feet is a puppy: Harvey.

'This was my brother's hideout,' Tegan tells me. 'He used to come here with Haley. It would drive Mum nuts when they'd disappear. They let me come along sometimes. Just me, never Kevin. He'd tell on us right away.'

She takes a pair of batteries from her pocket – she removed them from the TV's remote control earlier – and expertly loads them into a small cassette player. She's resourceful like that. It's something we share. She presses play, and a raspy voice begins to sing.

Tegan has a box of tapes on her lap. Each tape is carefully labelled with a list of songs on one side and a drawing on the other. 'Look, he did his own album art. Isn't it cool? He was going to be an artist when he grew up.'

She hands me a tape with a drawing of an eye made of concentric circles. 'I have all his art stuff under my bed. Mum doesn't know. When I move out, I'll take it with me. I bet you could be a really good artist. You have that way about you.'

I like this, but I'm distracted by the caravan and its contents. It is a mausoleum. I wonder if the cups have been in the sink since Andy died. If the last person to lift them to their lips was him. Does the air circulating in here contain his last breaths?

'What did they do here?'

'Get high, I think. Mum blamed everything on the drugs. But that's just 'cause she doesn't want it to be her fault.'

'She's so nice to me,' I say.

I fear Tegan will punish me for not taking her side without question, but she just shrugs. 'She's nice until she's not. It's almost worse that way. Fake nice.'

'Maybe she just can't be nice all the time,' I say.

'Andy took Haley to a party when she was fifteen.' It's Tegan's turn to tell me a story. 'Some bloke put something in her drink . . . They had to call an ambulance, make a police report, this whole thing. Mum blamed Andy, said he'd gone off the rails and now he'd ruined his sister's life, too. They had this big fight about it and Mum threw him out. Kevin and me were with Nan by then, so I don't know what happened, and Haley won't talk about it, but by the time we came back Andy was gone. Mum found him in his car. And now she won't let anyone drive it. Won't get rid of it either. We just have to look at it the whole time and think about what happened.'

She plucks out her eyelashes as she talks and brushes them away. Soon she won't have any left. We need all the wishes we can get, but I don't want to interrupt her.

'We didn't go to the funeral. They didn't give us the choice. Haley said Mum didn't want anyone to know she had a son who killed himself. She'd rather say he disappeared. They shut his bedroom door, as if we wouldn't notice he was gone. Like he never existed.'

I cannot imagine what it is to lose a brother. I have only lost a father, and even him, not for ever. In theory I could get my father back, if I knew where to find him. He's out at sea in my imagination or in the top right-hand corner of my brain. He might be somewhere else by now. He might be in a city on shore and have a new family with another daughter whom he tells bedtime stories instead, none of which I can imagine or want to. It's good enough to know he's out there somewhere. But Tegan has lost a brother for ever, which is a loss impossible to calculate. It does not equal one thing or another. It is not greater or less. There is just the fact of it.

The song switches over. There is a guitar, a few bangs of the drum, and then a voice that hooks right through my hips. It's rich and deep and I want to sink into it. Tegan sings along, faltering on the words, and then her lips move without words to fill them.

'Who is it?' I ask.

Tegan wants to lie, pretend that she knows the answer, and it makes me love her all the more.

'I don't know,' she says, at last, looking at the list of band names on the tape. 'We'd have to start at the beginning to work it out, I guess ... '

'Why don't we? It'll be fun.'

Tegan smiles. This was a different sort of test.

In the close confines of the caravan that was once Andy's, with the wind blowing past the windows, we listen to the quiet purr of the cassette player rewinding to the start, back to the beginning. We lie on the small bed, side by side, reading each track name and artist aloud, and spending the song trying to remember.

THE COSTUME BOX

We dress up as Tatiana and Tallulah. As the women we might one day become. Tegan wants us to take our missing-girl photo. The photo we'll give to the police if either of us disappears. She also wants us to send a copy to Eric666. These two ideas seem incompatible to me, but not for Tegan. She can keep two truths in her mind at any one time.

We find a box of costumes in the attic and a hanging rail full of clothes. Tegan pulls out a fur coat, the size of a wolf.

'Are you sure we should take that?' I run my fingers through the fur cautiously.

'Why not?' Tegan replies, and it's clear in her tone, she knows the answer.

We take it all down to Tegan's room and dig through our options. A taffeta tutu. A black wig, matted as a rat. A flamenco dress. Each costume is a character we try on for size. We create ourselves anew. Tatiana is a Gypsy and a mystic. She wears dark eye make-up and lipstick, because here the rules don't apply. Tallulah pulls a black tube skirt up over her boobs like a dress. She finishes her look with the fur coat thrown over her shoulders.

'When I'm grown-up I'm only ever going to wear high heels,' she says, slipping into a pair that must be Brenda's.

We spray Tegan's hair to make it big until our heads rush from the fumes. We paint our faces like we're preparing for war, except for this war we must be beautiful. We must be terrifying. We must be women. I stuff my bra with socks, believing in some small way that when I remove the white cotton balls later, in a feat of animism, my fully grown breasts will be bursting in their place.

When we finish we stand in the mirror side by side, like we did on that first night, like we always stood with me to the left and Tegan to the right, our eyes meeting only in our reflection.

I fetch the disposable camera Mou gave me for Christmas and we take turns posing for each other.

'We need one of us together,' Tegan says, and pokes her head out of the door. 'Kevin!' she shouts.

'No, don't!' I think about our grappling in the dark and feel a hot wave of embarrassment.

He appears in the doorway, as if he was already there, waiting. In his presence, I'm no longer fabulous. No longer Tatiana, Gypsy, mystic. I'm just a girl in old clothes that smell of mothballs and hairspray.

'What are you freaks doing?' he says, staring.

'See?' I want Tegan to throw him out.

'Sissy, ask him to take a photo of us. He won't do it for me.'

'Tegan!' But there is no escaping her will. 'Please. Just one,' I say, not looking directly at him.

Kevin takes the camera as if it's a chore, but he's pleased to be included. Tegan drags me onto the bed, and we lie on our fronts, resting our chins in our hands like Hollywood starlets.

The snap of the camera.

'Come on, Siss!' Tegan goads me to get into it. 'I mean *Tatiana*!'

Snap!

'On the chairs, like this,' Kevin says, arranging two chairs back to back.

We try to pout seriously, but the effort makes me laugh, and Kevin laughs, too. It's the type of laugh that makes you laugh harder.

'That was a good one,' he says, our poses punctuated by the wind of the film between shots.

'Wait, you need to look the part,' I say, and I find a bowler hat to place on his head, incorporating him into our world with a smile that surprises me.

We take photo after photo. We are dancers. We are snake charmers. We are make-believe. We are proper girls. Almost grown women. We pull on shoes to march outside and pose among the trees. We are a mad-glad costumed troupe, marching.

Snap!

'Fabulous, *dah-ling*,' Kevin calls out, getting into character. On the way he's assumed a pink kimono, which drags behind him in the mud. I pick up the ribbons and tie them in a bow. He tips his hat at me and I blush. It's hard to reconcile this boy here in his pink kimono and bowler with the boy who grappled with me on the dark landing at night. I could like this daytime boy. I like knowing he likes me, certainly. The elastic pull of his attraction makes me grow taller, grow brighter, beautiful even.

Tegan and I lie on our backs in the woods, and Kevin stands above us, the camera pointing down. 'Scream,' he instructs, so we do, our wails echoing into the world around us, sending a spray of birds from the trees.

Snap!

This is the photo I'll later frame for Tegan's birthday, and never give her. Our lipsticked mouths are wide open, our painted black eyes screwed shut. You can hear our scream through the surface and it is the call of the wild inside. A call to the future. Come faster, it says, come sooner, come closer, come brighter. It is the last cry of childhood. It is a scream of rapture, of readiness for the world that will soon be ours.

Snap!

The film ends. The birds settle back on their branches. We collapse in a bundle, limbs tangled around one another. Kevin is lying with his eyes shut, and I find myself examining his face for traces of Tegan. Their appearance is similar, but their expressions are uncanny: the clench of the jaw when serious; or the haunted, vacant look when silent. Kevin opens his eyes then and catches me looking. He sits up, grabs my face in his hands and pulls me in for a kiss. It is a dry kiss, our mouths pressed together. There is nothing I like about what is happening to my face except for the idea it has. And then it's done.

I turn to see how Tegan will react. She's watching with the strangest expression, a mix of intrigue and distrust. Kevin has my lipstick print against his lips, garish and red as the meat sauce from our first dinner. He pouts at me, playing the jester, the fool, and I laugh, and then I laugh harder. It was my first kiss, here, all together. My laughter is interrupted by Tegan, who shoves Kevin so hard he topples over.

'Leave off!' she snarls, and I'm thrilled to be claimed. Thrilled to be hers. I didn't like the kiss anyway. It was cold and thin-lipped. She grabs my hand and drags me away.

*

IT IS DARK by the time we get back to the house. Our clothes are damp and heavy, and our bare legs sting, whipped by wet branches and brambles, but we're elated by our adventure. We're shivering from the cold and our hands burn from the warmth inside like a thousand ants crawling beneath our skin.

Brenda is already in the kitchen.

'Where've you been?' Brenda shouts. 'Leaving me to handle all your dinners on my own.'

Brenda takes us in, struggling with our wet shoes in the doorway. 'Look at the state of you!' she says, coming over, and I can smell the wine on her breath from where I'm standing. She grabs Tegan's arm while she's still removing her boots, and pulls her over to stand under the kitchen light, wrong-footing her so Tegan stumbles.

'I'm sorry, we lost track of time,' Tegan says, but Brenda isn't having it.

'You're wearing my coat. It's ruined.'

Tegan looks down at herself. Leaves are matted in the fur, like an animal that rolled in the mud. 'I found it in the attic.'

'Is nothing precious to you?'

Brenda yanks it open to reveal the black tube dress, 'And what's this?'

'It's a costume, Mum,' Tegan protests.

But then Brenda pulls at her hair. 'Using my hairspray, too,' and pinches her cheeks, 'And you're made up like a tart,' and a small slap across the face, more of a tap really, but enough for Tegan to bat away her mother's hand. Then the grabbing and tapping continue, until she takes Tegan's head in one hand, and with the other, she rubs at her face, as if to rub away the make-up, but it only blackens her cheeks and her eyes, and reddens her chin. She is making her into a clown, into a horror story.

I want to defend her. We're not dressing like this for real: we're dressing like this for play. There's a difference still. At least, I think there is.

'Mum, get off!'

'Girls like you end up raped,' she says, but Tegan can't respond with Brenda's palm still in her face.

I step forward to intervene, but they are locked in an embrace I can't untangle.

Kevin is now standing in the doorway, his bowler hat in his hands, like it's a funeral.

'Get off!' Tegan screams, pushing her away.

The dog, tied up in the yard outside, starts howling.

'Take it off!' Brenda says at last.

Tegan takes off the fur coat and hands it over, but this doesn't suffice.

'All of it. I won't have you dressed like this in my house.'

Tegan is confused for only a moment.

'I said, take it off!' And she starts yanking at Tegan's dress.

'Stop it!' Tegan cries, and I want to push Brenda off her, to stand between them.

Kevin has turned away. He is facing the wall.

'Fine!'

Everything is quiet now.

Even the dog has stopped whimpering, as if he, too, has felt it.

Brenda is testing Tegan. Like Tegan tests me. She wants Tegan to refuse to undress in front of us, and then to beg, so Brenda can forgive her and that will be a victory. But instead Tegan pulls the black tube dress over her head, and just stands there in her underwear, cold and unflinching.

'Can I go now?' Tegan drops the dress on the floor.

'Get yourself cleaned up, then.' Brenda uses the same tone

she uses every night. She picks up the clothes from the floor, as if they're merely dirty laundry. 'Come down when you're done and help me with the table.'

WE SIT EITHER side in the bathtub together. The steam rises between us and I bat it away to see her more clearly. I don't want her out of my sight. I want to protect her.

'Mou says it gets easier after this bit.'

This is what Mou told me when the girls bullied me in the changing rooms at school. I have no evidence that Mou's right, and she doesn't act like her life is any easier, but it's something to say, and maybe that's the same reason she said it to me.

'When?' Tegan sinks into the water.

I don't know. I want to give her answers I don't have. 'When we're older.'

'Why can't we be older now?'

I wipe Tegan's face with a flannel. The mascara smears will not come off. Brenda rubbed it deep into her skin.

'Here, let me.'

She rubs her face so furiously that I take the flannel away to stop her. She cries then. She cries until the bathwater trembles around her. I hold her to stop her shaking but we shake together instead. Her body is an extension of mine. Her tears also. I drink the bathwater where they fall to keep what's ours inside. I don't want to wash away our not-yet-women sorrows. I understand these are tears we'll later remember, which will serve us some purpose that may never be clear. I lick a tear from her cheek. It's ever so slightly salty. I lick one side and then the other, and it makes her laugh.

'Weirdo,' she says.

'Pervert,' I say.

She smiles. 'Do you see now?' she says, and I nod though I can't understand. I think of Mou, her hand on my chest, feeling my feelings.

We wash our bodies – I'm careful to keep the webs between my toes hidden – until we're clean enough for dinner, then stand in water so dirty it's murky and brown.

I want to tell Brenda she's wrong. We're not real grown women. We are Unreal. Un-grown. Un-snatchable still. So she can't blame us. But soon we will be real, I think, and who decides for us?

Brenda is frightened and she hates us for it. She loves her girls and hates them for it.

THE RITUAL

The idea for the ritual is mine, but Tegan runs with it. I have a vague notion that we should hold a ceremony in the woods at the altar, but from there, she seems to know exactly how it should go.

During the day, we gather handfuls of herbs and dried mushrooms from the jars on Nan's shelves. We take her *Flammulina velutipes*, too. It lives on the dead; that must be dark magic. It's orange and bright as a warning. I read that magic is all about intention; it's like making a really strong wish, which I'm practised in. It was wishing that brought me Tegan. She wishes to be grown-up so she can leave home. I wish to be delivered safely from childhood to whatever comes next. I'm ready to know now what I'm becoming.

We collect our ingredients inside a metal milk bucket, the closest to a cauldron we can find. Nan keeps a bottle of gin behind the TV. We put that in, too. We each take a swig and feel it burn. It's good that it burns: there's a threshold we must pass, and pain is part of the equation. We prick our fingers with the thorn of a bramble, and squeeze in a drop of blood.

'I wish we had period blood or something really gross,' Tegan says. 'I bet that would work.'

'How about spit?'

Tegan shrugs and we both spit in the bucket.

After dinner, we dress up for the occasion. Tatiana and Tallulah resurrected. These costumes that only yesterday were worn in play are now the garb of our pending transformation.

'What if Brenda sees?'

But Tegan won't listen.

Defiance is key to magic, too.

With the house now quiet, we steal away and walk through the woods to our altar. It's a route we know well, but by night the trees are a portal to another world. Here, I am Tatiana, in purple taffeta, with lips as dark as blood. And Tegan is Tallulah, her fur coat wrapped tight around her shoulders, a wolf's embrace. The trees tell me just yesterday they saw a mad-glad costumed troupe parade past here. Ssh, they say, and we remain quiet. They saw a girl kissed for the first time, too. Ssh, I say, and they don't tell.

We place our bucket on the stone altar. The herbs, the gin, the *Flammulina velutipes*, the two drops of blood, one mine, one hers, our spit, all coalesces. We gather leaves and twigs from the ground. There are no rules for a ritual such as this, but we don't doubt its power.

'Wait,' Tegan says. She pulls out a few eyelashes and drops them in. 'Does it count as a wish if you pull them out yourself?'

Finally, I place my smoky quartz beside the bucket. We light a candle in the midst of our potion, and the world around us darkens, like when the curtain opens at the start of a show. We join hands, and I stifle a giggle, feeling a little self-conscious, but only for a moment. We close our eyes the better to imagine our futures, and they are bright and blinding as the flame. We turn slowly in a circle around the bucket. Three turns clockwise, three turns anticlockwise. And a chant forms on our lips, like forgotten knowledge, dislodged from our hips.

'By our power,' I say, no longer thinking, 'we will be strong.'

'Grow us older,' Tegan adds, as we keep turning, 'make us one.'

The meaning of the words doesn't matter, only the repetition, an incantation. The air around us closes in and the trees lower their branches to shield us. I begin to feel a strange tingling all over, as if my body is foreign or is becoming mine for the first time. *By our power . . .* we keep going . . . *we will be strong . . .* We start skipping to keep up with the pace of our song, *Grow us older,* we sing, *make us one.* The silver trunks sway as we dance, and the wind whips around our bodies, warning of the women who danced here before us and were turned to stone. The wind whispers, *Beware.* You are leaving somewhere safe for somewhere dangerous, but we don't listen.

The flame of the candle flickers and catches a corner of a leaf, and in a flash, a fire starts, fuelled by oxygen and alcohol and our desires. We stop. Our words caught on fire. Tegan drops to her knees and I feel the damp earth against them, as if they're my own. She blows on the flame to urge it higher.

She was never afraid.

With her, neither am I.

We gather more leaves and twigs, anything dry, to throw into the bucket, and coax the flames further. We are no longer in the woods we ran through this morning: we're in the woods of our imaginings. We throw in the rest of it. We throw in the bits of Mou's mind that are broken; the parts of Brenda that are cruel. We throw in the girl snatcher and all of the men who might one day hurt us; we throw in the man I bit in the car park at Asda; and William, too; I throw in Peter when Tegan isn't looking and I'll never tell her. We throw in the faces of strangers who fear us for being girls, and the faces of strangers who stare at us for too long. And the gin-rich flame grows higher, burning through our fears, fuel for our metamorphosis. It smells of camomile and the earth. Of hopes and desires. We are drunk on it. We are free.

We join hands again and pick up our dance. *By our power,* we shout, *we will be strong.* The others dance alongside us. The missing girl stands from all fours. Julie Hendry goes to the ball and devours the art teacher. *Grow us older.* The girl who turned into foam on the sea, she murders her love. The girl who turned into a tree walks again. *Make us one.* The nightingale, at last, sings a song for all the girls, of all their stories in symphony around us. It goes: Girl, creature, animal, woman. Girl, creature, amphibian, myth. We are changing and what we're changing into is of our making. In this story we get to choose.

The fire is reflected in Tegan's eyes and I have lived this moment before. It's what I saw when we looked into the mirror that first time and infinity looked back. The spell is working. I want to scream, and I don't care who hears me, because we were right. There is a power that is ours. I feel invincible. I want to reach across the fire and pull Tegan towards me. I jump over the flames, and she jumps too, and we leap back and forth, our feet making a rhythmic beat against the ground as old as the drum of first forgotten Eve. The soil beneath us belongs to her. It is her flesh and her blood. The hill we walked on is her formless body, the rocks in the ground her ancient bones. When this goddess is angry she shakes all over and the earth moves with her. We shake all over and the earth moves.

Tegan shrieks and falls to her knees. I run over, terrified of what we've unleashed.

'What happened?'

She looks up at me, alarmed, and turns to show me. Her tights are singed.

'I caught on fire.' The Lycra is torn and blackened around the edges. She put out the flame when she sat down.

'Are you burned?' I ask.

She shakes her head, and starts to laugh, and I laugh, too, and then we pull off her singed tights, tangling ourselves as they unravel like a pair of twisted snakes. We pull off mine too, still cackling, our legs now bare as the tree trunks around us. Our feet should be cold, but we feel no pain, just the sheer delight of our existence. I pull my taffeta over my head and she drops her fur coat to the ground. We fall into its furs, a wolfskin bed on the forest floor.

Tegan untangles herself from me, and motions for me to pass her my crystal. In a glance, I know what she wants to do with it. The quartz is soft and round. I'm used to turning it in the palm of my hand when I'm nervous.

'It's part of the spell,' she says, sensing I'm cautious or might not want to give it up, but she's wrong. I'm not afraid. This was always part of the ritual, even if we hadn't realised it. It's crossing a T or closing a circle in the sand. I hand it over, and, just like that first day, she disappears it without a sound, except this time, it's my crystal inside her. This time, I understand. It's our final offering to the future. To first forgotten Eve.

Tegan breaks the moment open with her laughter, sitting up to collapse her body into mine. I laugh, too. Laughter is so easy again. The embers have died down completely, and a thin chilled mist settles on our half-clad bodies. The stars through the bare branches are dazzling.

I feel no shame then, only wonder. Still, I'll tell no one about what we did that night, not my future boyfriends, or lovers, or best friends. I will keep it always between us, and in that way it will remain ethereal, luminous, a touchstone for my future desiring self and my future desiring body, which I will come to know only slowly, and much later, after all is done and its damage reckoned with. But, for now, we are bonded by it.

Tegan sits up, tears in her eyes.

'Do you think it'll work?' she asks, looking right at me.

'It has to,' I say, pulling her in close, feeling the cold around us for the first time.

IN MY SLEEP that night I dream of Tatiana. I dream of the type of woman I want to be.

I do not imagine I have breasts.

I do not imagine I have had sex.

Tatiana walks in the blue light of the moon and can speak to the animals. She wears rings on her fingers and bells on her toes.

Tatiana is proud of her scars and each one tells a story.

Tatiana knows the Latin names for all of the plants, which will make you sick, and which will make you better.

Tatiana's fingers crackle with expectation. There is a live wire through her middle that sends sparks flying.

Tatiana is adored and it doesn't even matter.

She feels no fear in the pit of her belly; her butterflies are tame and do her bidding. They circle her dark hair, a halo, moving to the thud-thud rhythm of her heart, one-two, one-two, one-two, to the beat of their feet in the woods, to the slow rise of her smile. And the butterflies are gone.

At night, Tatiana returns to the woods. She turns into a wolf. She turns into a frog, but only when she wants to. She turns back into herself at will. She turns into me.

MY EYES OPEN, and I grapple for air and understanding. A hand is clamped over my mouth and I cannot breathe.

'Ssh! Don't scream,' Kevin says.

We blink at one another.

I shake my head. I won't scream.

'Sorry, I don't mean to scare you, only I don't want to wake her up.'

I shake my head again. He seems satisfied. He removes his hand, and I take a breath and immediately hold it. He is lying next to me wearing just white pants. His pale skin shines in the night light. He lowers his head beside mine on the pillow and his breath is hot against my cheek.

'I liked kissing you,' he whispers.

I don't say anything, for fear of being heard, for fear of being kissed again. I look to Tegan's side of the room and see the curve of her back in the shadows.

'Can I get in? It's bloody cold out here,' he says, but he's already lifted the covers and climbed into bed beside me. 'Shove up, you're hogging the bed.'

I shift towards the edge. His skin feels cold against the warm softness of my own. Every cell in contact with his body is alive with dismay. I am wearing only my Tammy Girl pants and a T-shirt. I wish I had pyjamas. I remember my half-Greek legs and feel further embarrassed. I hope Kevin won't notice. He slips his arm around my waist, his fingertips brushing against my bare skin. His eyes trace my own, like he's looking for a sign, and I stay perfectly still for fear I might accidentally give it.

'I think you have the prettiest eyes,' he says, then hoists himself on top of me. His weight presses me down. It's happening just like I imagined and it's my fault because I let him kiss me. I invited this without realising. I remember our ritual in the woods and wonder if we cast the wrong spell. If we brought this on ourselves. I want him to go away and leave me alone. But if I push him out, he'll stop liking me, and I don't want that either.

'You're squashing me,' I say. I don't want to upset him, but I can't breathe. I try to roll him off me, and we jostle for a moment, but instead he shifts his hips between my own, and lifts his weight from my chest onto his elbows. He's between my legs now, wedged up hard against me, his hip bones like plum stones digging into my thighs.

'You ever imagine what it'd be like to do it?' he says. 'I imagined doing it with you.'

He kisses me again, and I let it happen like before, except this time his tongue slips into my mouth. It is nothing like how I practised with Tegan. My breath is shallow with fear, or is it desire? Are they the same? I'm afraid both of what he expects me to do and of failing to do it properly and disappointing him. I'm afraid it's too late to stop it. His tongue pushes deeper into my mouth and his hips with it. The space between my legs where our bodies meet commands my entire attention. I am barely aware of his tongue in my mouth any longer; I'm barely here at all. I'm watching us from above or from across the room, through Tegan's eyes. The only part of me still in bed with him is located at that point of danger. It's as claustrophobic as a locked door.

He lets out a stifled grunt and falls down at my side. The game is over. My body feels light and broken open. Slick and sticky where he's been.

'Next time, let's do it for real.'

I think of the foxes with teeth in their vaginas.

'Gotta go,' he says.

He gives me a peck on the cheek and departs. Next time we'll do it for real, he said. I let out my breath and shiver. I'm not cold, I'm shaking. When I look back to Tegan, she's facing me now. Her eyes are closed, and I hope she's still sleeping.

ANIMAL, WOMAN

I wake up feeling like the world has ended. I remember the fire, the light in our eyes, our dancing, and my spirit brightens. And then I remember Kevin, and something clamps shut inside me like a fist. I wonder if I dreamed it. But the weight of his body against mine. His hips, hard as plum stones. I throw the covers back in a hot wash of shame. There's a dimpled blue bruise on the inside of each thigh. It was real.

I walk over to Tegan's bed. 'Can I get in?'

I want her to love me. To tell me everything's okay.

She grunts in acquiescence and I climb in beside her, my head nuzzled against her back, her hair all over my face. I feel a dull ache inside me, and curl up tighter to meet it. The spell made me sick. Or maybe the gin.

'You're too hot,' she says, and pushes me away with one foot.

I put a perimeter of space between us. I want to take out the memory of Kevin's visit and bury it in the ground in place of the two Barbies.

*

WE GET UP to do our chores. It's a dismal day, leaving the kitchen dark. Brenda drags a mop across the tiles like she's pulling a woman around by her hair. It smells of old fruit, stale coffee, and bleach.

'Take the scraps out for the pig,' Brenda says, before we've even had breakfast.

I follow Tegan to the trough, and Harvey trots along beside us, wagging his tail. It's started to drizzle.

'Is that really Harvey?' I ask. His wet nose sniffs around my fingers.

'Yeah.' Tegan swings the bucket up to shake the food scraps into the trough. The sow watches wisely from the shelter of her pen.

'No, I mean Harvey from the photo you showed me at Haley's?'

Tegan looks at me then, cold as stone, and I realise she's cross with me. She knows about Kevin. 'No, stupid, it's a new Harvey. We just named him the same.'

The dog's muzzle is flecked with white hair. He's clearly old.

'Right,' I say, wishing I'd never asked.

'What – you don't believe me?' Tegan turns to face me. The bucket of food scraps now swings at her side like she might use it to hit me.

'Of course I do.'

'You think I'd lie about something like that?'

'Teg . . .'

'We were meant to pretend it was the same dog,' she says, almost shouting now. 'We're all meant to pretend.'

Her breath is quick; she's furious.

'Teg,' I say again, hopelessly meek.

I want to tell her it wasn't my fault. Kevin was uninvited.

The idea she hates me is too dreadful. But she empties the last of the scraps and walks away with her hood pulled up. It is a walk that defies accompaniment.

TEGAN DOESN'T TALK to me for the rest of the afternoon. She makes herself scarce. She's punishing me and the world won't right itself until I'm forgiven. I can't ask for it, though. She has to give it of her own free will, or I'll be indebted.

Kevin reappears in the afternoon after he's finished helping his dad on the farm. He's playing in the yard, whacking a ball with a bat in the rain. The ball is tied to a spinning clothesline. Each time he whacks the ball, the contraption spins around and the ball comes back to him at pace.

THWACK. Whoosh. THWACK. Whoosh.

He sees me through the window and gives me a manic wave, motioning for me to join him. He's acting like nothing happened. I don't respond, grateful for the thick stone walls of the farmhouse separating me from him. I scurry upstairs to Tegan's room and close the door behind me, fearful of being ambushed.

That evening, Tegan and I lay the table together for dinner in silence and sit side by side without touching. She doesn't make a face at me before Grace, or loop her hand with mine in prayer. I'm desperate but I try to hide it. I avoid Kevin's eyes all evening, but his presence is enough to roil me.

Tegan only talks to me once we are in bed with the lights out. 'So what – you fancy my brother now?'

An accusation flung across the dark room.

'No!'

'Maybe you're a good match. He's never had a girl-friend either.'

She knows how to be cruel.

'I don't fancy him.'

'Then why didn't you tell him to get out? Why didn't you shout? Or do something?' she says. And then she adds, already convinced of it, 'Did you have sex?'

I sit up to turn the light on so I can see her face. 'No! Don't be stupid.'

'I saw him on top of you.'

I don't want to think about it.

'What if you're pregnant?' she says, as if it's a foregone conclusion. 'What would you do?' She gets up and sits on the edge of my bed, looking frantic.

'What? I'm not!' I'm confused and alarmed by this turn of questioning.

Sex is putting one thing in another. And then I'd come apart in his hands.

'How do you know?' she says, looking for an opening to seize on.

I cover my ears with my hands.

'What if he did something without your realising—'

'Stop it!' I shout.

I can still hear her talking so I start to hum, louder and louder, except it doesn't sound like humming with my ears plugged, it sounds like a million bees in symphony inside my head. She tries to pull my hands away from my ears to make me listen, but then we're wrestling, struggling around on the bed, her grip tight on my wrists, and me still uselessly humming. My fists clench, ready to fight her for real, which she senses, because then she giggles, so I do, too, cautious at first, but soon we're full on laughing and collapse, out of breath.

'What are we even fighting about?' she says, clutching her belly.

I know the answer. It's the feeling like anger with soft edges. We're fighting because she wants to know I belong to her.

'Stupid Kevin,' I say instead.

'Stupid Kevin,' she agrees.

We never did it, I reassure myself as I try to fall asleep that night. Not for real. If he comes back tonight, I'll shout this time. I'll shout for Tegan and she'll drag him from my bed by his ankles and drown him in her long hair.

I WAKE UP warm and wet. This must be part of my transformation. This is what comes next after webbed feet, when I emerge from the dark soupy depths. But I wake up a little more, and realise something about this feeling isn't right. An old memory stirs like a rock turning over in a river, of being small and wetting the bed. Now I'm wide awake. I run for the bathroom.

Sitting on the toilet, feeling dizzy, I see it. There in the white cotton of my pants a stain spreads like rust, its centre dark and prehistoric. I am bleeding. I had that one conversation with Mou – the row of cotton missiles – but it didn't prepare me for this. I fold some toilet paper into a thick rectangular wedge and place it in my knickers, pulling them up and adjusting them to sit snugly beneath me. I'll be the first girl who bleeds to death, I'm sure of it. The first girl who dies becoming a woman.

Back in the bedroom, I pull back the covers to search for stains. I'm frightened I bled on the sheets, and then I'll have to tell Brenda. In the shadows, there's blood everywhere. I run my hands over the surface and it feels dry, but I can't be certain.

'Siss?' Tegan's voice behind me. 'You okay?'

'Just got up to pee,' I say, unready to share.

Tegan rolls over and I climb back into my bed. But then I have an idea, and I get up once more to pull on my jeans, even if they're muddy. At least I'll bleed into my own clothes and not on their linen.

Stiff and hot, I feel each release of blood and clench my thighs tighter. We beckoned womanhood and it came. First forgotten Eve answered our calls. I bled before I was ready, and I beckoned Kevin, too. As it falls into place, my heart beats faster. All of this is of our making. I am a dangerous thing, a witch, forever tied to the moon. Right now, though, I wish I could take it all back and just be a girl again.

WHEN I WAKE up, Tegan is gone. I remember what happened, and jump up to check my sheets. They're still white. The blood I saw was just fear and shadows. In the toilet, I replace the wad of tissue in my pants. It smells like iron, like the centre of the earth.

I wonder where Tegan has gone or if she's mad at me again about Kevin. I climb into the Tegan-shaped impress in her bed and long for her to return. She would know what to do. Everything feels serious, terminal, and for the first time, I long to be at home with Mou.

Lying in bed, I notice my body looks different now. Like the ritual accelerated my transformation. My rashes have spread, except they aren't rashes. I know that. I'm shedding. I peel back a layer of skin and, beneath, it's clammy and cold to the touch. I spread the webs of my toes, then force them apart with my fingers as if I can rip them open, but it hurts just like pulling hard on my ear. These changes are calcifying, becoming more real. There is no return from this. I get up and dress quickly, making sure to cover my whole body, and run downstairs to search for Tegan.

I check the pig pen and the cow field in case she started her chores without me. Then I walk to the clearing where just the other night we had danced and laughed, and I had felt so sure of myself. This sadness is weighty and adult and comes from deep within my belly, or some place lower, and it's accompanied by an ache, which I feel in my bones. A pair of wizened hands wrings out my innards. I crouch low to the ground, compelled by instinct. I am animal. Woman. One and the same.

SMOKE STREAMS FROM Nan's chimney. I peer through the window: Nan is in her chair, her hands folded on her lap and eyes closed, so still that for a moment I think she's dead. I knock on the door, and she calls my name, as if she knew I was coming.

'Dear girl,' Nan says, already putting the kettle on to boil.

I know the smell of my own blood, I want to say.

Nan gives me a patient look. Maybe she can smell it on me, too. Or feel the clench and release of my womb, like a dog shaking in its sleep from a bad dream.

Nan sighs. 'Is it a tiff?'

The words are impossible. I am bleeding.

Nan stokes the burning fire. 'She's a complicated girl, our Tegan. She'd sooner break things than have them taken from her.' Nan sits again, looks me over, and continues. 'If she's been cruel, it's only that she's scared of losing you. Too much loss in the girl's life already. Takes its toll.'

'It's not Tegan,' I say, at last, and by saying that I've paved the way forward.

The skin on her hands is loose against the bones, like a coat a size too big. At night, she slips it off and leaves it at the door as she goes dancing in the moonlight.

'I'm bleeding,' I say quietly. It feels better than saying I started my period. My period of what?

'Your first time?' She raises her eyebrows for just a moment, then returns to her unflappable gaze. 'It's no surprise. It tends to happen to girls when they're away from home, somewhere unfamiliar.'

I want to tell her about the ceremony. I want to tell her each herb we stole from her shelves and put in the pot, so she can tell me what witchcraft we did and how to undo it. Nan, we did this to ourselves and we can never go back.

'Well, congratulations then,' Nan says, without changing her pragmatic tone. 'A menstruating woman is considered sacred and powerful. That's why men have always thought us to be dangerous. Anyone who bleeds for five days and doesn't die, well, they can't be trusted, so they send us to a shed at the bottom of the garden or banish us to the woods where we can cause them no harm.'

'Five days?'

'Your first will be shorter.' She examines my face. 'You're in pain?'

I nod.

She takes my tea mug and throws the remainder down the sink. She starts pulling down jars of herbs from the shelf.

'Caffeine is no good for the cramps. You'll want some ginger root. Camomile. Raspberry leaf.'

The potion sits in a teapot between us beneath a knitted tea cosy the colour of margarine. I begin to feel comforted.

'While that's brewing, I'll see what I have by way of sanitary products, though we might need to go up to the big house.'

'No, please!'

'Every woman has one. It's nothing to be ashamed of, but it's no use me telling you that. It'll take it happening every month for you to get used to it. I've always believed it's a sure sign God's a woman-hating bastard like the rest of men.'

'You don't believe in God? I thought you were Catholic.'

'Doesn't make much difference if I believe in him or not.' She rifles through a box of medicine she pulled from the bathroom cabinet. 'I was married once. The fella in the photo you so liked the look of. He was handsome, I suppose. He died just a few years back. I found him on his knees by the bed, praying. At first, I thought he'd just fallen asleep mid-prayer, because his hands were still clasped, and his forehead was against the bed quilt. I went to shake him, and he toppled over, stiff as a plank. We'd not slept in the same bed for years, so I guess he'd been like that for some time. His heart gave out. We'd never much liked one another, but it didn't seem right, this dying in prayer. What sort of God cuts your life short when you're already on your knees?'

'How did you meet your husband?' I ask, grateful for distraction.

'Jack. His father was the farmer here and brought him into my father's surgery when he was maybe twenty-one and I was seventeen. The horses shied with the plough and he'd gone under. Torn off the back of him. I was training as a nurse at the time so my father sent me out after that once a week to the farm to change his dressings.'

'And you fell in love?'

She gave me one of her looks. The sort of look that takes in the whole of a person before deciding how much to say. 'No, I wouldn't put it like that. I found myself in the family way.'

I don't understand.

'I got pregnant. Not so much as looked at the man and I was carrying his child.' This idea is terrifying. I think of Kevin, and what Tegan said, and quickly bury it. 'We were married then, and I gave up nursing. Before Derek was born, the war began and he was gone, leaving me with the baby and the farm. Those were the happiest years of my life. When the men came back, those who did, we were booted off. Five years I spent turning this soil and milking the cows, and then it was back in the kitchen with you. That was when I started hating him and hated him ever since, until the day he died, and I realised what a waste it'd all been.'

'What had?'

'The hating. After a while it's habit.' She pauses, and then, remembering what she was doing, continues to rummage through the medicine bag. 'Pour some of that tea while it's hot.'

She pulls out a crushed box of sanitary towels.

'Bingo!' she says, pushing them across the table at me. 'Must have been from when I had my hysterectomy. They pulled my womb out through my vagina if you want a really scary thought about what a woman's body can do. There's instructions on the box. You're a smart girl, you'll figure it out. What you waiting for?'

In the small draughty toilet, I'm nervous to put my bum on the seat for fear of what might come up from the dark pipes below. The toilet bowl has been scrubbed down to the silver, as if some creature has been digging to get out. I imagine it scrambling up the pipes and then stop myself, because I'm grown-up now and too old for silly fears. I have real fears to contend with.

The instructions on the back of the box are faded and torn. There was one class in school for the girls on starting our periods and they gave us a kit with some pamphlets and sanitary towels, which we threw at one another in the corridor, then stuck to the locker of the girl who was least liked. The boys later discovered them and Ralph, who is always the joker, stuck the sanitary towel to his chin like a bandage and walked around as if it weren't there, attempting to chat to the girls while we fell about laughing or ran from him.

I dispose of the wedge of toilet paper in my pants, unfold a sanitary towel from its wrapper, and stick it on, pleased with myself, even if it's self-explanatory.

When I emerge from the toilet, I shift my pants every few steps. I'm sure it must show through my jeans, but I'm too shy to ask.

WHEN I GET back to the house, Tegan is reading *Top of the Pops* in bed. She looks up at me in the doorway. 'Where've you been?' she says, pretending to be reading her magazine still. 'With Kevin?'

I sit on the side of the bed beside her. 'I have something to tell you,' I say, feeling brave.

'If it's about Kevin I don't want to know.'

I take a deep breath. 'I started mine,' I say.

'Started what? Oh, my God, you got your period?'

Tegan throws down her magazine and pulls me in for a hug, and I fall down beside her.

'It worked!' she says, thinking the same as me.

I laugh and nod.

The boys on the wall turn to look at me. Matt and Brad and Jared notice me for the first time.

I'm no longer frightened. I no longer want to reverse what we've done. As long as we're in it together.

'You know girls sync up their periods when they hang out all the time.'

'Really? When's yours, then?'

Tegan looks away and something cautious flickers across her face. 'It was meant to be last week, but it skipped.'

'Is that normal?' I ask, and she ignores me, switching direction, like she does.

'Can you believe you have to deal with this for ever? What an actual pain in the arse.'

We lie in bed chatting about the world that lies ahead of us and what it all means. All the malice of yesterday has been forgotten. The future feels imminent and inevitable.

Tegan turns to me when our conversation has quietened. 'I want nothing to change,' she says. She has her hands in my hair, teasing out the knots that accumulated during our night in the woods. She prises apart strands with her fingers. I accept this persistent tugging. This prising. This teasing apart of my body, as if it's hers. I relish it, too.

'But you want to leave home and move in with Haley,' I say.

'No, between us. Everything always has to change, and I don't want it to.'

Her fingers are trapped in a matt at the nape of my neck. The pain is sharp where she's tugging.

'I want it to be like this for ever,' she says. She tugs harder. 'Promise you'll always be here for me if I need you?'

I promise.

The knot comes loose. There's a clump of my hair in her hands.

I promise. Again and again.

IT IS MY last day. Or half-day, even. I pack my bags quietly while Tegan sulks. She crept into my bed last night and circled herself around me. I only knew she was crying from her tears wet against my back. She wouldn't tell me what was wrong. Sometimes I feel like Tegan leads another life apart from the one we share together.

The heifer went into labour at 2 a.m. so Derek and the boys spent the night in the cow barn. A slippery sack of hoofs and a beating heart emerged with a smack on the concrete. I heard it in my sleep or dreamed it. Derek and the boys won't be awake to say goodbye, Brenda tells me at breakfast, and I'm secretly glad. I don't want to see Kevin, or worse, for Tegan to see me with him and watch my every move.

I collect my things scattered around the old farmhouse, whose damp sorrow I've come to recognise. I now know the creak in the floorboard on the walk to the bathroom. I know how to collect eggs and lay a table (forks to the left). I learned other things, too. I know what it is to be kissed. I know what it is to bleed. I know what it is to have a boy climb into my bed, unwanted. I don't want to think about that.

I'm returning different than I arrived. I'll tell Mou right away I got my period. I can already see the delight on her face, proud and maybe a little sad that I'm so grown-up now. Then, later, I'll tell her about the rest of the farm. She'll want to know how I filled each day. I won't mention the meat-eating or the sow that's a sex slave. The idea of home gives me a little glow, and I'm surprised at it. I thought I'd be sad to leave Tegan, but I'm ready to go.

Mou is due to collect me at 2 p.m., so Tegan and I have our final lunch together in the kitchen eating sandwiches side by side.

'I don't want you to leave,' Tegan moans. She picks up the crumbs from my plate with a licked finger. 'It's better when you're here.'

We visit the newborn calf in its stable. Big eyes and clattering feet.

'You can't get too attached,' Tegan says.

In the corner, Harvey has his nose in something awful. When he turns, his muzzle is red with blood.

We go back inside to check the clock: 2 p.m. has come and gone, and still no sign of Mou. A little worry knocks about inside me.

I try calling the house, once, then twice, but Mou doesn't answer and there's no space left on the answering machine.

'Maybe she got held up at work,' Tegan says.

'She works in a library. What sort of emergencies can they have at a library? Someone hasn't checked their book in on time?'

'Just trying to help,' Tegan says. For once, it's my turn to be short with her.

When Brenda comes home from work to find me still here, I feel embarrassed. I try calling home again.

'Maybe Haley can come and get you?' Tegan asks, hoping to manipulate the turn of events to her own advantage. But Haley has work that night and Brenda wants Tegan's help around the house. 'She's fine without me the rest of the time,' Tegan says, sulking on her bed. I don't want to hear it: at least her mum remembers she exists.

When another hour passes, I call the house again. Tegan can see I'm feeling wretched and I don't know how to explain. I sit on the floor of Tegan's room next to my bag. I didn't call Mou all week. It never occurred to me that I ought to. But she must have been at home alone and sad. Worse than sad, lonely. I've been careless. I haven't done my job properly.

Tegan sits beside me. She hands me the cuddly dolphin she gave me on the first day.

'For keeps,' she says, and I hold it in my lap.

'I'm scared something's happened to her,' I say, a lump in my throat.

'Isn't she late all the time? She's forgotten you before.'

She's trying to help but she has no idea of all the ways in which Mou could be hurting.

It's dark and we're laying the table for dinner when a car pulls into the driveway. I run outside to look, but I'm blinded by the glare of the headlights. I walk around to the driver's side, and there she is. Of course, she didn't start to worry until it got dark.

'Mou!'

I knock on the window, wondering why she hasn't switched off the engine or the lights. She rolls the window down. 'I'm so sorry, Sissy,' she starts shakily. 'I ... ' She doesn't even give me an excuse.

Brenda and Tegan come out of the house, expecting a greeting, but Mou won't get out of the car and I know it.

My bag is by the front door already. I grab it, while saying my goodbyes and thank-yous, rushing to get in at the other side. It's an inadequate farewell, rude even, but we have to get away immediately. 'Say bye to the others and Nan, please,' I add. 'And thank you to Mr Price.'

Kevin appears in the doorway. He gives me a little wave and I feel mortified.

'Bye, weirdo,' Tegan says, and I make sure to hug her.

Brenda approaches the car window and leans in. 'You're welcome to stay for dinner?'

'Thank you, but it's late,' Mou says, not meeting her eyes.

'I see.' Brenda gives Mou another once-over, less friendly than the first.

Then Mou winds up the window and we drive away.

I don't tell Mou my period started. I don't tell her anything about my time on the farm.

As we drive, the darkness engulfs the car. All we can see between the beams of the headlights is the ever-unfolding road ahead.

IV

(the passage)

IV

(one passage)

AMPHIBIAN

In the bath, I'm barely recognisable. My nuggets for breasts are pretty much the same, but the membranes between my toes have thickened, and if I look closely, I have patches of delicate scales in place of skin. There's no denying it now: other girls become women; I'm turning amphibian. I was not loved in the right way or at the right time or by the right person.

I sit up and feel a pain at the base of my spine. I reach behind me and it's just what I feared. A hard pointed lump, like a cyst beneath the skin: a fledgling tail.

Lying down in the water, I try to slow my fast-beating heart. I don't cry, because what good will it do me? I am changing, still; I am changing further. This changing hurts. The pain is different from before. It's no longer the pain in the back of my throat when I'm about to cry, but the pain of a sword passing right through me.

I traded one thing for another, and got something unwanted in return.

Puberty is vicious, just like Mou said it would be.

A thing with teeth, like a fox's vagina.

*

AT HOME, THE sentences are laid out all over the living-room floor, a trail of disconnected thoughts. It was this way when I came back from the farm, which means she was sentence-making while I was gone. Paper scraps stacked in piles with trophies and bird ornaments to weigh them down. Some are labelled with a number corresponding to a chapter or part of the eventual story, but they are not in the right order, as she has told me several times, as if that excuses what she's done.

She ransacked the bookshelf for material. The phone book, too, and the God pamphlets that come through the letterbox with warnings about the peril to our souls. The remnants are scattered all over, and I wonder whether she's been to work at the library at all. I try to follow the paper path, hoping it leads to a logical conclusion. As if the sum of the information might equal a whole.

'Where do I start, Mou?' I shout to her in the kitchen. 'Does it begin with, *All sanity depends on this*?'

I never told her I changed. I bled, which means I'm a woman now. A boy desired me, which means I'm a woman, too. But I'm growing a tail. What does that mean? Did one thing lead to another? Was it being desired that made me change? But it had started before then. Mou would under-stand how these events are connected. But I can't talk to her when she's like this.

Mou and I sit on the sofa to watch TV with a bowl of cereal on our laps. We have to tiptoe across the floor to get here because of the sentences. We've eaten sandwiches already for dinner, but Mou worried I was going hungry, and made me a bowl of cereal as well. The cereal is stale. I'm chewing cardboard Cheerios with milk a day past its Best Before.

Mou hasn't said a great deal since I got home. She hasn't asked me about the farm. She's trying to hide from me what's happening, and the only way she knows how is to stay quiet, as if I might not notice.

'Careful!' she says, indicating a certain precarious pile of scraps when I put my bowl down.

We're watching the news with the sound off, as usual. Sometimes the pictures are misleading. Sometimes something is happening that is entirely different from what it appears.

There is newly released video of the latest missing girl. It's the last footage of her seen alive. She is wearing her Halloween costume. A cape flaps behind her. A pair of devil horns on her head. She will never arrive at her party. I recognise the street, though – there's Chicken Cottage. I turn the sound on and Mou looks at me. I'm breaking the rules.

'That's Haley's street!' I say, in justification. I'll call Tegan later to warn her – she'll be thrilled by the proximity of danger.

A few seconds after the missing girl walks off screen, a man follows close behind: their suspect. The police have released a still of this man and I lean forward to get a better look. The image is black and white and blurry, magnified beyond meaning. A smear of a face without any features, just two dark pockets for eyes. It could be anyone. It could be any man at all.

'Turn it off,' Mou says quietly. 'It's too awful.'

THE BRUISES ON my thighs have healed. First they went purple as a plum, then yellow and grey. I was still when he climbed on top of me; I was not still inside. I was teeming like the sea.

I want him to do it again – appear in my bed at night, unbidden – and I'm terrified one day he might. Next time we'll do it for real, he said. Fear and desire are indistinguish-able. I don't know what happens next, except his weight on my body will be part of the story. And something will be lost in exchange for nothing gained.

I put my fingers inside me like Tegan showed me. For the first time since I buried the Barbies, I won't cut my pleasure short. I think about Kevin's tongue in my mouth; he's the only boy who's ever liked me. I swap Kevin for Luke Perry in the snug – he would kiss me gently – but then it's the face of the girl snatcher with black pockets for eyes. My fingers inch deeper, my hips rise to meet them, and I realise this new frontier of desire is enough. I banish them all from my mind: I banish Luke and Kevin, Peter and the girl snatcher. It's just me and my body, trilling and trembling. The grand expanse of its possibility lies bare before me and with it I break open, like a wave. There's no undulating pink light, no galloping horses. This time the other-other is deep green like algae and when I open my eyes I'm shaking all over, as if I'm terrified. I press my face into the pillow and cry. When the tears end, I'm exhausted and pass straight into the deepest dreamless sleep.

A KNOT THAT COMES UNDONE

In the morning, the kitchen is empty. I put the kettle on to make Mou a cup of coffee, and I eat a bowl of stale cereal while it brews. I stir in half a spoon of sugar – three times clockwise and three times anticlockwise, to undo any bad magic that might have been done by the first stirring – and take it upstairs to deliver it to Mou. This routine makes me feel adult, working in the kitchen alone. I take pleasure in each ordinary ritual: coffee-making, dish-washing. Tasks with a beginning and an end.

Inside her bedroom the curtains are drawn and Mou is curled on her side, unmoving. A muscle in my chest tightens, like a knot pulled taut.

'Get up, Mou, it's time for work.'

If I pretend everything is okay, then perhaps she'll pretend, too. If she pretends for long enough, she might trick herself into getting better.

I put the coffee on her bedside table and sit on the edge of her bed.

'It's your seven o'clock wake-up call,' I say, and the chirpiness rings false.

There is an outline of my mother beneath the sheet. If I touch it, she'll disappear, like a magician's trick. The sheet whisked away and – ta–da! – nothing there.

'Mou?'

The knot tightens.

My father tied knots in everything. He tied knots in dish-cloths and drapes, and once even in my hair, when he got me ready for school one day and didn't know how to do a plait. He taught me to tie my shoelaces. I only remember three knots he taught me and all of them are sturdy and secure. He didn't teach me the type of knots that pull apart with a single tug.

'Mum!' I say louder, shoving her outline. She doesn't disappear. She is heavy as a ship. She turns in the vast sea of her bed towards me, her face crushed by the pillow. There is a crease from her eye to the corner of her mouth.

'You're going to be late for work, Mou,' I say, standing.

The knot is so big I need a drink to swallow it. If I keep moving everything will go back to how it's meant to be. Everything will return to normal.

'Go ahead without me,' Mou says, rolling over. 'I need another twenty minutes.'

'Just get up!' I yank the sheet from her, but she pulls it back over her head and ignores me. She is an outline of my mother again. Or not my mother at all. The un-mother.

In the kitchen I down a glass of sour milk and retch.

I WALK TO the school bus. I must be careful not to arouse suspicion about Mou's condition – or my own. At school, Lydia is talking delightedly to Clara. The conversation is about one of the boys on the bus and whether or not Lydia told this boy that Clara fancies him. The boy is a bit fat, and, as it's commonly agreed that Clara is a bit fat too, they're seen as an obvious match to everyone except Clara, who is furious.

'You told him you were joking, right?' Clara hisses at Lydia, who, at a safe distance, is smirking.

'I tried!' She has clearly done no such thing. 'But once I'd said it . . . He's going to call you tonight and ask you out.'

Clara's jaw clenches. She's among the girls who have never had a boyfriend. She is smug and cantankerous with the boys, as if she's already decided she's of no interest to them.

Tegan listens to their conversation, her chair half turned towards Clara, head resting on one hand. The social interactions of the bus kids intrigue her as a world she has no influence over. Tegan never vies for power like the other girls. Her power is given to her freely and she wields it, but she stays out of things beyond her control.

When I arrive, Tegan doesn't turn to say hello to me, but her hand reaches out beneath the desk, inviting me to take it. We hold hands like this, a special greeting, more powerful for being silent.

Tegan asks me to go home with her after school today. We're walking down the corridor when she asks, so I don't have to look at her when I say no.

'I can't,' I say, and she sulks.

'But it's been ages,' she says, stopping short of asking why.

I haven't gone home with her since returning from the farm two weeks ago. The first few days back at school she didn't ask because she just expected me to come with her, like always. She'll only ask once, then punish me for not coming. I can't tell her it's because my mother is sick and if I leave her for too long she'll never get up again. That it's my fault she's sick in the first place, because I left her, and only my returned presence is holding us together. Or that every day when I'm at school, I'm afraid of what I'll return home to find. It's the dog-end of winter now, nearing spring. The most dangerous time, Mou often says.

'Maybe I'll just ask Hannah,' she says, but she's bluffing. Too much of Tegan is hidden for her to invite the other girls home. This is something we share without saying it. 'Please,' she says, and the word rocks me. I can't.

Later, as the bus pulls away from school, Tegan is at the back gate getting into Haley's car. I go to wave, but then I see Peter's driving. I slink back in my seat. As we pass, I turn to get a better look. She's laughing; a flush of hatred for Peter returns. But then I realise she isn't laughing – she's crying. Not just crying, her fists are clenched and her mouth is open in a wail, and he's just sitting there, ignoring her, as if her tears aren't his problem. It is the same mouth we made when we applied our lipstick. The same mouth we made when we screamed into the trees. I turn full circle to keep my eyes on her until she's gone.

THE HOUSE IS quiet and the lights are all off when I get home from school. I want to wish for my mother to be well, but I used up all my wishes on Tegan. Maybe that's why this is happening. This is the price I paid for Tegan to be my one friend. I think of Mrs Adebayo and how some people are so unhappy death is the only cure, and I'm more afraid than I've ever been in my life.

Running upstairs, I take two steps at a time, calling for Mou. I stand in the doorway to her room.

Her outline under the sheet is so still, she could be dead already.

'Mou?' I say again, and she doesn't move.

I lie down beside her and place my face against her back and hear the faint, familiar thud-thud of her heart. Someone trapped inside is trying to get out and that someone is happy and free. They're knocking on her chest like it's a door, waiting for an answer. In the long, rambling car days, she said she was looking for a version of herself she'd left behind. It was here all along, inside her.

'It's safe for you to come out,' I whisper into her back. 'Don't be afraid.'

WHEN THE PHONE rings later that evening, I hope it's Tegan so I can find out what's wrong. I can't say I saw her crying, though: she wouldn't like that.

I'm surprised when it's Haley at the other end, her faraway voice distorted and uneven. Tegan is upset, she tells me. She's been crying since she got home from school, and she won't say why.

'You're the only person she might talk to,' Haley says, and I can't turn her away.

In a house as silent as a tomb, I wait for Tegan to come over. Right now, Haley is driving Tegan to my house. There is time to tidy. To cover up for Mou. For both of us. I could do it, like I always have, but I stay exactly where I was when I hung up the phone. Waves of momentum ebb and flow inside me. I nearly get up three or four times, but something stops me.

Haley's car pulls up outside, but it's Tegan's footsteps alone that walk up the drive.

I open the door. Tegan has clearly been crying, but she walks into the house like she enters any space. Like she owns it. Like there's nothing in here that can scare her. It's an act to cover up her tears, which she won't mention, and I won't ask her about, and that's the only reason she agreed to come. We hug, but she pulls away quickly, fearful of the emotions it might unlock.

'Haley wanted me to come,' Tegan says. She wants me to know it wasn't her idea; that she would never have phoned to ask me.

'I'm glad you're here.'

She steps into the living room, gravitating towards the sofa and the TV, our usual ritual, but she falters. The books. The scraps. The bird paraphernalia. She steals a look at my face, assessing. She kneels down to run her fingers over one pile of sentences, and I resist the urge to stop her.

'What is all this?'

'It's Mou's. She calls it poetry,' I say, repeating what she's told me so many times. 'A poetry of chance, or something. Two random sentences come together and make something new.'

'How does it work?'

I shake my head. 'Each pile is a poem. Or a chapter. I don't know.'

I've thought about this moment so often. When Tegan comes into my home. In getting to know Mou, Tegan would see me more clearly, understand me like she never could before. I wanted to show off my mother. I wanted to share all that is special about Mou. Her laughter. Her chattiness, not serious or boring like other mums. They would sing along to Mou's records. That's what I always imagined. But that mother isn't available.

Tegan fingers the ornaments and trophies dotted about. She picks one up shaped like a small wooden flute. 'What is it?'

'A songbird whistle.' I take it to show her. 'Turn it here, and it plays the call of different birds.'

She blows. The ring of a woodlark. A jay screech. Then she blows and no sound comes out.

'This one is broken,' she says, and I shrug.

It's the nightingale, I think, that cannot sing.

'Where's your mum?' Tegan says.

I don't have an answer.

Instead of words, I lead her upstairs. We stand in the doorway to Mou's room and the outline that is my mother breathes in and out, lost in the endless turns of her mind. Or maybe she's just taken one of her blue pills again. Tegan doesn't say anything. Seeing it afresh through her eyes, I can't take it any longer, and I pull her into my room, and close the door. If Mou gets up, she'll think my closed door is worrying. But she won't get up.

I keep my room tidy without Mou having to ask. It offers respite.

'Is she sick?' Tegan says, and I start to talk then. I tell her about my father, at last. The story she asked for and I never shared. About the car days and the man in the car park at Asda, who attacked us. The taste of his skin in my mouth. About the last time my mother went to bed and didn't get up, and how, soon after, we moved house again. I tell the story from beginning to end, and for the first time, the pieces fall into place. We moved because the school discovered she wasn't well, I realise now. The moving, it wasn't adventure, like she said; we were running away. We changed our names then, too, from Savos to Blackmore. Mou didn't want to be found out. I tell Tegan it's a sickness and it's secret. I tell her how Mou and I are a team, just us. I'm trying to redeem her, but even as I'm speaking, it feels like a lie. And the whole time, Tegan listens, nods occasionally, puts out a hand to hold mine. When I reach the end, I take a deep breath, as if to continue, but nothing more comes out.

'I figured there was something wrong,' she says. We're sitting now on my bedroom floor. 'She should get help, Siss. That's what they said about my brother. That if he'd got help sooner ...'

And then she stops talking because she knows what comes next. Her brother unfurled like the yellow scarf. 'Sorry,' she says. 'I didn't mean it like that.'

There is more to say – the Germolene-smelling doctor, Grandma Jean – but it's too hard to explain. I'm proud I told her my story without crying. I take solace in being brave.

We sit for a moment in silence. Tegan fiddles with my crystal collection, now missing the smoky quartz. She never returned it to me. I notice she's losing her baby blonde hair, like childhood departing. The roots are almost brown, especially when she hasn't washed it, like now.

'Want to see something funny?' I say.

She nods.

I show her my snug. I was right. It fits two me-sized girls perfectly. I tell her to lie on her back and look up. She notices the sticker and laughs; it's good to hear.

'I didn't think Luke Perry was your type,' she says, and I shove her.

'It's not about him.'

'It never is,' she says, and we both laugh.

'Siss,' she says, and I feel it coming. After everything I've told her, she's ready now to share. I gave it all to her, my home, my mother, my biggest secrets, even Luke Perry. I'm ready for her confidence now, for her secret inside the music box. Our connection gives me a feeling of pure joy, which I'll remember later and regret.

'Siss, I think I'm pregnant.'

It makes no sense to me at first. Pregnancy is impossible. It belongs to the adult world of which we're not yet part. But Tegan isn't playing. She's tugging the few eyelashes she has left.

'Siss?' she says, when I don't say anything.

'How?' I ask, which is the wrong thing to say. 'You're too young to get pregnant,' I say, which is also a mistake.

'If I knew you'd be babyish about it, I'd never have told you.'

Tegan sits up in a huff, and I'm chastised.

'Who did you have sex with?' There's a wobble in my voice. Not on her account, but because she's kept this from me. She has a life apart from the one we share together, and I always suspected it.

Tegan shrugs, like she doesn't know or it doesn't matter.

When a drawing of a man puts his penis into a drawing of a woman.

We once pushed pillows under our jumpers to pretend to be pregnant, and then we pulled the pillows out when the game was over. I want to pull the pillow out and for this game to end.

'Are you sure?'

She shakes her head. She skipped her last two periods.

I don't want to be alone with this secret. It's like when she told me about Andy. I want to return to the world where rules are laid out in neat white lines. Becoming a woman is dangerous and we're unprepared for it.

'We have to tell somebody.'

'I'm telling you.'

'A grown-up, I mean.'

'Leave off, we're not kids any more.' She crawls out of the snug, like she's searching for air.

I crawl out after her. She's standing in my room with her back to me. How strange that this is the first time she's been here. She looks lost and afraid, and I remember what Haley said, how Tegan wouldn't tell her what was wrong. I wish she had told Haley instead. Anyone but me.

'If you're not going to help me, I'll just deal with it by myself.'

'Of course I'll help,' I say, standing close to her now.

'I wanted to tell you sooner, but you wouldn't hang out,' she says, to make me feel guilty, and it works. I could make her feel guilty right back. She had sex without telling me.

'You kept making excuses,' she adds.

'Now you know why.'

She turns to me. 'You can't tell anyone. Promise?'

I don't want to, but I promise. I will say it again and again. I promise. I promise. I promise.

After Haley picks her up that night, I sit in my room thinking about the baby. I saw a programme on TV that said at six weeks a baby is the size of an apple seed. I wonder if the baby inside Tegan's belly is the size of an apple seed yet or larger.

I STAND IN the doorway to Mou's room wishing she'd wake up. Not now, Mou. I want to shake her and tell her, please, not now. She's lying on her back, her breasts resting either side of her chest, flat and hard in the middle, her face pallid from lack of fresh air. I go to open the window, but the fact I'm here like this for her again makes me angry. I won't do it. Mou can get up and open it herself.

I lie down beside her and count the spiders in the corners of the room. One, two, three, four. Eight legs each. Sixteen. Twenty-four. Thirty-two. An egg sack, woven, white and fat with expectation, hanging like a silken jewel from the mother's abdomen. Hundreds more in there. Uncountable numbers.

I wish I could tell Mou about Tegan. Mou knows about getting pregnant too young. If Mou was well, she could help us. Mou, there's been a breach from an unknown source and out of this breach might come a baby. An unimaginable human baby. Perhaps there are more ways than one to make a baby. Perhaps the breach was made by us in the woods that night. Perhaps it doesn't involve only a drawing of a man putting his penis inside a drawing of a woman. We made a baby another way, an older way. Like first forgotten Eve who birthed the world without the help of a man. We made a baby from earth and fire. We danced with the spirit of the night and howled to the moon like witches. We committed dark magic and perhaps that's the same as sin. The girls who danced before us were turned to stone. The other girls, who were loved too much or not at all, they were transformed, also. They turned into a tree, into foam on top of the sea, into the nightingale that couldn't sing. A different fate befell us. We put a stone inside you and, like a seed, it bore a fruit.

If it's true, then this baby is of our making.

If it's true, then this baby is ours.

Mou rolls onto her side to face me, looking as if she's only just realised I'm there.

'I took a day,' she says, as if it's just one.

The spider and its sack slip away into a crack in the corner where it's safe. There are eight legs and a hundred babies fewer in the room. I cannot do that maths. I don't know any longer who to count.

'I dreamed someone was here,' she says.

'It was my friend Tegan.'

'Oh, she should stay for dinner.'

'Another time,' I say, too tired to fight her.

I cook the expired can of beans from the back of the kitchen cabinet, and bring it to Mou. She sits up for us to have a bed picnic, which gives me a little hope. She eats, but she doesn't say a word. I took some money from her wallet this morning to buy a loaf of bread from the corner shop, and it annoys me she doesn't notice that we have bread when we didn't have bread earlier.

When we've finished, she says, 'You're a good girl, Sissy *mou*. So grown-up now. I'm sorry, I'm so tired,' and lies down.

'What about the library?'

'I'll be better tomorrow.'

She rolls over and faces the other way.

That night before I go to sleep I place my obsidian on Mou's bedside table.

'Do your stuff,' I whisper, and I really mean it.

AN APPLE SEED

Tegan and I have a plan. Or it's Tegan's plan, really, and I promised to help her. We'll go to the pharmacy after school and steal a pregnancy test. She went before, but the test was too expensive and, she says, if you get pregnant at thirteen, they'll call the police. 'Why?' I ask.

'In case you've been abused or something,' Tegan replies vaguely. It will be my job to distract the shopkeeper while Tegan puts the test into her coat pocket. She's stolen from there before and never been caught.

I try persuading Tegan to tell someone, anyone, but she won't listen. If we steal the pregnancy test, we'll learn the baby is real and we'll have to do something about it. Tegan already believes in it. She says the baby is hers and no one will take it from her. She wants to make-believe about the impossible baby.

'If I have a baby will you help me look after it?'

Tegan and I are sitting in the Maze together. She told Clara and Hannah they aren't invited, and they went away disgruntled, hating me more. They've started hanging out with Charlotte and the Sarahs more often.

'Of course I will,' I say.

There are small green buds on the tangled shrubs that make up the walls of the Maze. I pick apart a bud to examine what it's made of. My fingers are sticky and there's nothing inside.

'Do you think I'll get thrown out of school? I'll be too busy with baby things, won't I?'

I don't know the answer to this question. I don't know the answer to any of her questions any more.

'I've had enough school to be a pop singer, I reckon.'

Tegan sticks her belly out, arching her back. 'See? I'm definitely fatter. I'm going to be huge after nine months. And my tits have grown. Can you tell?'

I don't see and I can't tell.

There are webs between my toes, I could show her. Or my tail not quite sticking out from beneath my school skirt.

'How's your mum?' she asks, out of nowhere. No one has asked me a question like it, so I don't have an answer.

'Better,' I lie.

AT THE PHARMACY, the pregnancy tests are alongside the condoms and the fanny deodorant that once made us laugh. Tegan knows where to find them.

'Tegan?'

'What?' Tegan is annoyed because she's afraid. When Tegan is afraid she can be most cruel.

'What about Nan?' I ask, still desperate for an alternative.

We are browsing the make-up aisle by a display of Rimmel glitter lip gloss. A large pair of plastic lips smile down on us from above. The glittering lips are amputated from any face.

'Nan could help,' I say. 'She trained as a nurse.'

Nan would know just by looking at Tegan whether there

was a baby the size of an apple seed inside her. And if there was, what we should do. Mou once told me that if I swallowed an apple seed a tree would grow in my belly. And then she thought better of it. She said adults tell lies to children when they don't have the answers.

I think of Nan's kitchen, the herbs stuffed on her shelves in great dusty bunches and the sweet camomile steam wafting through the cobwebbed air. Her reassuring hands wrapped in parchment-thin skin.

'You said yourself she's a witch,' I add.

'Are you going to help me or not? You promised.'

I nod. I long for an adult to save us. Even if that adult tells us lies because they don't have the answers.

The lights are bright in the pharmacy. There are no shadows here. No earth in which to dig our hands. This is not make-believe any longer. The plan is I will buy some make-up to busy the salesperson while Tegan puts the pregnancy test inside her school coat. I've always known she steals but I've never seen her do it. I wish I didn't know, because every move I make screams with guilt. I take one of the glitter lip glosses up to the counter, without looking over my shoulder to where Tegan is still browsing. There will be a moment when she puts the box in her coat and I don't want to see it. I pay with Tegan's fiver and the salesperson hands me the change. I turn to leave.

'One moment,' the lady says, and every cell in my body freezes.

The suspended glitter lips shout, 'She's a thief!'

'You forgot your receipt.'

Smiling weakly, I take it. I walk over to Tegan and we take the small number of steps needed to exit the pharmacy. Soon we will be walking back down the high street to Haley's house where we will be safe. We will take the pregnancy test out of the box, and follow the instructions, and it will prove there is no baby inside my friend's belly. We will return to school the next day and continue to be girls for a little longer.

Except it doesn't happen like that.

TEGAN AND I are sitting on folding chairs in a room behind the pharmacy. There is a poster on the wall describing the ways in which our pharmacist can help us. None of the ways listed are what we need. They describe other problems we've not yet encountered, like alcohol addiction and allergies. On the table beside us is the pregnancy test in its box. Clear and Simple, it says.

It was another customer who spotted us. He shouted, 'That girl put something in her pocket,' which was when Tegan and I ran. We could have outrun the pharmacist if it wasn't for Tegan's school shoes, hand-me-downs from Haley, a size too big with a platform heel.

The pharmacist folds his arms across his chest, and the salesperson, who turns out to be his wife, sits in a chair opposite ours. She says her name is Anya and introduces her husband as Mr Borham.

'How old are you?' Anya asks. She has a bird face, narrow and long, with a furrow between her eyebrows.

'Sixteen,' Tegan lies.

Anya's furrow deepens.

Mr Borham huffs and looks away.

'We don't want to call the police,' Anya says, as if there is an ultimatum coming, which she can't bring herself to deliver. 'What are your names?'

Tegan doesn't even blink when she says, 'Tallulah.' I will always follow where she leads, so I say, 'Tatiana,' in turn, mimicking her bravado.

I wonder whether Mou will get out of bed to be angry with me or whether she will be too tired to be angry.

Mr Borham opens Tegan's school bag, which they searched when they found the stolen merchandise in her coat pocket.

'Tegan Price,' he says, handing his wife one of the text-books. 'Same school as Baz.'

We know Baz. He's one of the boys in William's gang. He was the fat kid whose name I didn't know.

'Try calling the school. They'll have their parents' details. If they don't answer, call the police. I don't have time for this.'

Mr Borham walks out, and Tegan calls after him, insolent as ever. 'Or you could just let us go.'

Anya almost smiles and, for a moment, I hope it'll turn out okay.

'Which one of you is the pregnancy test for then?' Anya says.

'Oh,' Tegan says, acting dumb. 'My Ken doll got my Barbie up the duff.'

Anya is annoyed now.

I wish Tegan wouldn't be like this sometimes.

IT'S MISS STOREY who collects us. She isn't dressed in her teacher clothes. She's wearing jeans, a black cardigan and patent ballet pumps. Once the children leave for the day, she changes into the real Miss Storey.

She watches us in the rear-view mirror as she drives us back to school. Her car is small and clean with no rubbish on the floor. She's acted strangely towards us ever since she caught us playing Girlfriends and Boyfriends, and now here we are, shoplifters, criminals, confirming her worst fears.

I'm annoyed with Tegan. If she had been nice to Anya and Mr Borham, they might have let us go. We could have given them Haley's phone number, and then we wouldn't be here in the back of Miss Storey's car on our way to school where the headmistress is waiting.

'You're lucky they didn't call the police,' Miss Storey says, in the same quiet voice she always uses. 'They could have, you know. Just because you're kids doesn't mean the law doesn't apply to you.'

When we arrive, the school is empty of its children. Only the lights in the staff room are still on where a few teachers finish their marking.

Tegan and I are put into a classroom not belonging to us. A display shows the cross-section of a volcano, its interior bubbling beneath its skin, surrounded by photos of real volcanoes: Mount Etna, Mount Fuji and Mount Vesuvius, fat and impatient to erupt.

Miss Storey leaves to call our parents. Tegan turns to me and takes both my hands in hers. Her insolence is all gone. She looks at me, beseeching. 'You have to tell them the test was for you. Please, Siss. They can't know it was for me, or Brenda will find out and then she won't let me keep the baby. She'll make me get an abortion or give it away.'

In all the stories I know, the girls don't get abortions. They get murdered or married, widowed or blamed. They disappear or they change into something else. But Tegan is here pleading with me. She has never pleaded like this before. Even when she wants something I won't give her, she only ever asks me once, if at all.

'But I haven't had sex,' I say, which seems an insurmountable barrier. 'I've never even had a boyfriend.'

'Say you were confused, say whatever happened with Kevin . . . that you didn't know.'

I hate that she's brought up Kevin, as if she prepared for this moment. I take my hands from hers, but she grabs them back again, forcibly, and once she has them, her grip clamps down.

'How do you know you're even pregnant?' I ask.

'I just feel different,' she says, beaming, her eyes electric. I see the fire in them from that night and our reflections multiplied infinitely. The world has become strange again. Distant.

'Did we make this happen?' I whisper.

We haven't spoken about the ritual again, though it's always there between us, a memory ripe with wonder and shame.

'That night in the woods?' she asks.

I feel her mind racing. There's a part of me that's always aware of what Tegan is thinking and another part that, despite how well I know her, isn't able to stave myself against her. I nod, and she senses an opening.

'You said it yourself. I'm fated. Maybe this is what I'm fated for.' She's quiet, but forceful when she adds: 'It's our baby, Siss. She's ours. We can't let them take her from us.'

There are things that happened in my imagination and things that happened in real life and the lines are for ever blurred.

'Just say you'll do it. For me. This one thing. Please? Promise.'

I nod. I was never able to say no to her. She throws her arms around my neck and everything else from this moment onwards is not real.

*

BRENDA ARRIVES. SHE passes by the door to the classroom without looking in. She is in her pink nursing uniform. Miss Storey comes to fetch Tegan.

Twenty-five minutes pass. I count it on the clock. It passes more slowly than any class ever has, and at the end of it I still can't leave. Brenda passes the door once more in the other direction, this time with Tegan at her side. Tegan looks into the classroom. She is a volcano impatient to erupt. We do not smile. We do not wave. We simply look for as long as we can, holding each other's gaze. Everything is about to change, just as she feared.

Miss Storey returns some time later. She sits on the edge of the desk next to me. She is waiting for me to speak first, but I won't.

'Sissy, do you have a boyfriend?'

I shake my head.

'Or a boy you hang out with?'

I shake my head again.

'What made you think you were pregnant?'

I don't say a thing. I can't lie, but I my capacity for silence is greater than they can fathom. She leans forward, bringing her face close to mine, doing everything she can to look sympathetic.

'Tegan told us that something happened between you and her brother.'

'I don't want to talk about it,' I say. 'Please.'

It's a magic word. I conjured it from long ago when 'please' was the gateway to whatever I wanted. *Please*, I don't want to talk about it.

After the longest silence, Miss Storey says, 'We can't get hold of your mum. Is there anyone else we can call? How about your dad?'

I'm tired. I want to say: My mother isn't answering the phone because she's gone to bed again, and she won't get up until she's good and ready. I don't know when she'll be ready and neither does she. She's hibernating. She is resting her mother brain because her mother brain is like a bear. It grows fat through summer, and in winter, when the nights are long and cold, it retreats into its cave and forgets the world outside. When she emerges in search of the sun, she'll be weary and thin, and I'll be there to guide her back to the light like every other time. I do not say this. I rest my head on my desk instead.

MISS STOREY MAKES a phone call in the office, cancelling her dinner plans for the night. Miss Storey goes on dates. Miss Storey has boyfriends. This would thrill Tegan and me in normal times. We could imagine the men Miss Storey loves and whether they love her in return. But these aren't normal times. And I don't imagine these things now.

When the caretaker comes to lock up for the night, Miss Storey leads me back to her car. I send telepathic messages to Mou. Get up! Get up, before Miss Storey arrives.

When we park, Miss Storey notices the car in the drive and that all of the lights are off in the house. She looks at me like I'm hiding something, annoyed. She knocks once, and then again harder.

'Mrs Blackmore?' she calls, through the letterbox. 'Sissy, I don't know what's going on, but you're bright enough to know that if nobody is at home, I can't just leave you here. What do you normally do after school?'

'I get the bus home.'

'And you're by yourself all this time?'

I don't answer.

'Well, then, you must have a key. You can let us in.'

This is logic I cannot deny.

When I turn the key in the lock, I'm betraying Mou.

When I let Miss Storey into the house, I'm a traitor.

I didn't know what else to do, I tell myself later, when reckoning with who was to blame for what happened.

Turning on just one of the dozen lamps in our kitchen, I hope she doesn't see the others. I avoid her eyes as she takes in the room. The white plastic picnic set covered with lists and junk. The dishes in the sink from last night's beans and the empty pantry shelves. The trophies lined up around the sides of the room and the overgrown grass in the garden at the back. Daffodils are readying to remind us of spring. Change is coming, they'll say brightly, whether we want it or not.

If she steps into the living room, she'll find the sentences. If she reads them, she won't know where to start, and if she doesn't know where to start she'll think it's nonsense. I'll say it's poetry, for the second time in two days, but she won't believe me. I don't believe me either.

'I'll get my mum,' I say.

I catch a glimpse of Miss Storey's face as I run upstairs. I could tell her the importance of each of these items and what they mean to Mou and me. We have our own language. Our own system for things, I'll say. And it's just ours, which makes it special. But I'm not so sure any more.

In Mou's bedroom, I turn on the overhead light and shake her.

'Mou, you have to get up!' I hiss, as loudly as I can without Miss Storey hearing. 'Please, my teacher won't leave until she knows you're here. I'm sorry, Mou, please,' I say, shoving her hard now, until finally she opens her eyes.

She looks at me, confused, glazed. 'What's happened? Are you hurt?' She clumsily reaches a hand towards me.

'No, Mou, not now. You have to get up and come downstairs, please!'

'Okay, good. I just need five more minutes and then I'll make you something to eat,' she says, retracting her hand and rolling over.

'No!' I say. 'You don't understand, you have to get up now!'

When I turn, Miss Storey is standing in the doorway. She looks away, embarrassed. 'I'm sorry,' she says, and goes downstairs.

'Mum!' I push her once more, harder than I need to.

The worst thing has happened. Our greatest fear. For a moment there is some relief in it. A lightness to knowing that what's hidden is now in the open.

In the kitchen, Miss Storey sits on one of the plastic picnic chairs reading a list. I instinctively grab it from her and gather all of the papers into a pile, as if they're important business she shouldn't see. She reaches out a hand to stop me. 'Sissy.'

I sit down. It's a sickness, which means it isn't her fault. Miss Storey smiles softly. She no longer looks annoyed. 'Can I use your phone, dear?' I show her where it is in the hallway. I explain she has to crouch down to use it and stay very still.

I sit down again in the kitchen and try not to listen.

'The house . . .' she whispers, crouching like I showed her, and then mumbling. 'Who should I call? I can't leave her here . . .'

There's shifting sounds from Mou's bedroom, and then her footsteps. I go into the hallway, and she's standing at the bottom of the stairs, wearing her oversized T-shirt, her legs pale and bare. Miss Storey turns to see her, too.

'I've not been well,' she says, so quietly I can only just hear her. She coughs, and tries again. 'I took something for it, and it made me sleepy.'

She is gripping the banister like it's the only thing keeping her upright.

'I'll call you back,' Miss Storey says into the phone, and hangs up. 'I'm sorry to barge in like this,' she says to Mou. 'Is there someone I can call maybe? Who can help with Sissy while you're unwell?'

'I'll be better tomorrow,' Mou says.

Miss Storey looks at me, and then at Mou.

'I'm fine,' Mou says more firmly.

'I'll let you get back to sleep, then. If you could call the school tomorrow and we'll fill you in on what's happened.' Miss Storey smiles.

Mou doesn't move. Her body rocks gently, unsteady on her feet. Miss Storey must see it, too. She's reluctant to leave me. I clasp my mother's side to show Miss Storey I'm safest here. This is where I belong.

'I'll let myself out,' she says eventually.

She takes one last look at me, then slips out of the door.

As soon as she's gone, Mou slides to the floor. I wrap myself around her.

'I'm sorry, Mou,' I say, my voice muffled in the folds of her T-shirt. I nestle my head into her lap, my arms tight around her waist. I want her to hold me like when I was little, but she just sits there, both hands still gripping the banister. 'I'm sorry,' I say again, this time in a whisper.

We stay like that for what feels like hours, until she has the strength to go back upstairs. I get into bed with her. I haven't slept with her for years, not since I was sick when I was little. I had a stomach virus so severe she called the GP. He said not to bring me in unless it lasted more than three days, and so for three days I slept in her bed, vomiting up the small sips of water she gave me. I remember the shame of vomiting on the sheets. She carried me into the bathroom and laid me gently in a tub of warm water. On the third day I got better.

I wake in the night, crumpled in Mou's sheets. I dreamed of the sea again. I keep dreaming of the sea, as if my father is calling to me from the rigs where we left him. Mou is looking at me, her eyes wide open, glistening.

'What is it, Mou?' I say.

'I have the most terrible feeling,' she says, and then she's asleep again, as if she never woke up.

DAPHNE, PHILOMELA, JULIE, ME

The first missing girl is found. She's found with ligature marks around her neck. I don't know this word they use on the morning news, which I watch with the sound on, because Mou is still in bed. I want to know what happens to girls who are beautiful enough to disappear. Girls with ligature marks around their necks. A ligature sounds like part of a musical instrument. Or a muscle strung so tight it cannot move. Hannah had ligature marks, too, of a different kind, from getting a hickey to prove to us that Marlon loved her.

I wonder if I'll ever be loved enough to get ligatures.

The missing girl is found, but the girl snatcher is still on the loose. They say he was a stranger. They say he was someone she knew. She'd been dead four days when they found her. Which means she'd been alive all the months before. They found her face down in a river. She was trying to hold her breath long enough not to drown and drowned trying. Her lips were blue. She was blue and beautiful and strangled.

Perhaps it wasn't her body they found. She shed her human skin, and her soul flowed into the river to escape the girl snatcher. She turned into a water nymph, a mermaid, a siren. She turned into something half woman, half fish. She'll wait for ever listening for the footsteps of men in the water, perhaps a fisherman on a Sunday morning or some boys taking a dip on a summer's day. She'll swim up beneath them and entangle their legs in her long hair and drag them down. She'll tickle them until they drown. Or in another version of the story she doesn't win. She'll simply flow downstream and into the taps of the man who killed her. He'll drink her, take a bath in her essence, or boil her in a kettle for his tea.

I DON'T GO to school today. After breakfast in front of the TV, I tidy the scraps as best I can without ruining their order and I do the dishes that are stacked in the sink. Tasks with a beginning and an end.

When I bring Mou her coffee, she's sitting up in bed.

'Mou? You're better?'

Mou smiles, tears in her eyes. She strokes the back of my head when I sit beside her. She's about to tell me she's sorry.

'Don't, Mou,' I say, pulling away.

She knows I hate it when she talks about being a bad mother, as if we both know it's true.

She looks at the clock on her bedside table and gets flustered by a responsibility she'd forgotten until now. 'You should have left for school already.'

I feel a well of anger I don't recognise. 'Since when have you cared?'

'I've always cared.'

'What makes you so special that you can stay in bed day after day and I'm not allowed?'

'Enough, Sissy.'

We are both silent.

She places her hand on my chest to listen to my feelings and I bat it away. 'No.' I can say no to my mother now. My body was once hers, but it's slipping away. Once she would have known I'm changed. That I have webbed toes and a tail already.

'There's something you're not telling me,' she says.

I shake my head.

THERE'S A KNOCK on the front door. Mou sits still with her eyes closed. I play with my obsidian that's still by her bed, watching my face distort in its surface. It's made from magma, from the boiling earth, cooled too fast and turned to stone. Another knock, harder this time, more assured. She opens her eyes. I am prepared to ignore it for eternity. To stay here for ever.

'Answer it, please,' she says.

'No, Mou.'

'Tell them I'll be down in a few minutes.'

I'm not ready for this to be happening.

Miss Storey is on the doorstep. She's with a man and a woman who are smiling at me like they have bad news. I want to close the door in their faces. To shout and tell them to go away.

'Hi, Sissy,' Miss Storey says. 'You weren't in assembly this morning. Is your mum still unwell?'

Miss Storey introduces the man and the woman. Miss Russell and Mr Atkinson. I don't want to remember their names. Remembering their names would imply I might see them again.

There was a time when Mou made me practise what I

should say to a man and a woman such as these to make them go away. I would repeat the lines after her like a prayer and that prayer was for our future. The difference is that this time the man and the woman are here because of something I did, not something Mou failed to do properly, like she always feared.

'My mum said to show you in,' I say.

The man and the woman sit on the sofa in the newly cleared living room, and I bring Miss Storey a chair from the kitchen. This has happened before. Figures of authority with concerned faces came and went, their questions unanswered. I just never grasped what it meant until now.

Mou joins us of her own accord, and I'm surprised by her. She's brushed her hair, but it's limp and greasy. The bags beneath her eyes are deep ravines. She's put on jeans, though she's wearing the same T-shirt and no bra. She keeps one hand on a doorframe or a chair back to steady herself.

The man stands to let her take his seat. I expect Mou to refuse – like when Mr Durant offered to mow our lawn – but she accepts and I'm disappointed.

'Sissy, will you give us a few minutes,' she says. And then, when I don't leave, 'Sissy, please.'

I go up to my room and lie in the snug looking up at my sticker of Luke Perry, wishing Tegan was here.

'Luke, if you protect my mum, I'll set you free,' I say, but Luke doesn't answer. There's no one here to help me, real or imagined. I pick at the corner of the sticker with my nail, until his face tears in two.

When they call me back downstairs, Mou has been crying. Not quiet tears like this morning, but heavy tears that left her face scarred. The ravines beneath her eyes have deepened, so deep they've become treacherous.

The woman asks me some questions, as if she's making conversation, but I know these questions are to trick me into telling her something I don't mean to, so I refuse to answer.

She asks me to pee on a stick.

'She can't be pregnant,' Mou intervenes. 'She hasn't started her period,' and Mou starts to cry again. I feel guilty for never telling her, and doubly guilty for being embroiled in this lie.

'All the same,' Miss Russell says, as if she already knows better.

She stands by the door to the bathroom. I'm embarrassed to hand her this stick, wet with my urine, and then embarrassed when she takes the stick with her back into the living room, where everyone can see. She glances at her watch and then we wait quietly. Girls bleed after they first have sex. I bled after Kevin visited me. Maybe he and I did it for real. A kernel of doubt. I could be pregnant. Stranger things have happened at sea, which is an expression I've always liked because it makes me think of my father. I sit on the floor by Mou's feet.

After two minutes, Miss Russell smiles at Mou, and then at me, and says, 'Phew,' as if there's nothing to worry about, when really everything I have ever worried about most is happening right now.

Then it's Miss Storey's turn.

'Do you want to tell us what happened with Tegan's brother now?'

I shake my head.

'Did he do something to you, something that made you think you might get pregnant?'

I turn to Mou. She reaches out and takes my hand in her own, but she looks away, like she can't bear to see me.

I shake my head again.

Miss Storey looks around, and tries another tack. 'I saw you and Tegan playing a game in the playground once and told you not to play that any more. Do you remember?'

I remember us playing, the rush and the throb. Was it wrong to feel so much? I think of how we sleep, entwined and symbiotic as vines. She showed me the place deep inside us. Was it all wrong?

'Did you play something like that with Kevin? Did he get carried away maybe?'

'Tegan and I were just messing around,' I say, feeling a new shame rise through me. 'It wasn't for real.'

We didn't mean it. I want to say what a child says to undo whatever bad they've done.

'Sissy, if you don't tell us what's going on, we can't help you,' Miss Storey says. 'That's what we all want here. To make sure you're safe. Your mum, me, Mr Atkinson and Miss Russell. Tegan, too. She's worried about you.'

I try to think of Tegan acting worried, telling Miss Storey and Brenda that I said Kevin had done something that might make me pregnant. She is so convincing that I believe her. I could tell them he climbed into my bed and put his hand over my mouth so I wouldn't scream. I could tell them about the two bruises on my thighs, his hips hard as plum stones. I could say I fancied him and I was afraid. But I don't say these things. I don't want to get him into trouble, and that impulse wins out.

'We just kissed,' I say, my face hot with embarrassment. 'Tegan got the idea in her head it was something more. I know the difference,' I add, though I'm not convinced of it any longer.

'We're going to have to ask Kevin, too, you know? You're twelve, legally still a child.'

'No,' I say, scrambling. 'He didn't do anything. It was just a stupid joke.'

'What was?' Miss Russell asks, confused. 'You were playing a joke on Tegan? Or her brother?'

Only Mou knows this is something I would never do.

'We were just messing around,' I say again, knowing it
makes no sense. 'Tegan and me.'

'I think we're through here,' Mou says quietly.

'Mrs Blackmore . . .' Miss Russell tries to interrupt, but
Mou stands shakily, and the room watches with apprehension.

'She's not pregnant. She said nothing happened.
Interrogating her like this isn't helping.'

'We have to take these reports seriously—'

'I already said: enough!'

There's an awkward silence. And then Miss Storey and the
man and the woman leave. They talk quietly with Mou in
the hallway for a short time before they go, and something
is decided. When Mou shuts the door, she rests her head
against it.

'Mou, what's happening?'

She doesn't answer. She gives the door three short hard
bangs with her head.

IN FRONT OF the mirror in my room, I inspect my body. My
tail has grown two inches. I can reach around and feel where
it slopes over my bum. There's a fine mesh of scales on its
surface, like the skin of a salamander I saw once in a pet shop
in London. The petshop owner told me that salamanders are
poisonous. They used to believe if a salamander was dropped
into a well, it would poison all who drank the water. Or if a
salamander wandered into an apple tree, all who ate its fruit
would die. In the Bible, it wasn't a snake in the tree, they
say, it was a salamander. Shapeshifting, poisonous, uncertain.

Mou makes me go to school the next day, even though I don't want to leave her. I'm scared of what will happen in my absence. She says it's important that on top of everything else no one can accuse me of skipping school, too.

In assembly, the headmistress tells us not to talk about the missing girl, who's now dead. She says it's out of respect for her family and friends. 'What happened was a tragedy, but let's not dwell on the upsetting details,' she says. 'They are not a topic for idle school gossip.'

She wants us to pretend the missing girl and the threat she represents don't exist. Mou lied to me: girls *can* die becoming women.

Tegan seeks me out after assembly. 'That was a close call,' she whispers, looping her arm in mine as we walk to class. She's acting like we got away with something. 'What did they do to you, then? Don't worry about Kevin either. Mum's already dealt with him. That'll teach him for sneaking into your bed. Creep. Didn't I warn you?'

She sounds victorious.

There are no words.

'What's up? Did something happen? Is it your mum again?'

I feel a silence descending, like I'm sinking into the depths of the ocean. Koko told me that the bottom of the sea is dark and silent. At a certain depth, the density of water changes, and sound waves can't travel. The weight of it on top of you could crush you to death. That's where I am now. Crushed in the dark cold ocean deep where I cannot speak because there is no sound.

We take our seats in the classroom. Miss Storey walks in and seeks me out with her eyes. I look down at my textbook to avoid them. I hate her. She betrayed me with her niceness and long woollen skirts.

Tegan passes me a note in class. *What shall we call her? I'd like you to choose.* When I look up, she smiles. She's being gentle with me now, and I long to meet it. I write a list of names in my textbook. They are the names of all the girls from all the stories I've ever known. They are the names of the girls in my head, who for weeks now have been silent. We'll call her Daphne; we'll call her Philomela; we'll call her Julie; we'll name her after me.

I RUSH HOME after school, not even waiting to say goodbye to Tegan. I need to see Mou. I sit at the front of the bus, counting the turnings until we're home. When the bus hits traffic, I get off and run the rest of the way.

My house is full of people. Different people from before. A woman and two men this time, who are sitting at the white plastic picnic table with Mou. They all turn to look at me when I walk in and the woman and two men give me the smile people seem to give me right now. The smile that speaks of a sadness I might not fully understand. But they're wrong: sadness is something I know. It's in my bones, like Nan told me.

Mou leads me into the living room where we sit on the sofa together. She's showered and is wearing clean clothes for the first time in days, but she's fuzzy around the edges, like a nightingale's wings. She's struggling to put her thoughts in order. She pauses before she speaks, like she needs a moment in which to gather strength, search for order. Mou told me once that depression is a type of blindness. There might be good all around you, but no matter how hard you try, it's something you cannot see. Right now I have nothing good to show her.

'Are those people doctors?'

'I'm going to need you to be very grown-up for what's about to happen,' she says, and it makes me furious, because what else have I been? What else have I ever been? 'Grandma Jean is coming to stay for a short while to take care of you.'

'But we hate Grandma Jean.'

'Ssh! We don't hate Grandma Jean. And that's not the point.' She looks right at me. Her eyes are a little less glazed than before. She reaches to take my hand in hers with the slightest tremor. 'Why didn't you come to me? I thought you'd come to me if anything was wrong.'

'You've been sick,' I say, defiant.

'Is that why you didn't tell me?'

I don't answer, because I don't know how.

She sighs. 'Grandma Jean loves you and you shouldn't hate her because of me. She was angry that I fell in love with Koko and ran away, and then she was angry with me for leaving Koko and becoming a single mother, which was the only thing worse I could do than eloping. And she loves you.'

'You said that already,' I say. 'We don't need her. We're fine, just us. Tell those people to go away. I'm sick of all these people in our house. Why did you let them in?'

'We do need her, Sissy. I want to be a proper mother to you, and I can't—'

'Don't.'

'Grandma Jean is right. This isn't any way for you to grow up, and if I didn't see it before, now with this pregnancy—'

'I was never pregnant!' I plead.

'If I'd been paying more attention ...'

'I'm sorry, Mou,' I say, tearful because this is all my fault.

Mou takes a deep breath and tugs at her hair with the hand that's not holding mine and stops herself. The woman and two men in the kitchen are talking quietly. They're talking about me.

'I need you to be honest with me, Sissy,' she says, ignoring my tears to forge on. 'Are you having sex? It doesn't matter with whom, at least, not right now, but if you are, you have to tell me.'

In this moment, I must decide if I can tell her. Just us. But it isn't that simple any more. There's a baby the size of an apple seed in Tegan's belly and I must protect her. We forged her through the powers of our imagination. Through our powers. She's too precious to speak of aloud for fear she'll break open and there'll be nothing inside.

'Sissy?'

'I promised,' I say quietly, knowing this is wrong already, in the part of me that's grown.

'What did you promise? You might think you're in love, but you're too young to have sex. For God's sake, it's illegal. If someone is pressuring you . . . '

I never thought about sex being illegal. Sometimes when a drawing of a man puts his penis inside a drawing of a woman it's breaking the law. No part of the book said that.

'I'm not having sex. Please, Mou! It was all a mistake.'

'What was a mistake?'

But I'm crying harder now, and she doesn't want to push me further.

'Okay, okay.' She places a hand on my chest, as if listening. 'I trust you, Sissy *mou*.'

She pulls my head towards her own. Our foreheads are touching when there's a knock at the front door. One of the people in our kitchen, who I don't know, opens it and a new pair of footsteps enter. Mou's tears quicken and so do mine. I'm frightened. Mou was right. Something terrible is about to happen. Grandma Jean is standing in the doorway. She's older than I remember. She has a beige tartan suitcase, which she places on the floor by her side, and a rain jacket the same shade of beige over her arm. Her ashy hair is beige also. She gives me a wan smile, not wanting to interrupt.

Mou stands. She's trying to walk away from me, but I won't let go of her hand.

'Mou, no,' I say, because I already know she's leaving me. 'Mou, it wasn't your fault.'

The woman and two men are in the room now, too. I hate them. I want them to leave us be.

'Be good for Grandma Jean, please,' Mou is saying, and I'm shaking my head back and forth so furiously the world has turned blurry.

'No,' I say, again, louder. The woman and the two men, I understand now what they're here for. They're here to take her away, like the Germolene-smelling doctor. 'Don't make her!' I shout. 'Please, I don't want her to go.'

Mou turns back to me. 'Sissy, no one is making me. This is my choice.'

'Then don't!'

She shakes her head.

'But I need you.'

'This is for the best,' she's saying, her face wet with tears. 'I love you,' she says, prising my hands from hers, 'I'm so sorry,' and then she's up again, and the two men are either side of her, escorting her away. Grandma Jean has an arm around me so I can't keep after them.

'No, it's a mistake.' I'm shouting now, I'll do anything to stop this happening. Anything. And there's one piece of truth that might make a difference: 'It wasn't for me!'

She stops and turns to look at me, and with that small

ounce of hope I keep going, believing for the shortest moment I can exert my will to prevent Mou from leaving. 'I never thought I was pregnant. I never had sex. Nothing like it. The test, it wasn't for me. It was for Tegan. She made me promise not to tell. Please, it wasn't for me.'

Mou nods, then shakes her head, and they keep walking. The front door is open now, and then closing, with my mother on the other side.

SHEEP

Grandma Jean is ironing my school uniform. We don't own an iron, which means she brought it with her in her beige suitcase from wherever she came. She is awake and well-pressed, also.

'Morning, dear,' she says, and smiles gently.

Her lipstick is the exact same colour as her lips. I wonder, when she wipes it away at night, if there's a blank space where her lips should be.

'Let me look at you. I didn't get a proper chance last night, and it's been such a very long time.'

She holds me by the shoulders and looks me up and down. I'm still wearing the T-shirt I sleep in with my legs bare, just like Mou and I always do. I fear my tail might be showing. If Grandma Jean finds out there's something wrong with me, she'll blame Mou for my body's mistakes. I tug my T-shirt down as far as it'll go.

'Aren't you tall,' she says, as if it's something else I shouldn't be.

She navigates me to the table where there's a bowl waiting with cereal and fresh milk, ready to pour. Grandma Jean slept in Mou's bed last night. She brought her own set of sheets, too. Mou is not in her bed waiting for coffee. I don't know where she is or when she'll be returned to me. And everything that is happening now is my fault. It's Grandma Jean's fault too, if only by virtue of her being here.

'I don't want you to worry about your poor mother,' Grandma Jean goes on, while returning to her ironing. She has an air of triumph about her. 'We've been through this before, of course, but she's finally seen some sense and let me help.'

Mou says Grandma Jean is the type of woman who wears ivory cashmere. She says it like an insult.

'I've missed you terribly these past years, you know?'

She hands me my uniform, now folded.

'Are we not feeling hungry this morning?' she asks, seeing my bowl untouched.

CLARA AND LYDIA are talking about a girl in the year above who agreed to kiss a boy in the caretaker's cupboard at the school disco. Her name is Naomi. She has the biggest boobs in the school, so everyone knows who she is. The boy says Naomi gave him a blowie, which means she's a slut. (A blow job is another thing a girl gives a boy and she gets nothing in return.) It doesn't matter if she gave him a blowie or not. She was a slut before she even stepped into the caretaker's cupboard on account of her big breasts.

'Charlotte saw her crying in the lunch hall,' Clara says, frothing with glee.

'What do you think?' Hannah asks Tegan. 'Do you think she did it?'

But Tegan isn't paying attention. Her focus is on me, as if she senses my betrayal.

She sits on the floor by my desk, resting her chin on my knees.

'Do you remember the note in the music box, the one we hid together?' she whispers.

I nod. The secret she never told.

'Come to mine after school today. I'm ready for you to read it.'

She scans my face for a reaction, but I can't meet her eyes and she sees it. She stands, hovering over me.

Miss Storey walks in and claps her hands for our attention. 'In your seats, please!'

As the class settles, Miss Storey singles me out again, except this time, her gaze shifts from me to Tegan.

I wonder which betrayal is worse: my betrayal of Mou by letting Miss Storey into our house; or my betrayal of Tegan by breaking my promise. I'll never know her secret now.

'Tegan, can you go to the headmistress's office, please?' Miss Storey says. 'Mrs Greidinger is waiting.'

Tegan looks up, then directly at me. I feel the power of her venom. She is stone cold. She is playground Tegan, capable of anything. Everyone has turned to watch her, except me. I broke my promise. I told a secret I wasn't supposed to and everything I'm most afraid of is happening.

'Tegan!' Miss Storey says. She isn't soft with Tegan like she is with me. Even her quiet voice takes on an edge.

Tegan stands and the class is silent. When she passes my desk, she scratches her nails gently along its wooden surface, a warning.

Miss Storey closes the door behind her as if the matter is settled.

She draws a diagram on the blackboard, a series of lines, dashes and circles. Her chalk is worn down to a stub. I can taste the dust in my mouth like I'm choking. She writes an alphabet for a language I don't speak. We have to draw a household circuit that will set off an alarm if a burglar enters our house. I cannot imagine the house I'm protecting or how the lines on the page correspond to the real world. Nothing makes sense any longer.

Tegan's desk is still empty. Every minute the loss grows greater. Whatever is happening down the hall will not be reversed. Whatever I've done, there's no going back.

TEGAN DOESN'T RETURN after class. The subject of Tegan's removal occupies Clara and Hannah throughout break. They gravitate towards me, because they sense I might have answers.

'Maybe something happened to her family,' Hannah suggests. 'Like a car accident.'

'That's horrid.' Clara crosses her arms.

'Why's that horrid?'

'Why are you always so dense? Someone's obviously told.'

'Told what?'

'Hannah, really?'

Hannah looks down at her shoes.

'Told on her for what she does down on the courts with William,' Clara says, defiant now in Tegan's absence.

I wonder if they're talking about what she did with the stone or something else I don't know about. It wouldn't surprise me any longer.

At lunch, I sit in the toilet cubicle to hide from their questions. On the wall someone has written NAOMI SUCKS DICK(s). The plural was added later in a different marker. Someone else has written, SHE CAN SUCK MINE. Naomi has become foam on top of the sea. Girls are falling by the wayside. Maybe that's where all the girls in my head have gone. They were taken while I wasn't watching. Snatched or turned to stone.

AFTER SCHOOL I slip away from the bus queue to walk to Haley's. I want to see Tegan and make sure she's okay. I want to sit on Haley's sofa and watch TV and drink tea and tell each other secrets that never get out. I want things to be just like they used to be. We'll turn thirteen and fourteen, our breasts will grow, our hips and tummies, too, which will curve ever so slightly out; we'll have boyfriends and lovers, whom we won't always remember, and heartbreaks that will make us forever sad; we'll take exams, find summer jobs, leave home and stay in touch. Tegan will sleep on a futon bed, because it's fashionable, and I'll keep every Christmas card she sends. I can see it all, as if time has collapsed in on itself and older, wiser Sissy is looking back on me, smiling. Older, wiser Sissy wishes she could whisper a story in my ear, which will make everything easier, but she's too far away for me to hear. It is a fantasy so ordinary it feels quite new to me and I keep playing it over and over in my head until it feels like a memory.

I walk through town. There are still posters of the first missing girl lining the street, on the lampposts and in shop windows. Whose job is it to take them down? Who decides it's over?

When I get to Haley's I ring the bell like I have so many times before. I'm buzzed inside, expecting to see Tegan's head peering around the apartment door from up the stairs. The door is closed. I knock, waiting a few moments before Haley opens it. Without make-up she looks like the girl she was in the photos Tegan once showed me. No warrior dashes of bronze across her cheeks.

'Can I see Tegan?'

'Sweetie, you're a good friend, but—' Haley is interrupted by shouting from inside. I can't make out the words until Tegan bursts through the door, past Haley, and runs at me.

'Get out! Get out! I never want to talk to you again!'

Tegan's fists fall fast and furious against my head and all I can do is shield my face. Haley gathers Tegan up to stop her pummelling me, all arms and rage and tangled blonde hair, but I don't feel the punches. Only the shock of her rejection. 'I hate you, you liar, you told! You told . . . ' she says, as I crouch on the floor with my arms over my head for shelter. A hand or foot emerges from Haley's grip, even though I don't fight back. 'You were never my friend. Never!' At last, Haley gets her to the floor and holds her down, and then there we are, the three of us in a heap of limbs and tender future bruises. All the fight drains from Tegan, and she weeps in Haley's arms, like I have never seen her cry. A guttural cry of unspoken grief.

'I told her,' Haley says to me. 'I told her it doesn't matter what you said, people would have found out one way or another.'

We sit, and it's almost like it once was on Haley's sofa when we were so close, except now those moments are falling away. They will never happen again. They will only be a memory I return to in the future.

Tegan's crying has slowed down, the ruddy pink of her cheeks flushed from the fighting and her hair stuck to her wet face.

'This is how it has to be, sweetie,' Haley says, into her ear. 'Brenda wasn't going to let you stay here after this. Let her blame me. It's better.'

Haley is crying, too. She helps Tegan up and back inside the apartment. Through the doorway I see a bag packed with Tegan's things, the poster of the Levi's man rolled up with a rubber band.

I wait in the doorway, quietly hoping if I stay long enough something might change before I have to leave. Longing rises within me, harbouring a shame powerful enough to make me close my eyes until it passes.

Haley comes back. I am sitting with my back against the hallway wall, my face buried in my hands. I want to show Haley how sad I am and for her to sit beside me and stroke my hair.

'Would you like a lift home?' she says.

'Can I stay? There was something she wanted to show me,' but Haley is shaking her head before I can finish. And it's all blank after that. We are in Haley's car driving away, and then I am walking up the path to the front door of our house and wishing more than ever that Mou was at home, waiting for me.

GRANDMA JEAN IS in the kitchen making dinner. The trophies are all gone. She's tidied the house and thrown away everything she doesn't understand. There's just one lamp remaining, shining moderate light on the room, and a few bird teapots lined up nicely on the shelf. It's an ordinary kitchen now, apart from the white plastic picnic set, which is all of Mou that remains.

'Sissy, lay the table please, dear,' she instructs. She never liked my name. She thought I should be called Sarah or Charlotte. 'That awful picnic set will have to go, too, of course. Maybe I can buy you a proper dining table while I'm here.'

I lay the table, forks to the left, like Tegan showed me. We eat chicken and peas; Grandma Jean doesn't care that we're vegetarians. She chews with her mouth closed, and so must I, which means we can only talk in the time between one mouthful and the next, for which I'm grateful.

'Is Mou coming home soon?'

'Is my cooking that bad?' Grandma Jean smiles like she's making a joke, and I want to throw my plate on the floor. Her smile flattens. 'I'm sorry. Let's take one day at a time, shall we?' And then she adds, as if it's a perfectly normal question: 'When did you last speak to your father?'

I look up, bewildered.

'He'd like to see you very much.'

'You talk to Koko?' I ask, and immediately regret it. I have betrayed Mou again. It was a trap and I fell for it.

Grandma Jean must see the guilt on my face, because next she says: 'I'm not the bad person your mother says I am, you know?'

She reaches her hand towards me on the table, which I don't take. Her nail polish is clumsily applied, like she was shaking when she painted them, and for a moment I wonder if I have her all wrong.

'She doesn't say you're a bad person,' I reply. 'She says sometimes we do terrible things to people we love.'

'I see.' She retracts her hand into her lap and considers this. I think I've wounded her. 'I didn't always get it right, that much is true, but I wanted what was best for your mother. For you, too.'

I ask if I can be excused and I go straight to my room.

That night, under the covers, I pull my tail up between my legs to get a good look at it. It isn't dainty like the tail of daydreams. It has heft. It would make a pleasing smacking

268

sound against skin. There is power in a tail like this, and for a moment I admire it. This new body is capable of the strangest feats.

TEGAN IS BACK at her desk the next day. She will leave no room for anyone to ask about her absence. I wonder if the adults know now. Did she tell them what she told me? That the baby is ours. She's of our making.

As I walk over, Clara is talking about a girl who got fingered on the back seat of the bus. The girl didn't care that everyone knew it was happening. Clara doesn't know the boy's name – the fingerer – but that girl, she's also a slut. Tegan laughs and asks for all the details. She's holding court with dazzling menace.

I'm waiting for Tegan to look over so I can know if I'm forgiven. I'm so focused on her that I don't notice at first Lydia is sitting at my desk. She looks up and smiles.

'Siss! How's it going?' she says, her curls bouncing smugly.

I'm standing where she stood just a few months ago. She has reclaimed the space I took from her. It was never mine. Tegan has her back to me, pretending to be entirely absorbed by Clara's story. Pretending I don't exist. I want to bang my fists on her desk. My mother is gone, you can't leave me. My mother is gone, because you made me lie.

I walk to my old desk at the side of the room. The Siamese Fighter Fish I once loved turns in circles. This wasn't what I wished for. I made a wish for Tegan to be my one friend and I wished for nothing more. Where did I go wrong? Was it telling Mou's secret? Or the spell we cast in the woods that night? Was it something I did with Kevin? Or further back, burying the two Barbies in the garden, and then breaking my promise to first forgotten Eve. Maybe it was wanting a thing I couldn't have, and believing it could be mine. Or just wanting.

My tail grows half an inch longer. It happens when I least expect it.

AT LUNCH, TEGAN, Clara and Hannah file out together, looping their arms in a single line of defence. Clara looks back over her shoulder, thrilled at my expulsion. They disappear into the Maze, and I follow, unwilling to give up what's rightfully mine. Unready for more to be taken from me. Tegan spots me loitering around the entrance.

'Hey, Siss, what you doing?' she calls out. 'Come over here, will ya!'

Her smile widens and she stretches out her hand. I was never able to say no to her. I wanted it so much all along. I take her hand, and she shuffles up so I can sit by her side where I belong. The gravel is damp and dozens of tiny stones score my skin. Tegan's grip tightens. Her fingers are cold when they have always been warm, and it gives me only a moment of warning, the suspended time between tripping and hitting the floor.

'How's your mum, Siss?' Tegan says flatly, her smile gone. I see in her face what's about to happen. She wanted me close to witness her revenge. Tegan turns to the others. 'Poor Siss, her mum is sick.'

'What's wrong with her?' Hannah asks, preparing her judgement.

There is no forgiveness for an unordinary parent.

'Mentally sick,' Tegan explains, drilling a finger into the

side of her head. 'They might have to put her in the loony bin and then Siss will go into foster care.'

And just like that my mother's mind unzips like a carrier bag on an open street, its contents spilling out for all to see.

I try to stand.

'Where you going? Sit down!' Tegan yanks me back down beside her. Her hands were always stronger than mine. She reaches across my body as if in a hug, but it's a vice-like embrace. All these months, entangled, and now she's using it against me.

'Siss had a bit of an emotional breakdown on me the other day, so we should be nice,' Tegan says, and then she laughs, 'but you should have seen her bawling,' and she pulls a face that parodies despair. She knows just where to hurt me.

I wrestle my body free, and get up abruptly. Tegan falls into the space I left. 'Don't get mad, Siss!' She giggles, dusting the gravel from her palms. Her performance is flawless. 'I'm only saying!'

I am both betrayer and betrayed.

'What?' she says, responding to the anger on my face. 'It's true, isn't it?'

'At least I don't tell lies about my dead brother!' I shout, because it is the worst thing I can think of in that moment. 'He never killed Harvey, did he? It's the same stupid dog you always had.'

The others quieten, looking to Tegan for a cue. For a moment she looks like a child again, like she did on the floor of Haley's hallway in tears. But then her face hardens.

'What are you even talking about? You're a head case, just like your mum.'

I stumble out of the Maze.

Just before I leave, it's Tegan who says it: 'Fuck off, sheep.'
Elsewhere in the playground a child screams.
It is me screaming.
I am making that sound.

BUTTERFLY WINGS

In the days that follow, I return to my routine before Tegan and I were friends. I walk the perimeter fence of the playground at lunchtime, the same circuit I once did. My tail moves from side to side as I walk. Its weight is reassuring. At home now, in the bath, I can unfurl it to its full glory. Or I can tuck it away where no one can see. I wonder if I'll soon leave girlhood behind completely.

William has taken up teasing me again. He follows a few feet behind, sometimes bleating. I don't fight him. I don't do a thing. He has no idea what I'm capable of now.

It's been a week since our fall-out. Since Tegan and I stopped being best friends. One morning, her desk is empty. I think about the baby and worry. There must be baby shopping and baby appointments and baby things I can't imagine, all of which Tegan will do now without me.

In the lunch hall, Miss Storey approaches my table. She kneels on the floor to bring her face close to mine. She speaks quietly, not wanting the other kids to overhear, even though no one sits near me.

'Have you spoken to Tegan since yesterday?' she asks. 'Was she planning to go anywhere? To meet anyone?'

I shake my head. Miss Storey smiles and walks away before I can ask her any questions.

I'M CALLED INTO the headmistress's office before break is over. When I walk in, Miss Storey is there and, unexpectedly, Brenda. She hasn't styled her bouffant. Her hair hangs limp around her face making her look suddenly old. Haley is here, too, her eyes puffy.

'Don't worry, you're not in trouble,' Mrs Greidinger says. 'We just want to talk to you, as Tegan's best friend.'

'Tegan's fine,' I say, even though I have no proof of this. My first instinct is to defend her still.

'You've spoken to her?' Brenda says. It's not a question, but an outburst. 'Where is she?'

Someone has pushed forward a chair because I'm now sitting, but I don't recall getting here.

'Tegan didn't come home from school yesterday,' Miss Storey says. 'She never got on the bus.'

And then Brenda again: 'Who is she with, Sissy? Is it the father of the baby? Is she with him?'

'Who?' I say, trying to understand what's happening. Nothing is clear.

Haley is biting her nails with vigour.

'This isn't some game. Tell us, for God's sake!' Brenda says.

In a large display cabinet on the wall, decades-old insects have been delicately skewered and left for dead. They've pinned the butterfly down by its wings.

Mrs Greidinger is talking now, she's talking about my mother, and how upsetting it must be, and how nothing I say will get Tegan into trouble, but I don't want to listen. I look at the butterfly in its casket instead, its wings pinned for eternity. There is a hairline crack in the glass, and with the flow of oxygen comes inevitable decay. Dust gathers in the bottom of the frame.

'Listen, sugar,' Haley says, trying for my attention. 'She wouldn't tell us who the father is, and if we knew that perhaps he could help us find her.'

'There is no father,' I say. The baby is ours. We emerged from the dark mythic woods of childhood dancing and full of knowledge. One of us bleeding and the other carrying a baby.

'Okay . . . Well, has she met any boys on her own? You're both so grown-up, I forget you're not just part of our crew. Maybe one of the lads you met at mine?'

'Just Peter.'

'Who's Peter?' Miss Storey asks.

'My best friend,' Haley says. 'He babysits sometimes when I'm at work.'

'When you're at the strip club, you mean,' Brenda interjects. Haley won't look at her. 'When you leave her alone while you take your clothes off for money.'

'Isn't that what you always wanted for me?' Haley shoots back with venom.

Truths have emerged in my absence. Haley had secrets, too. She kept hers hidden in that small suitcase she pulled along behind her with a broken wheel.

'Have you told the police about Peter?' Mrs Greidinger asks, to steer the conversation back.

'She's not with Peter,' Haley says. 'He went to work a season in Ibiza with his girlfriend. He left a week ago.'

'This is on you!' Brenda stands, her chair falling back clumsily. 'She was meant to be safe with you.'

Haley returns to her nails.

'I said already, there's no boys,' I say, wanting to protect her. The adults all look at me. 'Tegan didn't even want a boyfriend.'

This feels good. This feels like something solid. But their faces tell a different story.

'Please, Sissy,' Haley begs. 'For Tegan. Please.'

I shake my head again. 'I promised,' I say.

This is another thing Tegan kept from me and I can't admit it.

THE FOLLOWING MORNING I'm late for school because there are two policemen in my kitchen. They are sitting at the white plastic picnic table with Grandma Jean when I come downstairs for breakfast. She's made them tea. Grandma Jean calls me over and I sit beside her while they ask me more questions. I'm glad for her stoic presence so close at hand.

'I don't know anything,' I say, and they look at me like I'm lying.

'She must have been frightened when she found out she was pregnant?' the policeman with the gentler face asks.

'Not really.' I'm shy in front of Grandma Jean. This is not the impression Mou would want me to give.

'And how about the dad? Was she worried people might find out?'

Only one policeman does the talking. The other takes notes, and this note-taking distracts me. I want to know what he's writing down. I could tell them the story of the girl who changed into a tree. The man never loved her. I know that now. That man, he was like the girl snatcher. Once she'd changed from a girl into a tree she could no longer run from him. Once she'd changed, he could just take what wasn't his.

'You know it's not breaking a promise if you tell a policeman? It's the law. Policemen are the only people you can tell secrets to without getting into trouble.'

When I remain silent, the policeman who hasn't spoken yet leans in. 'Have you heard about those girls who went missing?' I nod. The gentler policeman looks annoyed at this. 'We have to be careful about young women like yourselves out there on their own. You wouldn't want your friend to end up like that, would you?'

'I told you, I don't know anything,' I say again, except I say it too loudly, because I am standing and shouting with my fists by my ears.

EACH DAY WITHOUT Tegan, I grow more afraid. The search escalates quickly, because the girl snatcher is still on the loose and he operates around Haley's house. He does his snatching at dusk. He likes his girls almost grown. Her wish came true. She became the missing girl. She will be beautiful for ever.

I give the nicer policeman the photo she wanted on her poster.

'She wanted you to use this one,' I say.

Tegan in the black dress and Brenda's fur coat, pouting.

The policeman doesn't take this how I intended. He asks, less nicely, if we're playing some sort of prank. They use her school photo in the paper instead; she hated that photo. It's another way I have let her down.

With Grandma Jean here I have to come straight home from school. And with Tegan gone there is nowhere else to go. On these evenings alone, I am filled with a longing so enormous it dismantles my very being. I want my mother home. I want to press my forehead into hers. I want to make a bed on the sofa together. I want to hear her talking to me from the other side of the house. I want my best friend back, too. I want to sleep entwined and tell each other stories until the day we die. Nothing can rescue me from the enormity of this longing. I can't play Mou's records; I can't lie in the snug; Luke Perry is gone. There is nothing that offers distraction. When I look in the mirror now, a different sort of creature looks back. I hide my despair from Grandma Jean, because to show it would be to admit Mou's failure. I can't rationalise this, but I'm certain loyalty to Mou requires me to act like everything is okay. I go through the motions of each day without really being here. In silence.

While undressing one night, I find one of Tegan's long blonde hairs wrapped in my collar. Another day, I find one in my mouth and gag. Half was already swallowed, and I feel it extracted from my insides, as I pull it out. I can't understand it. It's like she's with me even when she's gone.

HALEY COMES OVER unexpectedly that weekend. The search has continued for several days. She's waving a pile of small blue envelopes at me, looking frantic. I'm sitting in our overgrown garden in a lawn chair Mou pulled from a skip that smells of mildew. The sun is glinting through the clouds, in imitation of spring. I'm wearing long sleeves and jeans still to cover up what's happening to my body. I imagine the moment Tegan is returned to me. This will be our first summer as friends. We can make daisy chains and wear them as crowns. We'll lie in the grass drinking lemonade while playing make-believe with our future.

'Do you know who these are from?' Haley says.

I pluck the long grass around the chair, looking anywhere other than the letters. I recognise the tight handwriting even from this far.

'I found them hidden in the bedside table in her room,' Haley says. 'They're addressed to Tatiana and Tallulah. That's the two of you, right? That's what you call each other?'

I gather the plucked grass around me.

'Sissy, did Tegan ever meet up with this guy, this Eric?'

Haley removes each letter from its envelope and drops them into my lap, as if any one might force me to speak. There are more letters now, so many more. I catch a few sentences. *Tell me the things you'd like me to do to you . . . your boyfriend will never know . . . send me another photo.* I brush them away and slide from the chair onto the lawn. I feel suddenly sick. 'Is it illegal?' I ask.

Haley looks confused, and then desperate. She takes me by the shoulders, 'Did she meet him? Tell me!' and then she starts to shake me. 'What did you two do?' I keep looking at her as she does, and I'm trapped for a moment in her quaking embrace, until Grandma Jean runs over to stop her. Haley collapses and cries then. She was always immune to the world around her, all of it, except Tegan.

'It's all right, dear,' Grandma Jean says, kneeling down, resting a hand on Haley's shoulder. Her beige trousers will be dirty. She'll have stains on her beige knees. 'It's all right,' she says again.

The three of us are there in the long grass, quiet now, the first daffodils dazzling around us.

'I tried to be careful,' Haley says, speaking not to Grandma Jean, not to me, not to anyone. 'I know how Andy felt now. That's why he did it. Because of me. I know now . . . '

'Best to get back home,' Grandma Jean says quietly, into Haley's ear. 'Just stay by the phone, like they said.'

As Haley walks away, I call after her: 'Is Tegan going to have a baby?'

I feel very young and afraid all of a sudden, like the game of pretend has come to an abrupt end.

'It hadn't been decided,' Haley says, and then she's gone.

THAT NIGHT I ask the universe for one more thing. I ask first forgotten Eve, closing my eyes in prayer. 'Return Mou to me,' I whisper. If Mou is returned, I'll tell them everything I know. I'll tell them about Eric and Peter, William and Kevin. I'll tell them all the promises I made and the secrets I kept. I'll tell them about the note in the music box, too, which I never read. If Mou is returned to me, it will be a sign that this is the right course of action. It will be certain. Otherwise I'll keep the promises I've not yet broken.

THE RIVER

On the bus to school, Marlon and Hannah are sitting in front of me when a short boy with a squashed face leans across the aisle towards them.

'Is it true Tegan was pregnant?' He says it with glee despite using the past tense already.

The boys on the bus all know Tegan, even though she only occasionally takes it now.

'That's what Baz said,' Hannah responds, also gleeful. 'He overheard his parents talking about it. He said that's why she ran away.'

I tap Hannah on the shoulder and she turns around.

'Traitor,' I spit, and mean it. I want to punch her in the face. I might do, and she knows it.

'Don't go mental,' she says, and I hate her. I've always hated her. 'Wasn't me who told and, anyway, *everyone* knows.'

'Tegan once offered to show me her fanny,' another of the boys declares.

'Liar!' I shout, and now everyone is listening. I don't disbelieve him, even if I'll never admit it. She might say such a thing – it sounds like her – but she'd demand something in return and whatever that *something* is he's not telling.

'And did you see it?' another boy further back asks.

'Told her, "Nah, thanks."' He raises his hands as if her fanny pulled out a gun.

I hate them all. They're talking about Tegan the way they talked about Naomi. The way they talked about Julie Hendry, too. She is the girl in school whose name everyone knows. She will always be that girl. The equivalent girls in the years above know her name, too, like a club of girls who will always be talked about. They picked her out before she was fully grown. She was chosen. Fated, just like I said she was.

Chris turns in his seat further up. 'She could really be missing,' he says.

The kids on the bus are seemingly chastised and settle down.

Chris catches my eye as he turns in his seat. 'I'm sorry, Sissy,' he says, and I realise none of them ever call me by my name.

It also hits me for the first time that Tegan might be gone for ever.

Out of the bus window, I instinctively scan the streets for her. Mostly I try not to think about the baby inside her belly, and if, by now, it's bigger than an apple seed. I don't know what comes next. If it's a baby the size of a walnut. Or a baby the size of a human heart.

At other times, I think about what the baby might look like. I can't tell anyone it was us who made Tegan pregnant. Sometimes the universe gets mixed up. Sometimes, when you ask for something, you get more than you bargained for. That was what happened that night. We danced her into existence, like first forgotten Eve.

*

THE POLICE SEARCH Eric666's house. I see it on the local news. They found fibres of Tegan's hair in his car. A pretty news anchor reports that Mr Weston, as they call him, claims to have met Tegan Price in person just once: the day she went missing. When he realised how young she was, he dropped her back at home. He releases a statement through his lawyer to say he's cooperating with the police investigation. They show a clip of him walking into the police station. He looks vaguely like he did in the photo he sent us. Not quite an old man pretending to be a boy, but not the young man he said he was either.

In his apartment they find the photo of Tegan we took together, the same one I tried to give the police. She cut out her high heels so you can't see that they're too big for her. 'Girls like you end up raped,' Brenda said. The picture she wanted is on the news now and I focus just on that.

They display his headshot beside the blurry image from the CCTV of the girl snatcher. They speculate whether he groomed the other victims, too. I'm unfamiliar with this word: grooming. They're about to explain when Grandma Jean walks in and turns off the TV, my questions unanswered. She always wanted to know what he did to them. In wanting, did she bring it on herself? Will she be found face down in a river, beautiful and blue and strangled? There is no solace for these thoughts, no remedy. I'm holding my breath again and remember to let it out.

NOW IT'S THE spring term, we have swimming instead of PE. In the toilet before class, I carefully tuck my tail away, fearful I'll be found out.

The chlorine burns my skin in the water, but I keep

moving. I swim like I'm trying to die drowning. I gulp water as if it's air. My head barely rises in a furious front crawl, my paddle feet propelling me forward so fast that when I finally hear the scream of Miss August's whistle all the other kids have stopped to stare.

In the changing rooms afterwards, I'm stretching to pull my Tammy Girl bra over my head when I first see them, gaping and pale. A wound that's unbloody. I look over my shoulder to check no one is watching. With my arms back at my sides, they're harder to notice, but I run my fingers along my rib cage, until I find them and prise them apart like a pair of cold lips. Inside, pink tufted membranes flutter and recoil. Gills. Two sets of gills either side just beneath where my breasts should be. I take a sharp breath in shock, and see them opening and closing. The damp air enters my lungs without passing my mouth. I could swim to the bottom of the ocean now without drowning.

I dress quickly. I have perfected the art of changing under my clothes, a shuffling akin to shedding a skin. People can't know the wrongs my body is committing.

'I don't like getting changed in front of her,' Clara hisses to Hannah in their corner.

I keep facing the wall as I pull on my school skirt before removing my swimsuit to conceal my tail beneath.

Clara barrels up to me. 'Is it true?' she says.

Hannah and Lydia are watching. They're waiting for my reaction. Clara is their emissary. I squeeze the water from my swimsuit and pack it into my PE bag before I turn to her. I cross my arms over my chest, feeling newly vulnerable. 'Is what true?' I say, to make this end faster.

'Tegan told us the real reason you fell out.' Clara is enjoying herself and her newfound power in Tegan's absence. She is making sure everyone hears what she has to say. 'She said she caught you masturbating in bed on a sleepover.'

I laugh. It's the only thing I can do. You can't be mad at a missing person. You can only be mad at yourself that they hated you when they disappeared. And if you never see them again, they'll hate you for ever.

'She also said—' but Clara doesn't finish her sentence because I'm swinging my PE bag around to meet her head. There is a satisfying thud. The other kids gasp as she stumbles, but then I'm on her, crushing her face against the wet tiled floor with satisfaction. I'm surprised I'm strong enough to overcome her, until I feel my tail unfurled behind me, pinning her to the ground with force. I jump up quickly to hide it, and Clara turns back to me, horrified, her hair messy, and one side of her face swiftly bruising.

'See?' she says, to the assembled group, clutching her cheek. 'Did you see that? I told you there's something wrong with her,'

But I'm already scrambling out of the door.

I KEEP WALKING. I walk straight out of school, half running, because I don't want to be seen. I run all the way to town, stopping on the bridge to catch my breath, and look down at the river, the same river where the missing girl was found. It's swollen from rainfall and bursting its banks. That's where I belong. Somewhere silty where I can go unseen until this transformation is over. I long for it. To be immersed. To disappear.

A man shouts at me from across the street, 'You all right, love?' and I run on, through the other side of the town, and along the stretch of road to the cluster of houses where I live.

My lungs burn by the time I reach home. I cannot take in enough air. I unlock the door and kick off my shoes, ready to run upstairs where I will hide until Mou is home, and I will be safe. I can pretend Tegan isn't missing, and she and I are still best friends, and my body isn't changing and none of this is real. My thoughts evaporate when I see a man sitting at my kitchen table.

He has his back to me. His shoulders are broad. A shock of dark curls, like storm clouds. I can't catch my breath. Beyond the man, Grandma Jean is standing at the counter, making tea. She's surprised by my presence, home early. She takes a few steps towards me and the man turns in his chair, following her eyes to where I stand in the hallway, my schoolbag at my feet and my face pale.

The man stands. His height. The smell he carries with him, turpentine from cleaning his hands and the cedar oil he used in his hair. These smells are for ever with me. They are with me now.

'You remember your father,' Grandma Jean says.

The world around them has narrowed down to this moment, and this moment is too small. I shake my head.

'Sissy,' the man who is my father says. 'It's really wonderful to see you.'

I shake my head again. I think about the bursting banks of the river. This is the end, I think, without knowing what is ending and what will begin in its place. I cannot. I cannot. *The basking sharks ate baked beans for breakfast,* he'd sing, *out on a broad blue sea*. It returns to me, and if I say just that, nothing more, those words will bring him back to me, as he was then, sitting on the edge of my bed. But the incantation exists beyond my reach and I say nothing. The kitchen recedes, as I walk upstairs and away, as if he's not there. As if none of this has happened. If I play pretend for long enough the imaginary world might become the real and the real be the imagined.

I crawl into my bed, the weight of the duvet reassuring on my body. I am still in my uniform, so my clothes tug and pull tight. I cannot. I cannot. The height of Koko creaks within me. Too tall for our house. The height he gifted without my asking. He must duck his head to pass through the doorframe, and a love I am unready to remember turns and yawns inside me.

FEVER

A sickness comes as if I willed it. A headache first, and then a fever takes hold, pulling me down, deep into the bedding, beyond its feathers and springs, through the floorboards of the house and its foundations, into the burning centre of the earth, and it is there I sweat and cry and wait for time to unfold.

The girl who turned into foam on top of the sea and the girl who turned into a nightingale come to sit with me. All the other girls in my head are back, too. None of them can speak any longer, but I understand them. They can't tell me what to do or where to find Tegan or when Mou will be returned to me. But their presence is reassuring. I tell them I have webs between my toes, and with a shrug, they tell me not to worry. That sort of thing is normal right about now. I tell them I have a tail, and they say, how lucky.

The girl who turned into foam on top of the sea leaves a wet patch on the bed beside me. She's parched and thirsty. She didn't become foam in the end, she says, in a voice so quiet it's ethereal. She ascended. She turned into air. She's desperate to tell me more, but it's so very hard to hear her.

She was turned not because she wasn't loved in time, she says. She was turned because she dared to love at all. She desired the prince and was punished for it. She desired. That was the sum total of her crimes.

The nightingale says nothing. She sits on the tip of my finger. She is not beautiful like I'd imagined her. Not like the girl who went missing. She is plain and small, yet defiant. I realise this is how she stays safe. She is unnoticed. I stroke the feathers under her chin. They're dripping blood. She is the softest thing I've ever touched. She is so soft, she disintegrates between my fingers, and then I'm alone on a bed so damp it feels cold.

I WAS NEVER turning into a woman, not really. I was turning into this creature I am now. An amphibian with a tail and webbed feet. I am becoming the frightful thing I first envisioned. I am full of fright.

I swim to the bottom of the ocean where the cold dense weight could crush me. I can breathe through my gills, like the water is air. I can see in the dark of the deep. I can change colour. I can change into anything I want. At the bottom of the ocean Koko is waiting. I say I'm sorry I ran from him. He tells me he's sorry, too. I tell him I swapped my legs for a tail because I don't want to be silent. I swapped my legs for a tail because I want to love whoever I want whenever I'm ready. He can't hear me. We're too deep under water and there is no sound.

'Where's Mou?' I ask, but I'm back in bed drenched in sweat. It's the middle of the night and no one is here. I tear off my uniform until I'm just in my pants and vest. I remember what happened and roll over. I want to slip away again, back to the other place.

The next morning when I haven't got up, Grandma Jean comes into my room.

'Did he go?'

Grandma Jean nods and sits on the edge of my bed. 'I didn't mean for you to meet like that—'

'I'm sick.' I don't want to hear whatever she might say.

She puts her hand on my forehead. I imagine it hot and clammy. She feels the wet cotton of my under-clothes, now cold.

'Okay then,' she says. 'I'll let the school know.'

She fetches me a glass of cold water. By the time she's back my sickness has settled deeper. I beckon it on with all my might.

I'M BACK IN the woods. The forest bed is dotted with blue-bells as far as I can see. Tegan and I lie on the damp ground where the woodland animals can speak to us. Beetles, their bodies shining and black, emerge from the earth to tell us of the dark days in the forest when we were both gone, and squirrels scamper down trees to sit on our chests, wiping our brows with their tails.

'The baby is hungry,' you say, clutching your belly, and the squirrels and the beetles fall to our sides. I clutch my belly, too. You groan in pain and the noise comes from my mouth. I want to help you, but I don't know how. We're here together in the woods and the baby will come when it's ready. You cry out like a cat in search of its mate and I cry out, also. All the girls who went into the woods to become women cry out with us, and it's a howl as loud as the night. You vomit then, and the forest and its mushrooms and its bluebells fly out of your mouth, a volcanic eruption. I wipe my face clean.

'It's coming,' you say, and we both know it.

I begin to tell you a story from the future, but you can't hear me. 'When I was a girl, I went into the woods . . . ' I say.

'What if I die, Siss? What if I'm already dead?'

I gather you in my lap and stroke your hair, just like Haley did on the hallway floor.

'We will give birth to this baby and she'll be a girl,' I whisper. 'An unimaginable human daughter. She will be half of you and half of me. She will have your snaggletooth smile and my muddy skin. Her eyes will be grey like the sea. She will laugh like the symphony we make when we're happy, which sounds like a stream meeting a river and knowing its way. She will walk on her own from the beginning and speak in a language only we understand. She will be a leader, fearless and followed by women, and we will fall to our knees in prayer.'

You scream and I scream, also, because the baby is coming fast now. Its head emerges from between your legs and it looks like light coming through an open window. I pull the baby out with my own two hands; it's brutal and necessary, and we tumble together onto the forest floor. She is perfect. She is everything we hoped her to be.

It is night now, and there is blood on the ground beneath us. I smear a streak across our cheeks to mark our passage into this new world.

You and the baby are sleeping, and I am naked beneath the stars. My skin is burning despite the cool night air. The baby is the same colour as the moon, the light reflected on the surface of her skin like scales. Like me. She is our wilding, our feral nature realised. She is compensation for the rest of the girls who came before and died becoming women. For the girls who were changed into trees, and birds, and stone. She is a gift, conciliatory and wise.

Nan has come to visit. The lines in her face make a map for my fingers to follow and they lead me back to the woods, back to the caravan. The morning light silhouettes her head.

'Your mother will be back soon,' she says gently, in a voice that isn't her own. She's wearing beige lipstick, which feels all wrong.

'The baby?' I say. 'Where's the baby?' but she doesn't answer.

'Shush now,' she says, and it all slips away.

WHEN I WAKE up, Mou is sitting on the side of my bed with a cup of soup and a spoon.

'You look better.'

'Are you real?' I ask, and she smiles.

Last time I saw her, she gave me a root vegetable to hold as if it were a baby and I realised she wasn't really there.

'Yes, Sissy *mou*,' she says, and I reach out to touch her face. Her fingers wrap around mine. She is real. I cry and she gathers me into her, pressing her forehead to mine. 'Sissy *mou*,' she says again, crying also. I have her back. She's been returned to me.

'Never leave me,' I say, burying my head in her shoulder. She goes to speak, but I stop her. 'Don't promise,' and she nods.

She gestures at the soup and I shake my head. I'm not ready for eating.

'Mou,' I say again, and she shifts closer. 'Are you better?'

'Getting there,' she says, and the air about her flutters. 'I had a very kind doctor called Mr Gosh.'

I smile. She knew I would like that. Then I remember all the things that happened between her leaving and my falling sick.

'Tegan?'

Mou shakes her head sadly and holds my hand tight. 'Try not to think about that just yet. You've been very sick.'

'For how long?'

'Four days. Your fever broke on the third but it was like you didn't want to wake up.'

Four days, plus the days before, it must be over a week now that Tegan's been missing.

'They're still searching,' Mou says, guessing what I must be thinking.

She's made a little camp bed on the floor next to me.

'Grandma Jean was meant to leave when I got back, but it's been a real help to have her here.'

'She read me stories,' I say, remembering flashes of the past days.

'Really? She used to read to me when I was little. I'd sit so still, scared to move in case she stopped.'

'She told me other things, too. She told me how when you were born you got stuck on your way out. She said even being born was difficult for you. I don't think she realised I could hear.'

'That sounds like something she would say.'

'Koko, he was here.'

'You were dreaming.'

'No, before.'

'We don't have to talk about Koko, if you don't want to.'

'If *you* don't want to, you mean.'

Mou tugs at her hair and stops herself.

'Grandma Jean asked if I wanted to see him,' I say. 'She said he's wanted to see me all this time.'

Mou is taken aback by this. 'Did Grandma Jean call him?' she asks. 'That's not what she said to me.'

'Is it true? Would you have told me if I hadn't found out?'

Mou sighs and rests her head on the pillow next to me. She takes a long time to answer. 'Koko used to make me freshly squeezed orange juice for breakfast,' she says at last. 'He'd do it before I was up, so there would be juice waiting for me on the bedside table. Now whenever I think of him my tastebuds pinch shut. Isn't that the funniest thing? When he came into my life it was like he turned a light on in a room, and each time he left it went dark. I guess that's hard for you to understand.'

She examines my face and sees I understand.

'Maybe not so hard. You're heartbroken yourself,' she says, with one hand against my chest. 'You love Tegan very much.'

I feel guilty then. I told Tegan her secret and now everyone at school knows. I want to tell her what happened and for her to forgive me. But if I told Mou, it would make her hate Tegan, and I'm not ready for that.

She goes on, 'We fought a lot, though, and one time he said I wasn't fit to care for you. I was so frightened he'd tell someone about my being sick and they'd take you from me. So the next time he went out to the rigs, I packed up the car with you and left. Looking back, I wasn't very well then. I hadn't been since you were born. Once we'd settled in London and I was doing better, I tried to put it right with him, but he was furious, threatened to sue for custody, and seeing him started it all up again. The school got involved that time too, so I packed us up and we moved again. I guess he was right ... ' The story has upset her, but she gathers herself and lifts her face to me, defiantly. 'But I don't care if he was. They're not having you.' She smiles through her tears.

'No, Mou.'

Mou gets up.

'Will you stay?' I ask her, and she nods. She turns out the light and climbs into her camp bed.

I stare at the ceiling and imagine meeting my father once more. I remember seeing him in the ocean deep. I remember my journey as if it all really happened. The ocean and the woods and the baby on the forest floor.

Mou must have been thinking her own thoughts because, after a few minutes, she turns the light back on, gets out of bed and walks across the corridor to her room, where Grandma Jean is sleeping. I get out of bed and follow.

Grandma Jean is staring at the ceiling, also. Three sleepless generations of ceiling-staring women. The bed sheets are uncrumpled. Her clothes are folded neatly on the armchair. I wonder how a woman who conducts herself with the neatness of a sharpened pencil can be the same woman who made my mother.

'Mummy, I need you to answer me truthfully,' Mou says.

Grandma Jean does not sit up. 'Yes?'

'Did you call Koko? Did you invite him into my home to see my daughter?'

Grandma Jean removes her arms from inside the covers and folds them over her chest. 'Susanne, I did.'

My mother's body shakes beside me, a motion so slight only I can feel it and perhaps the spiders still waiting in their web. Mou takes a deep breath to contain the same anger that had caused her to hit her mother across the face with a coffee cup all those years ago, the repercussions of which have reverberated throughout her life. It is an anger I share. I felt it when I struck William with the stone and when I attacked Clara in the changing room.

Mou breathes out slowly. 'Why would you do such a thing without asking me?'

'He's your husband.'

'He's not. We never got married.'

'Is that so? I was sure—'

'We lied.'

'Oh ... Well, he's the father of your child and that's reason enough.'

A long moment passes.

'I expect you shall ask me to leave now.' Grandma Jean props herself up with great effort. Her eyes, bare and bleary, her second mouth removed on a piece of tissue and thrown into the bin.

I take Mou's hand. I don't know what she's going to do, but I want her to know I'm right here. She stands there for some time without speaking.

At last, she says, 'I forgive you.'

There is no softness in this forgiveness. It is forgiveness forged in stone and handed to another like a weight to be carried a long distance.

'Well ...'

'Goodnight,' Mou says, and she closes the door.

WHILE I WAS sick, they dug up Eric666's London garden in case she was buried beneath his paving stones. They trawled the length of the river, too, where the last girl was found.

On the evening news, there's an interview with the shopkeeper from the hamlet near Tegan's house, the same shopkeeper who sold us a packet of biscuits and a pint of milk with the single wisp of grey hair. He saw Tegan get out of a man's car on the day she went missing, corroborating Eric666's story. He assumed the man was a friend's dad until he saw the papers. The news anchor reports that Mr Weston has now been released on bail. They recreate a timeline of Tegan's last day: leaving school early around 3 p.m.; meeting Mr Weston in town shortly after; being dropped off within the hour, witnessed by the shopkeeper; and then she disappears.

The news anchor creases her eyebrows to look purposefully worried. 'The search and rescue team are relocating to the area surrounding where Tegan was last seen, not far from the Prices' family home—'

Mou switches off the TV, as if she can protect me. But I don't need to hear any more. It's not about Eric666. It never was. I imagine Tegan calling him in desperation. Waiting after school in town, alone and determined. I imagine the scene between them in his car after he refused to take her back to London with him. I can see it all. Her being dropped off, distraught, furious, and coming up with another plan. I know where Tegan is now and I can't believe I never thought of it.

After school, I stay on the bus all the way to Buckland Dinham, like Tegan once told me, and then I take the number 68 to the hamlet near her house. I get off at the bus stop by the village shop, where the news anchor just stood.

I'm not certain I'll remember the way, but I try to follow my feet without second guessing. The bridle path winds out of the village, and into the woods. The trees are no longer stripped bare, but covered with the first burst of buds. It looks like a different landscape from how it was in the depths of winter. I stop often, unsure if I've walked in the wrong direction. I come to a clearing and rest on an outcrop of stone. I saved half my lunch sandwich from Grandma Jean, wrapped in its foil package. There are parts of Grandma Jean I'm learning to enjoy. She brought her cat, Mephistopheles, to live with us while Mou gets back on her feet; Mou pretends to be annoyed, but she likes him, too.

I eat my sandwich and listen. I hope to hear the music from Tegan's little tape deck or the sound of her singing from afar. But there is only the quiet tide of the wind. Tegan will for ever exist in those woods for me. There is a version of me out there still, too. She is a little less grown and a little less broken. She hasn't yet felt the full scars of womanhood.

When I stand, I realise I've lost my bearings and I can't tell which direction I arrived from. I turn in a circle and everything around me looks the same. I walk one way and then another, but at every moment, I am the centre of a world of endless trees. I walk on in the hope of recognising some marker. The sun is lowering in the sky, and Mou will worry if I'm not home soon. Grandma Jean, too. The woods have cast a spell to keep me for ever in their midst. But I'm not a child any more and I can't let my imagination run away with me. I shouldn't have come on my own. Perhaps I shouldn't have come out here at all.

Up ahead, I see a dash of colour between the trees and walk towards it. A wild violet blue. The closer I get, the more of it appears, until I reach a clearing and gasp. There are bluebells as far ahead as I can see. I step into their midst, forgetting to be frightened or that I'm looking for my lost friend. I disappear into the blue like it's the sea. I want to laugh with the beauty of it, the magic. It's then I see the caravan. It's easy to miss with new foliage climbing its sides.

I'm nervous now, because if Tegan isn't here then there's nowhere else to look. If she isn't here, then Tegan is truly gone. All this time, I never believed it. I kept waiting for the phone in the hallway to ring or for her to be at her desk one day, acting as if it was no big thing, lapping up the attention, the drama.

I walk up to the caravan in the footsteps of my former self, wishing I could be that girl still. Even before I get to the door, I see the padlock is open and I hurry my pace. Inside, there's stacked cans of baked beans and spaghetti hoops and a box of tea bags. A packet of biscuits, half eaten. When I turn the corner there she is, curled up on top of the covers, asleep. This is woodland Tegan, boyish in a bulky sweater with her hair greasy and unkempt. She looks like she hasn't washed for weeks. On top of the box of Andy's tapes, I see my smoky quartz has been carefully placed, and my determination wavers. I want to climb into bed and wrap myself around her, like we used to. For the membranes that separate her from me to melt away, and for us to be a single self, with a single beating heart. It will be just like my dream. We will stay here together for the months yet to come. We'll forage like Nan showed us, eating wild mushrooms and nettle soup and dancing beneath the full moon. We'll live here together, forest creatures, wildings, and when the months have passed, our baby will be born. She will be the physical manifestation of the spark that united us. She will be just ours.

I also know none of this will happen. That those things I believed to be true were in my head. The note in the music box, I know what it said, more or less. Perhaps I always did. There is no drawing of a man and drawing of a woman; there is no magic in my crystals either. No first forgotten Eve. Peter made her pregnant. She was ready when he said she was. Haley refused to see it, until she couldn't any longer, because I called her and told her where to find the note. Was that a betrayal, too?

I back out of the caravan quietly. If I stay a moment longer my resolve will unravel. The type of knot I never learned how to tie. I remember the way now; I have found my bearings. I run back to the village and follow the path towards Tegan's farm, through the meadow that is now bright yellow with rape flowers, and then down through the copse the other side. I don't go to the house, though: it isn't Brenda I'm after. Instead I stop at Nan's cottage. A spire of twisted smoke winds from the chimney.

Nan is already standing, as if waiting for me, when I walk in. 'It's better that it's you,' she says, pulling on her boots. She doesn't ask any questions, but walks beside me, like she already knows the way. I'm walking faster now, because the end is near, and I'm ready for it. Nan spots the caravan and overtakes me. She looks back before she opens the door. Her expression is sad, resigned even, like she knew where to look all along, and chose not to.

The next few hours are full of sirens, and flashing lights, and policemen, and tears. I hang back, waiting for Mou to collect me. Tegan is taken to hospital soon after, and Brenda goes with her in the ambulance.

We didn't emerge from the woods hand in hand like I once imagined. We didn't emerge carrying our unimaginable human daughter, forged from fire and stone and dreams. Tegan walked a few steps ahead of me, her hand gripped tight in Nan's. She didn't resist, like she might once have done. She seemed depleted, tired, Nan's scarf over her shoulders to keep off the evening chill.

Tegan looked back only once, enough to know it was me who had led them there. I broke one last promise, but it doesn't matter now. There are no deals to be made with the universe, no system of wishes. There is just the fact of our friendship and the fact of our betrayal, and all the murky waters in between. It was through these waters we swam to get here, like our amphibian ancestors emerging from the soupy depths, busy becoming.

I feel alone walking a few steps behind them. The wind picks up a song through the leaves, an ancient lament, and I sing it to myself under my breath. I listen for the chorus of girls, waiting for their voices to rise within me, but I'm listening for them still. I'm singing still!

v

(rebirth)

AIR

I found the Barbies I once buried in the back lawn. I saw their blonde hair matted in the mud. I washed the dirt from their crevices, where worms had worked their way around their joints and found no nourishment. I gave them to Mou to donate to the bird shop where she's working again, two days of the week. She has her job back at the library, too.

Once in a while, a woman called Tracy sits with us for an hour in our front room. Mou does her best to act Proper with a capital P. Before Tracy comes we clean the house and Mou makes sure there's food in the fridge. We don't wear our house uniform or make a bed on the sofa. Mou even brushes her hair.

Tracy tells me to behave just like I would if she weren't here, to pretend she's not even in the room.

'Why don't you leave, then?' I say. 'It'll be easier.'

She smiles as if I'm trying to be funny.

Mou covers her laugh with a cough.

A year has passed and I know my body better. I have clearly defined edges. I masturbate how Tegan showed me. I no longer kneel on the heel of my foot and wiggle around while holding a pair of Barbies. I will never tell a soul that's how I once did it. In fact, I'll barely remember. When I come, I don't see galloping horses or undulating pink light behind my lids. But the pleasure, it's mine. When I break open, only then, my boundaries are infinite.

My tail is still here when I need it, unfurling at will. Mostly I'm grateful for it. I never wanted to be like the other girls anyway. And it's a comfort to me: I can hold my breath now and never drown.

ANOTHER GIRL GOES missing before they catch the girl snatcher. They think there were other girls before the girls of ours he snatched. Girls in other towns with different faces, but the same name. They are all the missing girl. They are all beautiful for ever. They all have their picture on posters around town. There are so many of them and each has a story. More stories than I know how to tell. All these girls are sitting with me, telling their stories, and I can't work out which belongs to whom. They make a single sound like the nightingale's song.

Tegan is not among their number and for that I'm glad, even if we aren't friends any longer and never will be again.

I see her once more, before Mou decides it's time to move on. We're going to the coast, she says. Maybe I'll see Koko again. It doesn't seem so far-fetched any longer.

When I see Tegan, I'm waiting for Mou outside the library so we can walk home together when she finishes work. I recognise her right away, and my heart quickens. After the woods, we didn't speak. She didn't come back to school that term. I tried calling the house once or twice, but I always hung up as soon as anyone answered. Someone on the bus said she'd had the baby, but no one knew for sure.

Now here she is, and she's pushing a pram towards me. She sees me and pauses, and I think for a moment she's going to turn and walk the other way. But she throws her hair, now brown, over one shoulder, like she used to, and marches onwards, the pram rattling against the pavement.

She acts like there's nothing unusual about our meeting, like we saw each other just the other day.

'Do you want to meet her?' She nods towards the pram.

I'm frightened for a moment by what I might see, but tucked up in the blankets is an ordinary baby with fat cheeks and a cautious smile. Tegan reaches in to pull the blanket down a little further, so I can get a better look. The baby has muddy olive skin and one bright white-blonde curl on the top of her head. Tegan is watching for my reaction; she already knows what she wants me to say. It's a test, as always.

'She's beautiful,' I say, too frightened to touch her.

But this isn't what Tegan wants to hear.

'Don't you see?' Tegan says, imploring me to look again, look closer. She walks around to my side of the pram and stands beside me, her presence so familiar still. She looks at the baby herself, as if still astonished. 'Look! She has your eyes. Can't you tell?'

I see now she's right. The baby stares up at me with grey eyes the colour of the sea, like looking into a mirror. She looks like she knows me, like she's already mine.

'I named her Sissy,' Tegan says, but I barely hear her. Her voice is a whisper I might have imagined. It's only in my head.

Sissy reaches out her impossible hand towards me. I touch my finger to hers, and we stay just like that, frozen in time.

Our baby.

Our daughter of the air.

ACKNOWLEDGEMENTS

Firstly, thank you to my wise and brilliant agent, Emma Parry. I feel enormously lucky to have you shepherding me through this writing life. Thank you also to Rebecca Carter and the team at Janklow & Nesbit.

To my editor, Carla Josephson, and to Sarah Savitt and Rose Tomaszewska, thank you for seeing the strange beauty in my book, and for your smart and thoughtful edits. You made it a better, braver book, and I couldn't be more proud. To the entire team at Virago, thank you for championing *Amphibian* and for all your work to so beautifully deliver it into the world. I remember eyeing the apple on the spines of my favourite books as a young reader and I still have to pinch myself to believe that my book will be among them.

To my early readers and dear friends: Nicky Woolf, Julian Tepper, Jeff Bens, Hanna Putnam, Jack Stigner, Clemmie Seely, Hannah Marriott, my sister Caitlin, and my writing buddy Taylor Beck, for your many hours reading, for your feedback, and most of all for your encouragement. To Georgia Frances King, this book might not have happened if you hadn't picked up the pieces of me when I'd given up and pushed me onwards. Not to mention the many rounds of edits and ultimately, the title. Thank you.

To Kerri Arsenault and Drew Wood for again giving me space and time to write in your beautiful home – you might be stuck with me for each book here on out. To Paige McGreevy for all your support and inviting me to read an early chapter at Les Bleus. And to Eric Farber who hosted me at Curious Jellyfish.

To the friends and strangers who shared their stories with me, I am indebted to each and every one of you; you made this book richer and more real, woven with truths beyond my own.

To my family, for your love and support. You are my favourite people and nothing makes sense without you.

And finally, to my husband, Adam, for our beautiful lives together that make it all possible. And for bringing me endless cups of tea at my desk. There is no greater love.

CREDITS

p.102 Sylvia Plath, *The Journals of Sylvia Plath 1950–1962* (London: Faber & Faber, 2014)

p.150 'Fairytale of New York' lyrics by Jem Finer and Shane MacGowan © 1987

p.220 Doris Lessing, *The Golden Notebook* (London: Fourth Estate, 2022)